Humanicide

Henry Melton

Humanicide

Henry Melton

Wire Rim Books
Hutto, Texas

WRB

Printing History
First Edition: November 2015
ISBN 978-1-935236-63-4

ePub ISBN 978-1-935236-64-1
Kindle ISBN 978-1-935236-65-8

Website of Henry Melton
www.HenryMelton.com

Character images © 2015 by Djamila Knopf
http://shilesque.deviantart.com/

Printed in the United States of America

Wire Rim Books
www.wirerimbooks.com

Acknowledgements

I want to thank Jonathan Andrews, Shelly Barnes, Jim Dunn, Linda Elliott, Mike Lynch, Alan McConnell, Mary Ann Melton, and Tom Stock for helping me with this story, so long in gestation.

Dedicated to my grandparents Henry and Vivian Wheeler. During the long dry spells of my writing life, the memory of Grandma Wheeler's joyful pride in every little publication of mine was the single greatest inspiration to continue.

Contents

Cis-Terran Space

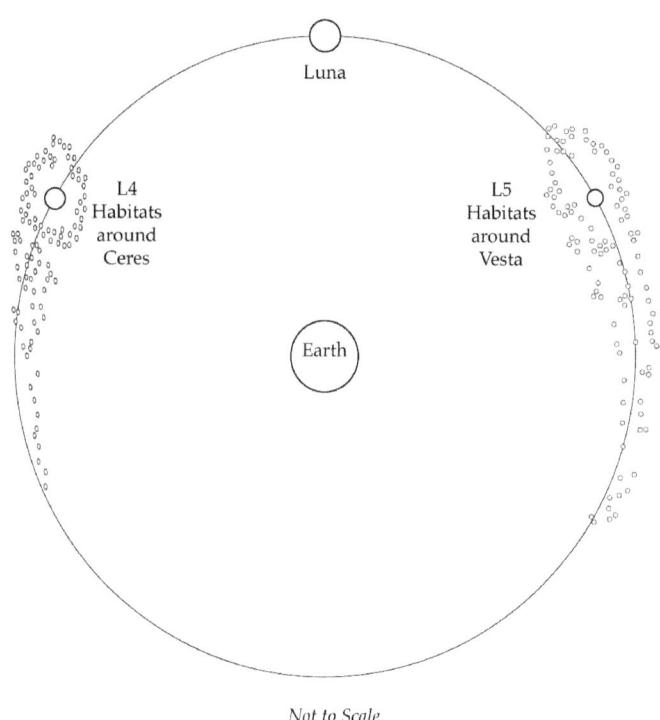

Luna

L4
Habitats
around
Ceres

L5
Habitats
around
Vesta

Earth

Not to Scale

Chapter 1

ALEXANDRIA HABITAT, L4 CLUSTER

Dr. Bet Nomad crouched down behind a shipping crate as the officer passed by. A transport had too few places to hide. But if she could just wait him out… He had to get back to his command station soon.

When the footsteps on the deck plate dwindled, she stood up and tapped on the meter-wide display set into the wall. She dismissed the chart showing the inventory and how it was placed. A few familiar taps and it went into auto-reflection. She stared back at herself. *I need to pay more attention to my appearance. I look too young today.*

She brushed her hair back into place. The screen showed the texture of her skin looking unnaturally smooth today, not at all matching her hair. No one was watching, so she opened her kit and added a few age lines. She needed to look at least forty to match her current bio report.

Satisfied, she tapped DOCKING VIEW. Opening like an abrupt rupture into free space, she raised her hand, fighting the illusion that she was looking into vacuum. She squinted, trying to take in the details of the long range view.

This view has to be from Alexandria. That's us. She laughed. *Our ship looks like a virus.*

I've got virus on the brain again. Concentrate. Today is public-relations.

There was a click on audio. "Dr. Nomad, report to Access G-4."

"I'm already here, Captain Che."

There was no answer. She was annoyed with the man. *Stick to piloting and don't try to entertain me. I'm cargo.* The hardest part of every new assignment was the first few hours and she didn't need his distraction.

The display was entrancing to her medical mind. *It's just like a viral attack. A tiny rod-shaped mobile capsule draws near to the membrane of a cell that is enormous in comparison. Soon it will locate a hatchway—a compatible spot of chemistry, and then inject its genetic cargo to hijack the cells life-force for its own ends.*

A smile attempted to twist her practiced, professional expression. *But that makes me the disease!*

The remote camera watched dispassionately as the transport lined up with the clamps at the hub of the slowly spinning city in space. Latches secured the ship and the walls around her echoed a low metallic clang. The transport ship was being lowered to the rim by the huge external elevator. The docks were at the habitat's full spin gravity. She could feel no difference—the transport's own local pseudo-gravity kept everything balanced.

Captain Che's voice echoed again, "Bet, it looks like you have a welcoming committee."

Her smile reverted to a scowl. He'd ferried her twice now. First from Blanco to New Lusaka, and now to Alexandria. *He's getting possessive.* She preferred to be invisible, and the voice of experience was nagging. He'd soon be a problem, but the best she could do for now was ignore him.

Better check out her greeters. Two assignments earlier, she'd bent a few of the medical restriction rules. Someone might have noticed, and cared enough to track her down.

She looked at her massive packing crate and shook her head. *I don't want to have to run again. Too much to lose.*

"Computer, do you have a visual of the loading dock outside G-4?"

The wall display changed.

Five young men stood on the ridged metal of the loading dock. One held a cluster of flowers—not the normal reception committee. But it was a relief—no one waiting with World Court Enforcement agent uniforms and restraining rods.

Still, they do look unusual. Bet watched as the men jostled for position among themselves. She would have been complimented by the attention, if experience hadn't warned her it was all wrong.

What did Central Medical say about me? Alexandria was the next posting on the rotation. She knew nothing about it. Just another independent habitat with barely enough trade to get it listed in the circulation.

Most postings greeted her arrival. There had been bands, parades, and dinner parties with the local leaders. Frequently, someone was responsible for getting her settled.

Five pretty boys is a little unusual.

There was nothing to do but go meet them. G-4 was the closest hatchway that could handle her gear.

When she palmed open the hatch, they turned in unison to look her over. The smiles were unanimous.

I don't look that good. Her natural appearance was younger than the look she crafted—a gracefully-aging forty-something, a look she could easily maintain with common cosmetics. She'd taken great pains to keep her hair and skin plain, and her clothes drab and professional.

Keep your eyes open. She strode out onto the elaborately decorated deck, wondered briefly at the Ancient Egyptian motif on the walls, and faced the group.

"Could someone, you, help me with this?" She pointed to one of them, the cheerful one with light hair. She deliberately snubbed the one with flowers. It was important to maintain her status, at least at first.

The exchange of glances and expressions among the others made their actions seem almost ritualistic. She had chosen, and the others drifted in pairs to help at the other access ports.

What just happened?

"Jeff Harris," he offered, with a short bob of his head.

"Dr. Bet Nomad, from the Circuit Medical Pool. Can you help me transport my gear?"

"No problem." Jeff Harris had nice white teeth, much whiter than the patients at her last posting. She wondered if it was genetic.

Bet returned his smile. He was too eager, but he was offering to help. "Now I have to find where I am to set up."

He pointed to a display mounted high over the cavernous loading dock, where a secondary set of large airlocks led into the interior of the space habitat. DOCTOR NOMAD was marked in green next to a map designator. "We've been waiting for you to arrive."

"I have module GH8443." It had taken some time to compact a traveling clinic into just one shipping module. It took her most of a day to set up when she had to do it alone.

Jeff worked energetically. She had her mental checklist and spent little time watching him. One thing was odd. He always checked the cross-corridors as they walked. He was looking for someone.

Habit made the half-dozen trips to and from the dock go swiftly. She used the time to absorb the feel of the place. Someone had tried hard to soften the reality that the Alexandrians lived all their lives in metal corridors. Decorations were everywhere.

Hieroglyphics, reddish brown on a sandy yellow background, must have been added as a decorating scheme many decades ago. In some cases, aged and peeling paint revealed the original hall signs. Another oddity was the text itself. Everything was done in phonetic cartouche style, rather than using the true meanings of the symbolic ideograms. Someone had taken a book and translated every sign along the main hallway sound by sound.

Strange décor for a tribe descended from Anglos.

...

The portable lab clamped firmly to the surface of the cabinet. She looked for a power connector. Jeff was down on his knees in an instant and located the charger. He coughed and said, "It's ready."

She gave the meter-wide cube a shake. Solid and unmovable—just the way she liked it. Although it had been decades since she'd suffered a mishap with it, her memory was long and there had been plenty of scares in space habitats. These Lagrangian outposts were huge—everyone just called them the Space Cities, no matter what their current population. When these were made, raw lunar rock was thrown into the orbit by catapult and solar furnace factories smelted the aluminum and other materials in place. There was no limit on how big they could be made. But that had been a long time ago.

I'm glad this one is big. The gravity feels real.

On smaller ones, where the spin was faster, every time she turned her head, she could sense that edge of corriolis distortion.

Not that Alexandria was a real city. The population was about five hundred from the few paragraphs she'd been sent—poor and unable to afford a resident doctor, thus her posting here.

Her assistant worked efficiently to help her turn an empty storage bin into a clinic. She sniffed. Machine oil. It must have held machine parts earlier.

In spite of Jeff's tendency to stay within touching distance of her, she was pleased by the way he worked. All of her equipment; drug cabinets, fold-up beds, and her nonstandard lab had come with her from the last station. The more they unpacked and unfolded, the more the place began to smell like home.

"Would you like me to show you where Centrum Park is?" Jeff asked, casually leaning against the bench, his thumb hooked in his belt, exuding male charm. "I know where the only good pasta shop is."

"Not today, I'm afraid," she said. "I've announced the opening of the clinic already, and I have to be ready for the first patients. I requested no official greetings until at least the second day. Set-up takes time."

And no flirtation on the job. She might be old, but her hormones matched her true face. One slip, and it'd take forever to get her emotions back under control. Celibacy was a firm component of this identity. She had to maintain it, for as long as she was Bet Nomad, circuit doctor.

Besides, if she could get rid of Jeff soon enough, she might be able to process the samples she collected on the trip from her last posting. She'd bet herself they would show evidence of the strange new virus she'd been tracking.

· · ·

"Where are you!" A woman's voice echoed down the corridor. Jeff looked up hurriedly, his perpetual smile replaced by a frown.

Bet tried to keep from smiling. *Uh oh. That's it.*

She yelled back. "Hello? If you are looking for the clinic, we are setting up in A-12."

Footsteps echoed on the metal floor and then a young woman appeared. Her forehead was lined with fury, and her eyes were red. She held a length of pipe in her hand.

"Mary! Put that down!" Jeff edged back behind the foldout bed.

She advanced, with eyes for the both of them, but her pipe was swinging toward him. "You rat! I should've known you weren't playing CoSan, not with your buddies busy unloading the transport."

Bet edged back, long practiced in the art of not being where weapons were aimed. The pipe was threaded, a dead giveaway that it was heavy. She intended to keep large masses of furniture between them.

"Now, Mary! It's not like that."

Mary's eyes caught a glimmer of the overhead lights as she turned on Bet. "So this is the lady doctor! Is she pretty enough for you? Is she fertile? Lady, I'm telling you right now, I won't accept a second wife in my home, and I'm not giving him up!"

But the glare in her eyes was for her husband. "Slime bucket!"

Jeff slapped the alarm button, after jumping toward the hatchway, dodging his wife's swing.

Events cascaded quickly then. There were dozens of people on duty at the dock, and the alarm brought the sounds of shouts and hasty footfalls. Bet, who'd seen more domestic fights that she cared to count, kept her distance, and her mouth closed.

A wide, sweaty man with no hair and a scar on his face appeared in the doorway. He grabbed the pipe like it was nothing. A woman looking as muscled as he arrived next and grabbed Mary's arms, and shouted, "Behave yourself, girl!"

Mary struggled, and the woman slapped her hard. She twisted Mary's right arm up behind her. "You had your chance. Don't make it any harder." In total control, she moved the girl quickly out into the hall.

The big man scowled at the other on-lookers who had arrived to watch. "Get back to work."

A couple of them gave Jeff a nod and a grin that Bet wasn't supposed to see, then left.

After the room cleared out, Jeff's cheerful smile was gone. "Sorry about my Mary," he apologized. "I've got to go." He headed off in a hurry after them.

. . .

Mayor Fortuna Degrassa arrived early in the morning shift. She offered a vase of cut flowers and an ornamental scroll. Bet noted without comment the military style of her outfit, a home-tailored gray suit with three silver circlets on her collar—a simplified copy of Cluster Administration garb outdated by eighty years at the least.

"Are you ready for the grand tour?"

Bet was ready. This was standard, and she usually learned something useful during the official greetings, even if it was only where they didn't want her to look.

"I'm sorry you got caught up in their little argument. Don't judge us too harshly," the gray-haired Lady said, bringing up and dismissing the Mary Harris incident before Bet had time to mention it. They walked a hallway that curved upward out of sight, but not before it was almost lost in the distant haze. To the side were ballast tanks where many millions of liters of water were used to balance out the irregularities of the storage bins.

Even here in the interior, there were signs of a massive Egyptian decorating effort. Cleopatra reclined on a barge on the Nile, an asp in her hand. There was also the unmistakable sign of uncounted small dirty hands passing on their way to the roped-off swimming area.

"We are a small community. We all know everyone's business." She gave a polite little cough. "Too much togetherness. Perhaps, in medical school, you had case studies of isolated populations?"

Bet Nomad laughed, wondering at the Lady. *She treats me like I'm fresh out of school. How old does she think I am?*

"I've been there," she said. "I'm older than I look."

"Aren't we all!" Lady Fortuna shook her head, suddenly looking tired and showing a true age much older than the first impression she gave.

Bet continued, "I have been posted at several stations where a single family dominated the population. Usually they are smaller groups than Alexandria, but I certainly understand the dynamics. This place must be older than the first settlement wave."

The Mayor nodded, with a frown. "We were pretty much abandoned when Vesta was moved in and took all the industry. Still, a major storage facility is one of the better places to be in with a depression setting in."

"You had food," she guessed. Bet remembered dark times of her own.

The Lady Fortuna nodded. "The stories are still told! There was food, but it was hardly a balanced store. To this day, strawberry jam is banned." They laughed.

Bet seized a comfortable silence as they walked along a long narrow corridor.

"I suspect the girl from yesterday has a sprained shoulder," she said. "I want to see her soon. Your team leaders were efficient."

The Mayor said nothing, but she looked away to hide her frown. Bet was satisfied. Most postings hadn't seen a doctor in decades. *Let her know now that I have authority on my own.*

· · ·

The tour followed one of the lateral corridors. Bet noted extensive gardens, probably productive enough to keep the community self-sufficient. There were plain signs of abandoned garden areas. The population must have shrunk over time.

There appeared to be little industry. Alexandria was still in a convenient orbit for temporary storage of items boosted from Earth or Vesta and transported to Mars. Lady Fortuna gushed over the metal craftwork done by their local artisans, but Bet knew the difference between a studio and a factory. They must export very little.

· · ·

"This section is one of the oldest. It's an abandoned shipment from the first days of the Martian settlement." Lady Fortuna opened the ornate hatchway and they entered. "Our pride and joy."

Bet couldn't make out how deep the warehouse area was. The far reaches were lost in the dark. The Lady commanded, "Lights." In a ripple, row by row of bookshelves were illuminated, stretching off into the distance.

There were more books here in one place than Bet had ever seen. Someone had constructed half-pillars to decorate the walls in bas relief. They were scaled down copies of the pillars in the Valley of Kings. She even recognized the markings.

It was plain, now, what had been the intent.

"Wow. 'The Library of Alexandria.'"

The Mayor smiled. "When Mars was declared terraformed and lands were opened up, all the nations were competing with each other to make their new colony the best. That is, before Balday beat them out in the race to become the planetary capital. Dozens of new cities ordered complete duplicates of their hosting nation's libraries. The publishers joined forces to try to meet the demand and established this warehouse off-planet. Then the technology changed on them."

"Surprise," Bet said in deadpan.

"Right. Mars developed its bio feedstock much faster than anyone expected, and it was no longer worth shipping actual books when they could be printed locally from a data feed. The whole warehouse was written off.

"We renamed the habitat after that, when people started realizing we had the best library of physical books in the whole Solar System. At first, there was hope to attract tourists, but that never happened. Oh, we had scholars and politicians visit for a few years, until the novelty wore off, but after that … it was just too expensive for people to come here. We can move planets around, but we still haven't gotten personal transportation cheap enough for tourism."

Bet reached out and brushed a faint layer of gray dust off the spines of the nearest books. They were all in perfect shape, probably never touched except by the person who initially shelved them. There were titles here she'd never seen, but it was a random collection. If there was an index scheme, she couldn't detect it.

"That was one of the reasons I signed up for the Circuit Medical Team," said Bet. "I'd never get to travel to as many places any other way. The Project is good at moving tens of thousands of people at once, but little ships bother them."

Lady Fortuna sniffed. "They're specialists in keeping everything under control. At least you found a loophole. I never have."

PRIME CITY, CERES, L4 CLUSTER

William Mason's earpiece vibrated with the alarm. A touch on the thin band of metal at his temple dampened the sound level. Across the open air cafeteria, a dozen other people dressed in Project greens made the same motions.

Jay sneered, as he lay sprawled on the bench across the table from him. "I told you not to wear that thing while you're eating. If they want you, they'll page you."

Mason nodded, not that he agreed, but just to keep the peace. Jay's optical telescope on Ceres farside was currently in daylight, and he had nothing more important to do than kill time picking arguments with Project people. Mason knew better by now not to react to his jibes. Hurriedly, he shoveled a few more bites in.

"I forgot I was wearing it."

Florina shifted in her seat next to him, "I just thought you enjoyed being a Project Controller so much you had to share it with us."

"Yes," added Cinca in her low, rich voice. She handed Jay his order. "I think he does. Do you … sleep with that uniform on, Mason?"

He looked up and couldn't help noticing how good she looked in her waitress uniform. She was the reason he ate in this astronomers' dive.

Just then, the overheads spoke. "William Mason. Please report to your duty station."

Mason was grateful for the excuse to wipe his face and exit the table. Cinca was forever trying to get under his skin—just because he took his job seriously!

. . .

Project HQ had a dozen subsidiary control centers, mostly in Earth orbits, but this was Central Control. He straightened his shoulders as he entered the maze of work cubes. *There is nothing to apologize about. I am proud to wear the uniform.*

Through the transparent ceiling, both Luna and Earth were gibbous, with tiny Vesta riding the midpoint between them. The Earth was massive and beautiful, but every day Luna looked more and more mysterious under its turbulent clouds. The three worlds never moved in the sky, but their changing phases and the bright clouds of Luna and the Earth were a constant fascination to him.

I love this place.

Ceres was Earth's second largest moon, riding the central location in the leading L4 cluster. In its long history, it had been called, briefly, a planet, then demoted to the largest of the asteroids, then elevated to a dwarf planet. No one called it that any longer. It was a moon. Here was based Project Prime, the nerve center of the grandest effort of the human race. Hundreds of lesser habitats rode in loose orbits around it. Another similar cluster rode the L5 stability point 120 degrees off, on the trailing side of Luna, circling Vesta. None of the habitats were as large nor as important as Ceres—not even Vesta, no matter what its inhabitants thought.

The Eye of Humanity. He'd heard Ceres called that before, with two different interpretations. The astronomers had their big eye built in the Kirnis crater on farside. Mason preferred to think it meant Prime.

Ceres was large enough to be spherical from its own gravity, and Prime was built on the equator. Central was at the hub of that city, and the domed roof above him was the largest window ever constructed. Project Prime controlled every tractor/pressor beam in the Solar System, whether directing traffic for every spacecraft or directly controlling the huge beams that connected planets together like invisible chains.

The Terraforming Project was destined to change every planet or large moon humanity could touch into a world where people could walk without spacesuits. Mars was long done, a successful proof of concept, and Luna was close enough to completion that it was the center of every political conflict on the news.

"Come in, Mason." His section boss was the Lord Stephen Smith. "Have you heard?"

Mason shook his head. "Did the World Court rule?"

He fingered his beard and coughed. "No, that's still out. We have something a little more interesting. North Polar has detected an unregistered object on radar. I want you to shake it out."

Mason smiled. "My upgrade is approved?"

The man nodded and reflected his enthusiasm. "Your station has been authorized to control the two kilogram beams, but use them cautiously, or Phenig will revoke it. Get me hard data by shift end."

"Will do."

. . .

Two Kilograms. "That's not the force of the beam," he remembered his instructor from fifteen years ago, "that's the capacity of the energy cell." Two kilograms plugged into $E=mc^2$ packed a lot of energy.

Mason walked into his soundproofed, transparent workstation and slammed down into the swivel chair. He tapped his headset.

"Give me every level 3 or higher radar contact from North Polar in the past couple of hours. Screen two."

The wall turned opaque and text appeared. The listing was long enough to scroll on the floor-to-ceiling display. The item he wanted was there, plain as day, highlighted in red. He tapped it with his finger.

"Give me everything we know about this one. Use all screens."

The other walls became a maze of information. He swiveled in his chair, soaking it in.

"Metal." He had a bad habit of talking out loud to himself, but he blamed it on the silence of the work cube. Luckily, the computer's ears were smart enough to detect when he was talking to it, and when he was just muttering to himself.

It had to be metal. The reflection was strong enough and showed none of the splatter he associated with a radar echo off of rock or even a naturally formed iron meteor.

He glanced at the orbital map, and rotated it in 3D with his fingers until he had a good sense of just how far away it was from North Polar, an automated radar station balanced on a pressor beam a million kilometers above the north pole of the Earth.

Time to flex my muscles. "Order South Polar to get a confirmation ping." There was a pause. If he didn't have the authority, he should have heard it immediately. But if it did….

It took ten seconds for a confirmation that the radar array was being re-aimed. The actual ping would take several minutes. There was no rushing the speed of light.

. . .

Mason could no longer see the surface of Luna, and he missed it. The Lunar atmosphere was nearly a thousand kilometers deep now, and most of it was clouds. Stirred constantly by the spin beams, it never formed clear patches like the Earth. When he was a boy, he had watched as the fragments of Hyperion were herded down to impacts on the ancient gray surface. It had been fireworks on a grand scale. His father had died making that happen.

He turned back to the screens. No time for daydreaming now.

The computer was building a preliminary orbit plot, and it looked odd. "Plot the previous perigee. I want a date." The screen flickered.

"The one before that."

"Interesting."

He looked at the clock. The South Polar data should be in soon. With the information he had, it appeared that the intruder into Project-controlled space was in a long-period orbit, well out of the ecliptic. Of course, he didn't have enough information for a good projection, but it seemed that one orbit before, it had come past Earth well before the Terraforming Project had been established, and the orbit before that included the years right before the Star.

"You could be a spacecraft from the first space age."

There was a flicker on the screens and the computer spoke, "The data from South Polar has been included."

He could see it. All of the orbital traces tightened, as the computed course became more certain. The date ranges narrowed too. Two orbits in the past was the year before Betelgeuse went supernova.

...

"Lord Stephen?"

"Come on in. What do you have for me?"

Mason stepped into the office and stood at attention.

Lord Stephen rubbed his temple and waved him down. "You make me tired, just looking at you. Just give me the summary."

Mason held a slate that detailed his findings. His boss barely looked at it.

"Sir, I believe it could be a ship from the first space age. Radar indicates its outer layer is machined metal. I 'shook' it, just like you suggested, and got a good density reading. It's all consistent with a manufactured object.

"And now, if you will look at the orbit it came in on …."

He went on to describe his theory that it had been a ship launched via the chemical rockets in the ancient days. There were no good records of that time. Too much had been committed to electronic archives, and by the time humanity had recovered those abilities, the media were lost or damaged.

"So this is a golden opportunity. I have worked out a proposal to pull the intruder into a wide loop that will circuit the planet beams and bring it here to Prime for recovery and analysis."

Lord Stephen took the slate and looked over the analysis. "This looks like good work, Mason. I will turn it over to the Swiss for disposition." He didn't look Mason in the eyes.

"You are dismissed. Go home and get some rest."

Mason closed his mouth before he could say something impolitic. *He's doing this for my protection.* He bottled the anger tight. Not even an apology. Someone must be watching. He nodded and left.

A balding older man watched from a few hundred paces along the wall, standing casually in the doorway of his luxury office. When he saw Mason, he turned his back and closed his door.

Mason stalked past his own cube, heading for the exit.

Lord Phenig again! The Swiss faction on the Project Board was keeping a tight grip on him.

I am loyal to the Project. Haven't I proved it! Fifteen years of doing minor jobs—biting my tongue when they lie to me. Stephens knows my abilities, but every time I'm allowed to stretch, Phenig finds a way to put me back in a box.

I should have never come here. He looked at the Earth above. The terminator was over the Americas. Rio was already dark, were his mother was buried. Most of North America was still in the light. Would he ever go back home?

ROCKIES BACKCOUNTRY PRESERVE, NORTH AMERICA, EARTH

Kidd fell, and slid across the sharp rocks of the talus slope. He let his duffel fall away, tumbling down the steep cliff. He had to concentrate to keep from following the bag.

"Help," he shouted, "help me!"

There was no answer. The only sounds were the uneven howl of the wind through the high Rocky Mountain pass, and far off, the roar of spring melt in the creek below.

"Help!" He listened. Then, there was the one sound he had been waiting for—the clop of a horse hoof on stone.

Sprawled out as he was to keep from slipping any farther on the slope, he couldn't see the approaching rescuer, but from the sounds, he was getting closer. Kidd shouted repeatedly to urge him on.

"Hello down there? Are you hurt?"

Kidd pushed up a little, then stopped when he started to slide again. "No! Just scrapes. Help me."

"I've got a rope. Wait there."

Kidd grimaced. "I'm not going anywhere."

The rope that snaked its way down to him was braided leather—perfectly legal, but rare. He grabbed it and used it to inch his way up the slope, grateful for his own leather pants. These rocks would slash his skin to ribbons.

He pushed himself up over the edge of the cliff and rested, panting for breath. The two horses were panting white vapor, too. This mountain was one of the Fourteeners, and his lungs needed time to get enough oxygen.

"Here, drink this." The burly, bearded man held out a water skin. Kidd gulped down the sweet, slightly gritty water, probably from the creek below.

"Thank you. For everything."

"Glad to help." He looked over the edge where Kidd had been. "Are you a newcomer in the Backcountry?"

"Looks like it, after that stupid move! But actually, I've been on work teams up in the Montanas. This is my first solo."

He got to his feet and slapped his leather clothes free of the snow. He looked down where he had been. "My duffel is down there."

"Anything important in it?"

"Just my food." His face was grim. "My saddlebags have my clothes and other gear."

"Oh." The man held out his hand. "Well, my name is Trader, out here. I would be happy to guide you back to the portal. Guiding and trading, that's my job."

"Kidd. I'm an engineer."

"Let's get you down off this peak. You're freezing. My campsite isn't far."

. . .

"About the only food I've got is these tea pouches," Kidd said, as he rummaged through his remaining belongings. Trader was quickly bringing the fire to life.

"Tea? What brand?"

He handled the silk pouches. "Um. I'm not sure without the labels. I know this dark stuff has peppermint in it."

"New Spring?"

"Maybe. I never paid much attention when I was shopping."

Trader reached into his own bag. "Well, if it's New Spring, then you'll need this to make a drinkable pot." He tossed a little gadget to him.

Kidd caught the little egg timer and watched the white sand trickle through the glass as he held it in his hand. "Isn't this illegal in the Backcountry? They made me memorize the rules list. I'm pretty sure glass is on the proscribed list of manufactured items."

Trader waved his hand. "If you want to be picky. But think about it. Glass is just a kind of sand. The frame is plain wood. Grind it beneath your boot and there is nothing illegal about it at all. But a three-minute timer can keep you from a ruined meal or two out here, especially if you're as bad a cook as I am.

"Keep it, or destroy it, if it bothers you. My gift to you."

Kidd tapped the glass, dislodging a few white grains of sand still clinging to the sides, and then stuffed it into his pocket.

Trader smiled, then turned back to tending the fire.

Kidd casually fingered the hidden switch under the rough collar on his leather shirt, marking the previous few minutes as evidence. The audiovisual record of the next few days would be useful.

He constructed an appropriate smile. It was time to make friends with the smuggler.

...

"You've got to give up that habit," commented Trader.

"What habit?" Kidd leaned back against the rocks and tried to carve on a stick with his flint-bladed knife.

"You keep looking at your wrist, like you're checking the time."

Kidd looked again at the faint discoloration on his arm, barely visible in the flickering light. He laughed.

"I've been living under a deadline for years now. Forgive me if checking the time is instinctive. Building things is a matter of time and space and materials."

"So, Mr. Kidd, what kind of things do you build?"

Kidd smiled and stretched his arms wide. "Big things. Really big things. I was part of the Salt Lake City dome project. I also worked on the Butte Montana Pit mine preservation."

Trader laughed and slapped his leg. "Hey, I love the Bonneville Dome! There's a great nightclub next to the wall where you can see all the dolphins and whales and things swimming by. So you are a GAHSP man! What are you doing out here in a re-naturalized area?"

"Hey, I like scenic beauty just as well as the next guy. The Global Alliance for Historical Site Preservation isn't against nature. It's just that the Re-Naturalists have gone much too far. We have to remember our past, or risk making all the old mistakes again."

Kidd waved at the surrounding mountains with his knifepoint. "It's great that they've cleaned up the mine tailings and poured the poisons back into the mountain, but would it kill 'em to preserve an old mining town or two? Why rip up all the old rail lines and spend fortunes growing trees over the old jeep trails?

"And they aren't even consistent! Take the Lake Bonneville project, for example. Human pollution had absolutely nothing to do with the ancient Bonneville shrinking down to the Great Salt Lake. Why did they have to re-flood the basin, and drown half of Salt Lake City? And what's more, how in the world did they get the Berlin license to gene-tinker with the ocean life to let them live in the fresh water?"

Trader waited until Kidd paused in his tirade. Cautiously, the large man said, "Re-Naturalists do have a lot of money. And so does GAHSP, so I hear. What's your next project?

"And hand me that knife."

Kidd smiled at the obvious ploy, "Pardon me if I don't give out too much detail." He tossed the crude knife.

Trader grabbed it, and dropped it. "Ouch." He put a bloodied finger in his mouth. Then he picked the knife up by its leather handle to divide a wide chunk of dried meat.

"I'm just curious. I'm a lawyer when my annual permit runs out, and I'm always on the lookout for a new client. Does GAHSP need any more help? I could make you a good deal. I'll give you a full tour of the Backcountry instead of just taking you back to the Portal. All I'd ask is a recommendation to your legal department. What do you say?"

He handed Kidd part of the jerky.

Kidd appeared to consider his offer. "Well... I did come out here to do some serious thinking about the next project. It would be nice to have someone else do the worrying about where to set up camp, and where not to walk off the edge of a cliff."

Trader nodded, "It's done, then. I've got enough food for the both of us, and no one knows the Backcountry as well as I do. I'll take you places no one even knows exists. And, by the way, what is your next project?"

Kidd laughed. "Persistent, aren't you. But I guess it's okay."

He leaned forward. Trader did likewise.

"GAHSP has discovered a mothballed coal-fired electric generating plant, complete with smokestacks. We intend to re-activate it as a historical park."

Trader paled, and shook his head. "Never. You won't ever get permission for that. I don't buy into the Three Sins doctrine—especially now that they have gone violent. That group is just crazy, but their anti-tech message has made a lot of converts because people believe it. People messed up the environment, and God sent the supernova to set us straight. Then people tinkered with genes and God sent the Die-Off, and now people are tinkering with the planets, and God will send some new disaster that will put us back in our place.

"Smokestacks spewing gunk into the atmosphere is enough to get everyone up in arms. It'll never happen."

Kidd grinned, and said, "But, what if we build a tanstran dome around it—entirely seal it off from the outside air? It would have to be huge, maybe even bigger than the one on Ceres, because it would have to have enough oxygen inside to handle the furnaces. But when we're done, we will have the prototypical museum for the Techno age before the Star. With the electricity, we can run all kinds of other dirty industries, all inside.

"Then when people visit, they can see why we put all our heavy industries in space and worked so hard to clean up places like this. We need a museum like this! We can't just expect people to rely on cults like the Three Sins to keep humanity straight. People need to walk under dirty skies and smell the bad air for themselves."

Trader shook his head. "You think big, alright. But don't mention my name when they come to lynch you."

"Does that mean you don't want to do legal work for GAHSP?"

"I didn't say that!"

Chapter 2

ALEXANDRIA HABITAT, L4 CLUSTER

Bet recognized Mary Harris the instant she arrived at the clinic even though she looked entirely different. She wasn't swinging a pipe for one thing. For another she was dressed in gray work coveralls with a white cap low over her eyes. She had probably just come off her work shift.

Bet stopped dictating her log. "Yes. Can I help you?" The patient load had finally dropped off and she was trying to catch up on recordkeeping. Circuit Medical gave its doctors nearly total autonomy, but they demanded detailed records.

There were advantages of using the same computer year after year. Her portable lab was nothing more than a box with a chemical analysis unit that could work with samples much smaller than a single drop of blood, and a computer to drive it. Over time, it had learned her habits. It knew when she was talking to it and when she had patients. This time it noticed the change in her voice and automatically closed the windows where client details were visible. Years ago, when she first acquired it, she had to use keywords, then after time she'd gotten lazy, and it still kept up with her.

Mary Harris never quite locked eyes with her. She looked subdued. "Yes, I was told that you wanted to see me?"

Bet compared her with the wild-eyed fury she had been before, and turned her full efforts to making her patient feel at ease. She moved into the regular medical examination routine, bringing out the probes and checking her pulse and breathing. Mary gradually relaxed.

There were bruises, many more than Bet would have expected from her capture. Punitive bruises. The back of Bet's neck tickled. It was harder to force a smile when she finally asked, "I wanted to ask you some other questions."

Mary jerked her head, instantly tense. "No, I was told not to—"

"Nonsense, girl. You can talk about anything to me. I am a doctor."

"But Lady Fortuna said—"

Bet waved her hand and shook her head. "I don't care about Alexandria's rules. This is a doctor–patient thing, and it's been this way since long before space cities even existed. You can tell me anything, and I'm honor bound not to tell anyone what you said. I'm not interested in political secrets or anything like that.

"But I absolutely have to know what your problems are. What's troubling Mary Harris? You can tell me. I can't fix problems I don't know about. Did your husband do this?" She touched the bruise on her cheek.

"No! Jeff would never … It wasn't him!"

"Who was it?"

She looked down at her shoes and shook her head. "I promised."

Bet sighed. For some reason, she believed the girl. But how could she help?

Get closer. Bet relaxed the tension lines in her face. Making herself look any age was a skill she had perfected long ago. Subtly, she looked younger. She sat down beside her. She held the girl's hand, looked her in the eyes and said, "We can be friends. Tell me."

Mary's eyes welled at the edges as she gradually thawed. She looked down at the floor. "The beating was nothing. I broke the rules. I deserved it."

Bet didn't believe that, but the punishment was a side issue, really.

"Tell me, what's the real problem?"

There was a long silence, and Bet made sure her face was constant with expectation. Mary looked at her, and then down at her shoes again. Finally, she whispered, "I can't have babies. And now Jeff is looking for an outside-wife."

Bet leaned back. "And Jeff, Porto, Zon, and Bruno are all paying me so much attention because they think I could be an outside-wife for them?"

She nodded.

"And they want an outside-wife because their own wives can't have babies?"

Another nod.

Bet squeezed Mary's hand and tilted up her chin. She looked into Mary's eyes and said with a little laugh, "Well then, you can do me a big favor. I can't have babies either, and they are all just wasting their time. If you could spread that information around, I would be grateful!"

...

There was a blink on the door, and Bet went to deal with a middle-aged woman who complained of a sprained arm. Bet felt no evidence of it, but she treated the woman with a sonic and sent her on her way. The woman, Helva, seemed more interested in Mary, sitting on the bench, than with her own complaint.

Mary waited patiently. Bet suspected Helva just wanted to see if Mary was going to attack her again.

Bet closed the door when she left and sat down next to Mary.

"I think I know how you feel. I was a young bride once. I yearned to have children of my own. When I told my husband, it was ... unbearable to see the look in his eyes."

"Did he leave you?" Mary asked.

"No, he died." Bet ached to share more than she could, but it would do the girl no good to get into her own secrets. Mary could read her reluctance to talk, and was too timid to ask.

Bet changed the subject. "But let's see what your problem is. Some kinds of infertility are easily cured. I need to find out which kind has affected you."

Mary looked hopeless, "You can't help. We had other doctors, and they couldn't find anything."

"You've been examined before?"

"Oh, no. Not me, but they checked out my Aunt Elizabeth, back when she was young. I hoped that since my mother wasn't affected, that I would be okay, too."

Bet frowned. "This is widespread, then."

Mary put her hand to her mouth, "I don't know if I should say."

"Remember. Doctor–patient secrets. You have to tell me everything you know, or I might miss the one piece of the puzzle that would let me cure you. Aunt Elizabeth was infertile. Who else?"

Mary struggled to remember. Barrenness appeared to be a family shame as well as a social one. But each newborn was celebrated throughout the whole of Alexandria, and she knew every family.

"So, more than half of the couples are childless?"

"Oh, yes. Although when Lord—" She looked at the door, just to make sure it was closed. "When someone discovered that the men were fertile, that it was just the wives that couldn't have children, they started sending men out to serve on the transports, in hopes that they'd find outside-wives and bring them back here. It works, sort of, although Aunt Elizabeth has never forgiven Uncle Seth. I wasn't supposed to speak to my half-cousin Margaret either. When she was discovered to be barren a couple of years ago, I tried to comfort her.

"I wonder if I caught it from her?" She looked into Bet's eyes. "Can you catch … infertility by hugging someone?"

Bet put her arms around the girl. "No. I haven't ever heard of that happening, and I have heard about many medical problems. Don't worry that it's something you did. I have to examine you carefully, and then we'll have some idea of how to proceed."

…

She was grateful Mary was relatively unsophisticated about medical things. Bet's lab was much more powerful than the standard-issue one. Dozens of patients had complained when she tried to get the tissue and fluid samples necessary to make a good bio-assay and genetic analysis. She trained herself never to say the word "genetic", or any of the other taboo words like, "hereditary", or "inheritance". Too many families had ancestors caught in the Die-Off—when the someone developed a final "cure" for genetically altered life.

Bet remembered that time, especially during the witch-hunts, which put altered humans and genetic engineers equally at risk.

Bet knew that her possession of a lab that could do genetic sequencing would get her killed if it were ever found out. But many lives had been saved with her late-night proscribed labwork, and she knew she would never give it up.

When Mary left, with reassurances that her secrets would remain protected, Bet put aside her virus investigation routines and started analysis on the new problem.

What kind of infertility plague would work as described? And how many generations had it been growing in the Alexandrians? If she interpreted

Mary's family history correctly, it would leave the city completely infertile within another two or three generations. The Alexandrians as a people would be wiped out.

CERES BEACH, CERES, L4 CLUSTER

Mason trudged slightly behind Cinca, carrying both of their swim gear through the long curved tunnel to the Ocean. She showed an exaggerated sway in the reduced gravitational area. Ceres, like all of the cities in the Lagrangian zones, had large reservoirs of water. But unlike the constructed habitats that had been put into a slow spin to provide artificial gravity, Ceres had been a large asteroid—nearly nine hundred kilometers in diameter. Its own gravity had formed it into a sphere. Spinning was out of the question—it would tear the planetoid apart. Instead, the occupied zone of the city used an array of small tractor projectors beneath the dome, cycling at a high rate, to simulate Earth's attraction.

But out at the edge, where a huge cavern blasted long ago now held liquid water, there was only fringe coverage from the tractor beams. The planetoid supplied only three percent Earth-standard native gravity. He was constantly in danger of slipping on his own feet. Still, he liked to watch the easy way Cinca moved.

She'd been quick to sense his anger after the unknown ship had been taken away from him. When he had gone to her restaurant and splurged too much on bitter coffee, she badgered him until he told her the whole story.

. . .

"So these Swiss are out to get you because your father was killed?"

He shook his head. "No. It's just that the Three Sins people made him into a martyr. When the John Henry exploded and Earth had the comet storm, he was the first one to die. He was caught in the original beam while herding comets to Luna. It was his comets that were yanked toward Earth by the rogue beam. Then, when his best friend turned against the Project and joined with the Uruguayan rebels, blaming Dad's death on sloppy Project management, there were people here in Prime that needed someone to blame. Paul was out of their reach, protected by the rebels, but I was knocking at their doorstep, asking to join the Project to complete my father's work."

Cinca's wide black eyes had tugged more out of him than he had intended to tell anyone.

"Why did they even accept you, if they didn't trust you?"

He shrugged; it was a question he'd struggled with too many nights. "Prime needed a hero. Since Paul Lin had done the most to keep the comet storm from being a catastrophic, genocidal killer, he was their first choice, but he turned against them. Prime then latched onto my story—father killed doing his duty, mother injured in the tidal waves, but there I was, ready to support the Project. They had to welcome me in for public relations, but they never trusted me."

"So they kept you close and powerless." She was able to speak the contempt he felt, but could never really express. He nodded.

"You'll show them! I know you will."

...

A dozen people rested on the darkened shore, but there was evidence of more people out in the water. Ceres Beach was a tourist attraction for very rich scuba divers from Earth. Even before Ceres was moved into Earth orbit, a spherical cavity several kilometers in diameter had been blasted out. Later, tame comets, really fragments of shattered Hyperion, were landed with precision in the opening, and then the gap was roofed with a tanstran dome.

Once the water was melted with mirrors concentrating sunlight through the dome, it was seeded with the same cultured algae that were being currently broadcast into the swirling atmosphere of Luna. Before too long the mixture was tamed and the excess ammonia converted into a biological sludge down at the bottom of the reservoir. By the time Mason arrived at Prime, the Ocean was linked to the city, providing heat, humidity and gas balance to the internal atmosphere.

He set their gear down onto the fine-grained rubble next to the slowly lapping waves and took their tanks over to the compressor concession. Cinca spread out a towel and casually slipped out of her robe. He had to force himself to keep from staring.

He had grown up in Rio, before the beaches had been wrecked by the Wrath of John Henry. He remembered more skin from those days than he'd seen since, and at heart, he felt like a teenage boy when it came to pretty girls—a timid teenage boy.

Prime wasn't the best place for a young man to develop socially—not if he was intent on training for a controller spot in the center of the Eye. He had rigorously avoided girls into his mid-twenties, and by that time, he'd become a monk. These days, the idea of a girl being interested in him seemed too unreal to consider.

...

"Sunlight is less than ten minutes away. I've got a one-hour charge in the tanks," he said, "if I can keep from panting." He clamped his mouth shut.

Cinca flashed a shocked smile. "Don't tell me that was a compliment! I'll have to change my whole impression of you." She slipped the tanks over her skinsuit and fastened the connectors easily.

He couldn't come up with a response to that. The flirtation had come out on its own. He gratefully put the mouthpiece in and gestured toward the water.

Timing the entry was important. The waves were steep and leisurely, but they could still push you up against the rocks. Ceres was large enough and close enough that many of the habitats of the L4 cluster pushed against it with pressor beams to maintain their own orbital stability—and the Ocean was the only place on Ceres that sloshed. Surface swimming was nearly impossible. They pushed in through the surface of the water.

It was dark, and he snapped on his headlamp. A moment later, he turned it off again as the concentrated sunlight entered through the dome above. He blinked his eyes. They had planned to get under the surface early and beat the crowd that always arrived when the monthly sunlight illuminated the deep waters.

He waited while his breathing settled down. The view through the bright, crystal-clear water always fascinated him. He was only a few meters from the drop-off. The beach was a shelf of rock, secured with supporting metal girders, hanging over the edge of the infinite deep.

Cinca grabbed his hand as they drifted out past the edge. A school of fresh-water-adapted parrotfish drifted below them, a splash of blue against the gray rocks.

He could hear the snapping sound of their beaks as they munched on the algae on the rocks, and once again, he felt at home. Here, in the sun-warmed water, everything was like it had been when he was a boy. Down below the surface, it was no different than when he was on Earth. He kicked his flippers and pulled her deeper.

. . .

They pulled themselves out of the water with their tanks almost dry and exhausted by the swim. Cinca carried a net with several crystals she had chopped from the side of the wall. Neither of them knew enough mineralogy to identify them, but they were pretty.

"Thank God for no gravity," she said, as they shook the thick, clinging water from their suits.

"Here, let me take that." He lifted the tanks off her back and fitted them into their carrying harness. He secured his own and turned back to her.

She was drying her bare breasts with a towel; her dark eyes seemed to drill into his head. He turned away, his heart hammering in his chest.

She tossed a towel at him. "You had better dry off."

He nodded, sneaking a peak back at her a minute later as he dried his hair. She was back in her robe.

"Aren't you going to change?"

He shook his head. "I'm not that cold."

. . .

Cinca left him at the lockers. His Blue transit rail came before her Red, so she watched him looking back at her in the window as he left.

"Just a big puppy dog." She laughed. When he was out of sight, she walked back to the row of public comm boxes closed with soundproof hoods and mumbled a long string of digits.

This is my big break. She'd been wasting her time on this assignment for nearly a year. And now, a Controller who knew about the rogue ship just dropped into her lap.

The comm chimed a connection and she spoke into the blank screen. "Boron reporting. I may have the smoker we are looking for. William Mason, disaffected Controller. Check his history, especially at the time of the Wrath. This is the one who handled initial contact on Hydra. I will be putting him on a short leash. I hope to have him hooked by deadline."

The call ended with nothing more than a click to acknowledge that her report had been received.

Her lips were a tight line. *They won't be able to ignore me much longer.* She'd gambled everything on this assignment. It'd gotten her out of Constantine. No more the expendable courier carrying drug pouches. No more the complimentary girlfriend for visiting businessmen. *No more jerks.*

She'd hoped for more from the Three Sins fanatics, but in some ways they were just like the tribes where she grew up. At least now, there was a chance she could swing some weight of her own. Her invisible, and often silent, boss seemed only interested in what she could do to the Project, not what she could do to him.

The rail line stretching down the tunnel toward Prime drew her eye. She smiled again. Mason was different from the other men she'd known. She could almost feel like a little girl around him.

No, that isn't right. Her childhood had been a nightmare. She could barely remember it, and she tried hard to block it when it came back in her nightmares.

The red colored car came blooming out of the tunnel, and she shook off the fruitless thinking. She had a job to do.

ROCKIES BACKCOUNTRY PRESERVE, NORTH AMERICA, EARTH

Kidd watched Trader coming back with more firewood and mumbled, "Hurry." He had his index finger in his ear to conduct the sound waves from the hidden transducer, and the computer's voice sped up in response.

There was an unusual report from one of his agents on the Pacific coast, something he'd almost given up hope on. He'd have to hurry the smuggler up.

Trader settled down by the fire, and Kidd said, "I probably need to get back to the Portal."

"You don't like my company?"

Kidd shook his head. "It's not that. The Backcountry is fine … it just makes me too lazy. You promised me places no one has seen before. I need something exciting, or I need to get back to the office."

"Well, we aren't too far from Virgin Valley. We could set up camp there."

Kidd looked up, with a puzzled expression, "Never heard of it."

Faking ignorance was one of his most useful survival skills. In actuality, he had been at this very campground several times before, back before the highway was ripped out, back when the little valley contained the old mining town of Silverton. Now, all that was left was an alpine meadow carpeted with yellow flowers.

Trader grinned. "It's a popular place with the single women campers. One gal hiked out there a few years back and met up with the mountain man of her dreams. The story spread. You can just about always find some fem waiting for a real man to come along and play out her fantasies. They know it's only some advertising executive under those buckskins—someone who has to get back to his grind in a few days, but you both pretend and have a little fun."

Kidd grimaced. "I'm not that good an actor. Women see right through me," he lied, then gave an elaborate sigh. "Not this trip. Anything else?"

Trader frowned, and chewed on the edge of his beard. Kidd was satisfied. He would break soon enough.

· · ·

"You know," Trader smiled, continuing his fourth tall tale of the night, "they never noticed that the new bag was smaller inside than the last time they'd done a full check. I'm just lucky they quit doing X-rays."

Kidd nodded. "I noticed that. I wonder why?" He poked at the fire. The night sky was crystal clear above, and it felt like the cold of space was draining the heat from him.

Trader shrugged. "It wasn't cost effective, I guess. People try to smuggle things like warm synthetic socks, or something electronic, like a pathfinder. Rangers have to do an eyeball search for things like that anyway. It's not at all like the shuttle lines where they have to worry about bombs and guns."

"How do you get your stock inside? I've seen you trade more than would fit into the false bottoms of your saddlebags. I was surprised as that dentist we met when you produced a toothbrush. And these sandals you sold me." He wiggled his toes. "They aren't even contraband. How do you make a profit on things like that?"

Trader showed teeth. "You won't tell me where your smokestacks are hiding. Surely you can't expect me to spill all of my secrets."

Kidd just raised an eyelid. Trader loved to brag more than he liked skinning a sucker.

Trader gave a short laugh, and coughed. "Okay, I guess I have enough dirt on you that I won't have to worry.

"It was a few years ago—maybe three. I'd been doing the Trader gig for a couple of years and I was seeing how profitable it was for making contacts for my legal business. You can't imagine how useful it is to have a shared dirty secret when you are negotiating a big contract.

"Anyway, I arranged for a Meteor-Pak to come down … somewhere near here. That, plus an abandoned hunting lodge that somehow missed being discovered by the work crews, supplies me with a lot of my stock. If times are tight, I don't even have to bring anything in."

Kidd made admiring noises, Meteor-Paks weren't cheap. "I wish I could manage to spend more time out here. If it weren't flatly impossible to live out here full time, I'd consider giving up the whole GAHSP job and find a nice little valley."

"Umm."

Kidd looked expectantly as Trader struggled with his ego. All he had to do was watch.

"Well … it isn't totally impossible."

Kidd sneered. "Now this, I don't believe! You may be an expert in these woods, but I've had to manage work crews in restricted lands before. I know you can't get around time limits for backcountry access. I used political pull and even bribes up in Montana to try to get my men permits for more than the one-month work visa. Rangers may let some things slip by, but they're ruthless in keeping people to their visit schedule."

Trader kept his silence for a moment. He looked at Kidd, then off into the distance, as he thought about how to respond. Finally, he said, "I don't lie to you, GAHSP-man. I like you. Have I tried to scam you these past few days? I'm saying there are people living in these mountains."

Kidd said nothing. The skeptical look on his face didn't change. He had rarely challenged the tales Trader told, but he did know how the man would react.

"Okay." Trader got angrily to his feet, "Let's get moving. I'll take you there!"

Chapter 3

ALEXANDRIA HABITAT, L4 CLUSTER

Bet stared at Mary's genetic map, feeling echoes from long ago, when she'd stared at her own. She blinked, glanced over at the locked door, and then forced herself to concentrate on the job at hand.

The Die-Off had left her with life-long habits. She had been a young girl then, when her parents—the people she thought were her parents—abandoned her. Then came the chaos and the fear, hiding out from the witch-hunts.

To be different was dangerous. People with engineered genes were suspect, people to be avoided, people to be eliminated.

She must have been in her early teens when she realized she was *very* different. *There's no one like me.*

Enough of that! Privacy was in short supply. She had to make the most of the work time she had, rather than feeling sorry for herself. "Filter the map against the library, and remove all classic genes."

The detailed markup screen started dissolving away, leaving only the excess; unknown genes and random stretches of non-coding DNA.

"Remove all DNA patterns logged prior to the establishment of this station." That ought to get her down to reasonable candidates.

There was still a respectable list of DNA code sequences. It was as she suspected. Several generations living in a space habitat would have added quite a few mutations to its gene pool. No matter what the shielding, it wasn't as good as Earth's atmosphere. And with isolation, genes could be preserved and reinforced by inbreeding. Most of these mutations would be harmless, but if she could locate which gene had been altered enough to affect reproduction, she could at least guess which enzymes could be changed with drugs or diet to alleviate the problem.

"Re-run the filters against the remaining list, sort it by the number of mutations necessary to match."

This took a little longer, but it was still so much faster than it had taken when she had first learned the procedure, over a hundred and fifty years ago. The secretive Gnomes who designed the world's computers deserved everything they charged, in Bet's opinion.

The screen flashed, displaying the new list.

Most of the items on the list were non-coding DNA, or historically known genes with only a single mutation responsible for the difference.

The last one was colored yellow in contrast with all the others. "NO MATCH" it said.

"Who are you?" she asked of the big glaring exception.

The unknown gene sequence was huge, and the filters had rejected it entirely. This wasn't a mutation. It was a deliberately engineered gene.

Bet's hand snapped to shade the screen. "Off!"

She was out of her chair, standing on the other side of the room before she stopped to compose herself.

You were right to be worried, Lady Fortuna. If this was the culprit, and if it was indeed widespread among the Alexandrians, then that would make the whole city a proscribed gene pool. One hint to the outside world and the World Court would have a confinement team here instantly. The Alexandrians would lose all rights to their own future, and if history was any guide, all of them not already sterile would quickly be made so. No one would be killed, at least not outright, but sterilized and quarantined, there would be no more generations carrying this frightening biological code.

And they would find me too. She knew how the procedure worked. Everyone would be checked, just to make sure.

For her own safety, she should just wipe the code from the lab's memory and forget what she had seen. Other doctors had tried to help the Alexandrians. Surely that was enough.

. . .

From a century and a half before, Glenn's eyes haunted her. She'd been forty-five years old and barely looked fifteen when she found the man she would risk her life to love. Teenage hormones were overpowering no matter when in life they expressed themselves. She married him a year later and told him her true age on her honeymoon.

"It's okay Liz, I've been feeling guilty about robbing the cradle. So what if I'm the youngster now. That doesn't change anything between us."

At first, the only difference it made in their lives was that he became her partner in conspiracy, helping her look older with makeup and clothes. But he liked her young in bed.

After the first five years, they started trying for a child. After a frustrating time, it was clear that there was something wrong, something they couldn't risk bringing to a doctor.

By their twentieth anniversary, she grew very concerned about how old and tired and resigned Glenn had become. He no longer talked about children, but she saw the look in his eyes when he saw them. She promised herself that she would find the cause of her infertility and fix it.

She was a refugee from mainstream humanity, and to be a successful refugee demanded certain skills. It certainly would have been cheaper to send a sample of her tissue to one of the black-market geneticists still advertising on the Net, but that would have been too great a risk. She had to learn how to do it herself.

Glenn was eager to help. Only later did she recognize it as a warning sign.

There were only a few places where genetic sequencers were still used. One was in Geneva, where the World Court held its tight grip on all genetic engineering, the legacy of winning King Thomas's War. Another was in Lyon, where the only licensed manufacturing site for sequencers was located. The Net, anonymous as ever, advertised many illegal services, but she needed the hardware, and that was tightly controlled.

They moved to Lyon and found a small home overlooking the Rhone river. Glenn got a job booking traveling entertainers into the ancient Roman amphitheater, and she got a job sweeping the floors at the factory. It took several months, but one late night, she had access to one of the new machines for several hours. She put in her tissue sample and waited.

The look on Glenn's face when she told him what she found was burned into her soul. He'd taken a step back in shock, and that gap between them never closed again.

He claimed it made no difference, but she knew better. He had shared a life and a bed with a woman whose genes had been created in a lab. He was childless because of her, and there was nothing that could be done to change it.

Their sex life dwindled over time to nothing. The idea of adoption came and went. Glenn lost interest in her and their home life. She was careful to avoid him when he'd been out drinking. One night, after too much wine, he asked her what the coliseum was like when she was a child. He grumbled that her father was a microscope and her mother a petri dish.

He apologized the next day, but the night had left scars in her memory. He never struck her, but the words hurt deeper.

Sober, he was a man she still loved, but when he died in a cable-car accident three years later, she felt relief mixed with her tears. She never married again.

. . .

Bet stared at the lab, sitting dark on the shelf. Could she help Mary Harris? It was only one gene location, potentially something that could be repaired. What would her life with Glenn have been like if someone could've come to her aid with a magic wand to make her normal?

I chose the medical profession to help people. That's the only mark I'll ever leave on the world. I can help her. Maybe I'm the only person in all of humanity that can.

She sat down in front of the lab and whispered it back on. It was risky, and she'd have to be careful, but she had to try.

ARBORETUM, CERES, L4 CLUSTER

"Tell me about your mystery spaceship," Cinca asked, as they walked hand in hand through the Arboretum.

Mason looked up through the branches. This was not a place he frequented during the daytime, and it'd been a long time since he'd been in a real forest. "I don't know a lot. I know it's a ship. I shook it with a TP beam and it has to be partly hollow, but not so hollow as an abandoned fuel tank."

He shook his head in annoyance. "If I had known they were going to take it away from me, I'd have spent more time on it. I could've delayed a few hours, anyway. I could've gotten a lot better idea of what it was.

"But I was all anxious to prove how good I was, and threw away the opportunity just so I could look prompt and efficient. There are times I hate politics!"

Cinca smiled up at him, "You're better than they are. What did they do with it once they kicked you out?"

He shrugged. "I don't have a need to know, so it isn't in my databank, but if experience is any guide, they probably shoved it over into a low-intensity beam, like the solar flare screen, and in time it will probably be shoved out of the solar system."

He laughed. "I mentioned it to Mrs. Pearce, the lady who runs the place I live, and she thinks it's aliens."

"Aliens, like non-human?" Cinca laughed.

"Right. And what's more, she claims to have seen an alien spacecraft when she was young. She was a single-ship pilot when they surveyed the Jovian system."

"And how come I've never heard about it?"

Mason grinned. "She was alone when she saw it, and let a beam push it back out of the system."

"Why?"

He shrugged. "I asked that. She replied that we need to leave the dead alone."

"Well, I want you to get your ship back, and then if you find out it's not one of ours, be sure to tell me about it."

He found a bench and settled himself with a view to Luna. "It'll never happen."

She settled beside him, touching. "I think you could. You're just timid, and people push you around."

Mason gave a long sigh. She was right, and there wasn't anything he could do about it. He had made the commitment to work for the Project, to fulfill his father's dream. If it weren't for human pettiness in the mix, he could be content with that.

"Mason? What would it take to get the ship assigned to you again?"

He looked at her beside him on the bench. She seemed serious.

"I wouldn't worry about it. Something else will come up eventually."

She shook her head. "No. Let's change it now, while you still have a sharp mind. Don't let them keep you down in the mud until you are too tired to do anything but train the youngsters fresh up from Earth. You know that's what they'll do.

"Come on. Tell me what you really want to do, and I'll help you do it."

Mason was aware of a thud in his chest, his heartbeat kicking in loud enough to feel. Did he even want to buck the system? Or was he already worn out?

He looked up at Luna. The surrounding trees blocked most of the lights of the city and let the new world shine clearly through the dome. Beneath those clouds, he could still imagine the canal.

Yes, he did want to make a difference.

"When I was a child," he began, "my father was the man who created geoscaping. He was a comet man, herding hundreds of comets in from the Glitter Ring to impact Luna. It was all part of the process to build up the atmosphere and to assist the beams in breaking the tidal lock. He was just one of many doing the same thing.

"But he was the only one who realized what a tool he had in his hands! He used those impacts to carve landforms that people would use once the atmosphere and the oceans were completed." He looked into her eyes and saw that she understood what he was saying.

"My father's last project was a canal that would connect the isolated sea of Mare Marginis with the larger ocean of Mare Fecunditatis. He was almost done when the John Henry exploded. The comets that would have completed his canal became the Wrath. That's how it was left, the greatest canal in human history blocked by a couple of kilometers of rock. I went to work for the Project so that I could finish his job."

"Wow." Cinca murmured.

He remembered that night. He stood on a hill in the Amazon basin, overlooking the rampaging Xingu river, its banks overflowing from the storms that the comet impact had created. Through a break in the clouds, he'd seen the remains of his father's comet train stitch a line of impact flares across the face of the moon. His father's ship and his mortal remains must have impacted unnoticed that same night. His father had died for the Project.

"To finish my father's canal, I knew I had to be a Controller with TP beam authority, with permission from the Lunar Project Board. I've been trained for nearly ten years, and only once was I given beam authority, for nearly five hours, before it was taken back. My petitions for someone, anyone, to impact a mass on the blockage have been silently ignored.

"My father did more for the science of terraforming and geoscaping than any one of those idiots on the Board, but no one will do anything to see his project completed!"

Cinca said, "They want to keep him from being honored. They're afraid of the Three Sins."

He nodded. His chest was tight. Old anger was no less painful for being old.

"Well, then." She reached over and kissed his unresponsive cheek. "We'll just have to *make* them do it."

ROCKIES BACKCOUNTRY PRESERVE, NORTH AMERICA, EARTH

Kidd fingered his collar as Trader waded up to his hips in the deceptively deep waters of a beaver pond and spread a white cloth on top of the mound in the middle.

It'd taken two days. Trader had taken them over two passes and finally led them up a twisty creek. As Trader waded back, Kidd asked, "Now what?"

"We wait." He climbed out of the water, panting. "That's cold!"

They waited hours, while Trader paced back and forth. Kidd watched the birds and thought. He fought against looking at his wrist. Trader was right. It was a bad habit.

The first sign was a bird call. Kidd might have missed it if he hadn't been watching the antics of a stellar jay that accidentally landed in the same tree being used by a sharp-shinned hawk.

Trader had been waiting for that call. Worry on his face slipped away, to be replaced by his salesman smile. He pointed to the edge of a stand of aspens. "He's coming."

The newcomer was the picture of a mountain man. His long beard and worn-soft leather clothes made even Trader look like a camper fresh from the portal. He didn't smile. Kidd noticed that he made no noise at all as he walked, even when he obviously wasn't hiding from them.

Trader called, "Hello, Fred."

The man mumbled, "'Lo, Trader. Why'd you bring 'm?" He looked Kidd over with a critical eye.

"He's okay," Trader said. "This is Alex Kidd. He's been traveling with me for a few days."

"Told you not to bring anyone else here! You promised us," protested the man.

Trader dropped his voice and they spoke a few minutes. Kidd couldn't hear, but he could guess the content. After a bit, they turned to him. The mountain man looked sullen, but resigned to the situation. Kidd carefully displayed his disinterest in their conversation, but inside he was on fire. Fred had said "promised *us*"—he wasn't alone out here. Kidd had to see the others.

The frown finally eased off the man's face and he allowed Trader to introduce him. "This is Fred Gearson. He used to be a tool and die maker. Now he makes the best leather sandals in North America."

With Fred leading the way, they hiked a steep path up the side of the valley until a turn in the creek exposed a man-high square hole in the rock.

Fred gestured, "Used to be a mine, back in the 1800s. I found the old vein. Gold, but poor pickings. The restoration people had plugged the opening. Took me some time to clear it, without tools."

Kidd commented, "I admire your patience."

Fred gave a brief laugh. "No patience at all, I was freezing to death at the time."

Suddenly, there was a woman, appearing in the light from the hidden darkness within. Her buckskin dress was as worn as Fred's, but it was stained decoratively across the neckline in red. Her bright smile was perfectly framed by a head of long black hair.

"Oh Fred, I don't mind visitors, but did you have to bring Trader along, too?"

"Be kind, Clara," Fred said. "I already cussed him out a while ago."

Trader nodded to the two, "Alex Kidd, allow me to introduce Fred and Clara Gearson, permanent residents of the restricted lands."

From inside the dark, came a high-pitched voice, "Hey, don't forget me!"

A miniature version of Clara Gearson danced out, complete with the bright smile and the long dark hair. Kidd's head snapped around to watch. He fingered his collar.

Fred Gearson had a forbidding scowl for his daughter, marred by a corner of his mouth that wanted to twist it into a grin. He took a deep breath and introduced her, "This is Bonnie Gearson, who was supposed to stay out of sight. She's seven."

Kidd had eyes for the girl only. "I'm charmed, Bonnie. And I am glad you came out to meet us."

She giggled and moved to snuggle up against her mother's side. Both parents' eyes were on him. He broke off his examination of the girl with an effort, and addressed them, "Trader told me there were people living here. I badgered him into bringing me here to meet you. I have to hear your story!"

. . .

A well-ventilated campfire provided the illumination as they ate. Over a long meal of roast elk meat garnished with mint and a hundred tiny little strawberries the size of peas, they told him their tale.

Fred Gearson and Clara Weldon were losers on the outside. They dismissed that part of their lives with barely a word. Fred staged his own death one lonely vacation—a wintertime avalanche. The rangers had worked hard to find his remains, but all they could come up with were scraps of his clothing, mixed with his smashed backpack. The rules of the restricted lands made them content to find even that. Supposedly, there was nothing anyone, not even a ranger, could bring in that would leave any trace. Campers wore uncured leathers. They cut their food with stone knives. Even Kidd's teapot was unglazed pottery. So, the tools the rangers could use to find the body were limited. Fred Gearson was declared dead. Everyone was happy.

Clara Weldon was a Virgin Valley dropout. She had come to the backcountry for romance, but the terms she used for the two men who'd found her in Virgin Valley caught her a scold from her husband for talking that way at the dinner table. After her experience there, she had struck out on her own, and found her mountain man in truth.

"That was before I learned to walk quietly," Fred explained.

"You can believe that!" said Clara. "With all the noise, I thought it was a bear or something when he knocked loose some rocks on the hillside. I finally got up enough nerve and tracked him down."

"Tracked me and bagged me."

Clara shook her head sadly. "I should have kept him in the bag. I haven't yet trained him to keep his feet off the table."

Fred Gearson looked at his deerhide boots, as if surprised that they had propped themselves up there while he wasn't looking, and then sheepishly eased them down.

Kidd avidly listened to their tale, but more than half the time his eyes were on the little girl—watching how she reacted to her parents' antics.

Fred Gearson picked up the narrative, "By the time Clara decided she'd found her life's ambition in reforming me, I knew we had a problem. I was able to vanish in a snow slide, but she'd come in during August. There was hardly a snowbank left that was big enough to hide under. We had to come up with some other death."

Clara spoke, "So I got eaten by a bear."

Fred nodded, "We set her up a campsite a couple of days walk from here and left enough food out to attract a bear."

"We got a pretty, cinnamon-colored fellow," she added. "He really liked molasses."

Fred continued, "We left some strategically placed traces of Clara's blood around in the remains of the camp. And not three days after Clara's permit lapsed, a party of rangers rode up and found the camp. We did a good job—they didn't even hunt for the body."

Clara took over, "We did too good of a job! That cinnamon fellow liked that molasses and got it into his head that if he followed my smell, he might get some more."

"Took to following me around, too." Fred shuddered. "I didn't like that. We finally had to kill 'm. That was a job! No guns, of course. I rigged a deadfall. Clara was bait." He grinned at her.

"And we ate him!" Clara looked immensely pleased with herself. "I'm the only lady you're likely to find that ate the bear that ate her." Fred and Trader laughed lightly at what must have been an old joke to them. Kidd laughed big, but with part of his attention, he watched the child's tolerant amusement. For a child, she acted strangely. All her seven years had been spent with no company other than her parents. She had never seen another child. In some ways, she acted very much like a tiny adult.

After the meal, Trader and Fred retired to a storeroom in the mine where the Gearsons stocked the leather goods they made for trade. Kidd listened in for a few minutes, then drifted back to the table and offered Clara some help with her clean-up chores.

Clara watched carefully as he washed the first couple of dishes. They were unglazed pottery, like his teapot, but they were dishes and she had no desire to have a clumsy male break anything.

Kidd made a mental note that Trader must have been using the pottery as trade goods with the Gearsons. But his mind was on something else.

"Bonnie is a pretty girl," he commented to the mother after the youngster was sent off to gather some kindling wood.

Clara Gearson's face slowly flickered into a smile. She compressed her lips in thought, then said, "I think so, too." She looked at Kidd's face, which was cheerfully bland.

Kidd probed again, "She looks a lot like you. Fred is a lucky man. Bonnie will steal some hearts when she gets a little older."

That did it. Clara's smile dropped and she turned her face to the serious business of arranging her bowls on the bench against the wall.

Kidd appeared not to notice, but the evidence was clear. The mother, at least, was worried about the girl's future. Clara Gearson had given up the world for love, but what could her daughter look forward to?

He finished his work on the last dish and handed it to her. He commented, reflectively, "Bonnie reminds me of my niece Jennie. I guess I haven't seen her in three or four years. I used to send her presents. She was the first child of my sister, and for several years, she was the closest thing I had to a child of my own." He chuckled, "Not that I was able to visit her more than a couple of days a year, but she was special to me. I love children. My biggest regret about my job is that I've never had time to settle down and make a family of my own." He gave Clara a sad, wistful smile. "You and Fred have something very special—do you know that?"

Clara's eyes crinkled at the edges, showing tiny specks of light from the highly illegal oil-wick lamp on the bench. She nodded, "We know it."

Kidd stood quietly for a few breaths, then hesitantly asked, "Do you mind if I go help Bonnie gather that firewood?"

Clara smiled and said, "Okay. I'm sure she has been aching to talk to you anyhow."

Kidd nodded his thanks and eased his way out of the kitchen nook. His face hardened in thought. Around the corner, he grabbed up his pack and quick-stepped down the dark mine tunnel to the entrance.

The sun was behind the western mountain peak, but it was still an hour or more before darkness. He squinted against the light as he searched the slopes for his quarry—one little girl.

The foot trail led down toward the creek. He moved quickly, keeping his eyes open. As it was, he almost missed her.

She moved lightly, silently, on a higher trail, carrying an armload of sticks. Kidd was aware he'd never heard her footstep. She was growing up with skills her parents had struggled hard to learn. He took a deep breath, nerving himself for what he had to do.

He waved and climbed up to her. "Hello, can I help you with those?"

She dimpled and shook her head. In spite of her smile, she kept her distance—a little afraid of the stranger. He was some new kind of wild animal.

Kidd judged his chances. This ground was steep and rocky, like the place where he'd staged his fall for Trader. She was probably as sure-footed as a big-horned sheep.

"Well," he asked, in his polite-to-children voice, "will you take a few minutes to talk to me? Your mother said I could."

"Okay." She smiled and propped the stack against a rock so they were not likely to tumble down the slope.

"I've been wanting to ask you—do you have a middle name?" When she looked puzzled, he explained, "My full name is Alexander Foster Kidd. Do you have a name between Bonnie and Gearson?"

She shook her head and giggled, "That's funny. Trader has one name. I have two. And you have three. That's silly. Why do you have so many names?"

Kidd eased over and sat down on a large, flat rock. It put her at ease. He answered, "Oh, there are so many people where I came from that you had to have three names just to know who you were. It's better here. One name is good enough around here. Everyone knows Bonnie."

She sat down where she stood and wrapped her arms around her knees. Earnestly, she asked, "Is it scary, where you come from? Momma said it's scary over the mountains. It made her cry a lot. Daddy doesn't talk about it."

Kidd tried to put on a smile, but it didn't hold. "Yes, it is scary outside. I cry sometimes, too. If I had a nice family here like you do, I don't think

I would go back."

Bonnie's mouth pouted in quick sympathy. She asked, "But don't you have a lot of friends? Trader says he has a lot a friends outside. I would like some friends."

Kidd gave her a genuine smile, "Don't worry. I'm sure you'll find some friends."

Bonnie didn't appear cheered. Kidd glanced at the single patch of sunlight on the far peak. He hesitated, but there wasn't a lot of time. He had to make his move.

He got to his feet. He quickly reached out for Bonnie's arm. "Come on," he said. "Let me help you." He got a firm grip on her arm and suddenly, his foot "slipped" out from under him. The slope was steep and they both tumbled over. His firm grip pulled her off her feet. He had his eye on a sharp, splintered boulder. He forced her in that direction. For a brief second, there was a tumbling confusion, then a sickeningly soft thud as Bonnie hit.

Chapter 4

ALEXANDRIA HABITAT, L4 CLUSTER

Bet checked the blood samples one by one. She wished she had more, but most of her patients were conditioned against allowing it.

"What kinds of bugs do you have?" she asked of the lab. This one was from Mary's husband Jeff. The results were quick and exactly as she had suspected.

Three out of four Alexandrians, male or female, had the engineered gene and all of the affected had a free-floating loop of genetic material in their blood, more of a plasmid than a virus, that transported the gene. It was common in bacteria, but this was different and it readily interacted with human chromosomes.

Jeff, who had a sterile sister, fit the model. However, Patricia Harris, a cousin of Jeff, had the plasmid, but not the altered gene. She was pregnant with her third child. Her daughter Gem, the second child, was altered. Her first child, young Peter was clear.

It was insidious. Bet suspected it was sexually transmitted. A person contracting the plasmid would not be affected in their lifetime, but their children would be. One indiscretion could change them. Either Patricia or her husband could have caused it. Some time after her first child, they had the change, and then Gem was born sterile. With such a long latency between the infection and the symptom, she was not surprised the Alexandrians had missed the pattern.

The lab was working hard in the background running simulations of the sterility gene. She had to find out how it did its damage if she were to have any chance of reversing the symptoms. She wished it would hurry up. There was more work for it to do.

There was another problem—one she had been working on before she came here. In Jeff's sample, and in fact in every person's sample, there was an unknown virus. She felt very uneasy about it. Her last posting hadn't given her any motive to do this kind of analysis, but at the one before that, a metal separation plant, she had seen the same virus.

Then, she'd chalked it up as a simple cold variant. It hadn't really caused any problems there other than a mild cough, even though over half of those patients had it.

I'm just paranoid.

Still—the lab reported that Alexandria's version of the virus wasn't quite the same. It had changed, and the lab declined to call it a simple mutation. It needed serious analysis too, but the sterility problem was her first priority.

. . .

Mary Harris was wide-eyed as Dr. Bet explained the procedure.

"There will be a little blood, and some soreness for a day or so."

"And then I can have babies?"

Bet spoke carefully, "Maybe. I think so. But this is not something I've done before, and it's only a possibility. You will have to make the decision."

Mary nodded. Then after a few seconds, she laughed.

"Sorry! It just reminded me of what my Mother warned me about sex, right before I got married." Then her face dropped. "And she was wrong, wasn't she?"

Bet patted her hand. "I can't give you any guarantees."

She nodded, "But if it does work—then I will be cured?"

"No. I'm sorry Mary, but this isn't a cure. It is a treatment. Even if you do bear a child, any daughter of yours will be barren unless she has the treatment, too."

Mary stared past Bet at the featureless wall. "A daughter," she whispered.

She straightened up. "I'm ready. What will I need to do?"

Bet stood up. "Get undressed and lie down on the bench." She turned to her sanitizer and realized her hands were shaking as she picked out the tools she would need for the minor surgery.

I want to see it. I want to see the twisted little engineered thing. How could anyone be so evil?

The lab's detailed analysis of the sterility gene had spelled out exactly how it did its work, building a tiny ducted gland into the female embryo that would shift the grown woman's hormonal balance out of the fertile range.

What kind of a person could hate an entire people so much?

...

Lady Fortuna arrived at her doorstep less than ten hours after the surgery. Her eyes were steely.

"I have notified the Circuit Medical Administration that you have completed your job here. There is a freighter taking on a shipment right now. I want you gone when they leave in the morning."

Bet nodded calmly. She'd sworn Mary to secrecy, but she had not honestly expected her to keep her mouth shut.

Oh, well. It's not the first time I've been kicked out.

"I take it you are not happy with my medical service."

The Mayor struggled to find the right words for a few seconds, then said, "How could you? How could you give little Mary such false hopes? She would have had the whole place in an uproar if I hadn't put the fear of God into her."

"Has she complained about me?" Bet asked.

"No. But that doesn't mean a thing."

Bet straightened her back. She had a little height advantage over Lady Fortuna, and she was ready to use what little psychological advantage that gave her. Two hundred years of practice gave her an unfair advantage when face to face with anger.

"I disagree," she spoke softly, but clearly. "My contract with Circuit, and Circuit's contract with you, makes it very clear that I am responsible for medical care for my patients. I am not answerable to political officials."

Lady Fortuna glared. "I can send you packing. I can make sure you will never practice medicine anywhere in the cluster."

Bet locked eyes with her. "How?"

As that word registered, Bet continued.

"You gave Mary permission to visit me. Mary approved every treatment I used, in advance."

"I let her be treated for the bruises, you know that. Not—"

Bet smiled. "Not what? Be specific. A medical review board will need every detail of the ailment, and my analysis, and my treatment, if they are to pass judgement. I have confidence I am right. So does Mary. Where do you come in?"

There was silence in the room.

Lady Fortuna backed up a step and put her hand on the bench. "What do you know? What did Mary tell you?"

"I can't tell you that. It is bound information."

"Bound? Bound how?"

Dr. Bet Nomad reached into her pocket and removed a small, thin piece of metal engraved with text. It was worn around the edges. "I took this oath when I became a doctor. Read it."

. . .

"I SWEAR by the great Healer and God, according to my ability and judgment, I will keep this Oath and this stipulation: to reckon him who taught me this Art equally dear to me as my parents, to share my substance with him, and relieve his necessities if required; to look upon his offspring in the same footing as my own siblings, and to teach them this art, if they shall wish to learn it, without fee or stipulation; and that by precept, lecture, and every other mode of instruction, I will impart a knowledge of the Art to my own children, and those of my teachers, and to disciples bound by a stipulation and oath according to the law of medicine, but to none others. I will follow that system of regimen which, according to my ability and judgment, I consider for the benefit of my patients, and abstain from whatever is deleterious and mischievous. I will give no deadly medicine to any one if asked, nor suggest any such counsel; and in like manner, I will not give to a woman a pessary to produce abortion. With purity and with holiness I will pass my life and practice my Art. I will not treat my patients, except by skills I have mastered, leaving that to others to practice their Art. Into whatever houses I enter, I will go into them for the benefit of the sick, and will abstain from every voluntary act of mischief and corruption; and, further from the seduction of females or males, of free-men and slaves. Whatever, in connection with my professional practice

or not, in connection with it, I see or hear, in the life of men, which ought not to be spoken of abroad, I will not divulge, as reckoning that all such should be kept secret. While I continue to keep this Oath unviolated, may it be granted to me to enjoy life and the practice of the art, respected by all men, in all times! But should I trespass and violate this Oath, may the reverse be my lot!"

...

"This oath is over three thousand years old," Bet said reverently. "Doctors in all times and eras have sworn it, and the good ones have kept it." Bet drew her finger over the lines at the bottom. "Including this part about 'keeping secret what ought not be spoken of abroad.'" She retrieved the sheet and put it back with her things.

Bet drew Lady Fortuna's eyes with a gesture of her hand. "Now listen carefully. I will not tell you what is bound by my oath. Whatever information Mary gave me will never be divulged—not to you, nor to anyone else. The same goes for any other secret of my Alexandrian patients."

The woman looked sharply at Bet, trying to read her. "Is there anything I … Is there anything that Alexandria should fear to be known?"

Bet did not reply. As the seconds ticked away in silence, the Lady's expression slowly gave way to horror. The fear of genetic contamination could still not be spoken out loud.

It was a whisper, when she finally spoke. "Please. Please be gone tomorrow." And she left.

Bet didn't like playing the woman's emotions like that. Still, body language and silence were sometimes stronger weapons than a club.

She glanced around at her "clinic". It had a shorter run than most, and now she had to re-pack everything overnight.

Still, if Mary can have a baby, it's worth it.

PRIME CITY, CERES, L4 CLUSTER

Prime City, the only large settlement on Ceres, was only medium sized as space cities went. With a population approaching fifty thousand, it was well beyond the small hometown where everyone knew everyone else and everyone knew all the scandals.

Of course, it was a safe bet that a stranger met in the halls was an employee of the Project. The control center was Prime City's main purpose, and the reason Ceres was moved from the asteroid belt to Earth-Luna L4. Other than the astronomers taking advantage of the farside and its unique position shielded from Earth Space's radio and light pollution, most were Project support. They ran the housing, the restaurants, and the entertainment and retail centers necessary to keep the workers content.

Vesta, over at the center of the L5 cluster, was a manufacturing and commercial center, with a population close to twelve million, spread out all over that planetoid's surface. If you had a manufacturing process that needed gravity, Vesta was the place to be. All of the Lunar industries had to be relocated to Vesta when the terraforming started. It rankled the Vesta Chamber of Commerce and its population to be number Two in the Clusters—which is probably why the Vesta soccer team always included Ceres in its pre-season exhibition tour.

. . .

Mason grumbled, "I can't afford these tickets," as he paid for the center-front seats.

Cinca clung to his arm and smiled. "But you have to be here. You need to get out and be where people can see you."

She was worth seeing. Her costume was in the red and white of Team Ceres colors, and she looked extremely athletic. He'd always envied guys with beautiful girls clinging to them. It felt good, even if he was slightly embarrassed by it.

"Don't remind me. I should never have told you about my father." He handed the tickets to the gateman. He took the tickets, but Mason was amused to see that the man never looked at the slips of paper. He, too, was basking in Cinca's charms.

"Nonsense. How can you get Prime to recognize your father's contributions if no one knows about them?"

Mason shook his head. "I haven't had a moment's peace since the newspaper article came out. And it won't do any good. I doubt the people in charge in Berlin read the Ceres Prime Communicator anyway. I know I don't subscribe to it."

She led him to the concession stand, "But you are a hermit. Not everyone is like you."

"Hello there, Mason!" Someone in the crowd called out. He looked up, and there was some co-worker waving at him. He waved back. No name floated up to attach to the face.

Cinca was watching, a smirk on her face. "See?"

They went to their seats. There was a larger crowd here to see the local team beaten than there was during the regular season. Of course, the Vesta Vikings had more fans than Team Ceres. Ceres rarely made it on the Cluster Communications broadcasts.

Mason didn't enjoy the game. It was nice to have Cinca beside him, but he didn't really like crowds at all. The noise was too much for him. The louder the cheers, the more it drove him inside his own thoughts.

He hated what Cinca had done. Without his permission, she had gone to the news center and related his story to a writer there. He found out about it when he went in to work the next day.

Lord Stephen Smith had called him into his office and had asked him about the story.

"I knew your father, back in the old days—not personally, but he certainly made a splash when people realized what he had done with Triangle Island. He was a lot like you, very sharp. And like you, all too likely to upset the wrong people.

"William, I certainly hope you had nothing to do with this article. It's good that people recognize your father, but the people above me would be very unforgiving if a Controller took it upon himself to affect Project policy in the public press. It is not a good time."

Mason nodded. "The Spin decision."

"Right. The Project has accomplished great things, and has lent stability to the Solar System by regulating all TP beams. I am proud to be a part of the Project, as I know you are.

"But the instant we get court decisions controlling what we do with the world-beams, that's the day it all falls apart. We are dealing with great powers here. Too great. We can't tolerate contested control."

Mason nodded, not trusting himself to frame a coherent response.

Lord Stephen nodded, "I like you, Mason. You have my personal bond that I will get you a stronger Controller seat just as soon as I am able.

"But don't get yourself caught up in a power struggle. You are a gnat next to the nations suing in the World Court. You would get swatted without a thought, and there's nothing I could do about it."

. . .

Half way across the stadium, an elderly man edged his way next to a man leaning against a pillar. It was during the last minutes of the game, while most of the fans were on their feet. Robert Henderson suddenly noticed a familiar face move closer to take a place next to him.

"Hello John." He had to shout to be heard above the noise.

"Hello Robert. Like the game?"

"Yes. It's a welcome change."

"What?"

Robert moved closer, so he could shout in his contact's ear. "It's a welcome change. I was getting tired of the rain."

John frowned. "Olympia?"

"No. Luna." An ocean was being rained out of Luna's clouds. It never stopped. Robert led one of the scattered teams working to bio-engineer the newly forming ecology. He was an important part of the Project. People wouldn't come to live on dead worlds, even if they could breathe.

Robert suspected John would not have met him directly unless there was something up. No matter what his credentials, the Project Board would have his head if they knew he was in contact with the Olympia Secret Service.

It was a dangerous game, but Robert had no doubts. As much as he believed in the Project, Olympia was his homeland. His loyalty was clear.

John said, "Enjoy your vacation." He turned and pushed his way out of the crowd.

Robert glanced down at his feet. Among the clutter of temporary cups was an envelope. He reached down and stuffed it into his pocket. In the privacy of the bathroom, he glanced at the terse lines: WC DECISION SOON. MOVE TO STAGE 2 SOONEST.

He flushed it with a frown. His team was not going to like having their furlough cut short, especially when he couldn't give them the real reason.

. . .

"I won't do it!" Mason was adamant.

Embarrassed at his own voice, he shifted to a whisper. The restaurant was quiet and some people were now staring at them.

Cinca stroked his fingers. "Now Billy, don't be that way. I'm only doing this for you."

He grr'ed deep in his chest. She either didn't understand, or she didn't care what her schemes were doing to his career. "It's going too far."

She turned her head to the side. "But wasn't this unknown spaceship the reason you were so upset in the first place? With that story, Hester, at the paper, is sure the network will pick it up. It could even get distributed Earthside. You'll be famous. Your father will get his recognition. The Project Board will want to milk your popularity for its own ends and promote you."

Mason stared down at the table, and her hands. Their touch sent thrills all the way down to his toes. He pulled away.

"I am bound by my oath of service. I won't feed details of a current operation to the news vendors."

"But Billy, you've already told me about the operation. This is no different."

He looked up at her face, and saw a little edge, a little hardness.

"This is my career! I talked too freely before, and they could send me Earthside for that. If a hint of it reaches the news, then I'm done." His father had always been loyal to the Project. This was not something he would have been proud of. "I've already been warned by my boss."

"Billy, you can't just leave me hanging like this! I talked to people. People are waiting for you."

"And I had nothing to do with that! I didn't ask for any of it. This is your wild scheme, not mine. But it'll be my head in the noose. You don't know how the Board operates. I've seen it in action."

She looked away for a moment, and if he didn't know any better, he would have read the expression on her face as hatred. But surely it wasn't that.

Cinca composed herself before she spoke, but the words were tight and controlled. "Okay. You win. I'll just tell Hester it was a false alarm. I misread the situation. I thought you were serious about getting your father the recognition he deserves."

He clamped his jaw. He didn't want to argue with her, even when she showed her ugly side.

He glanced at his food. He didn't want it anymore, but it was impossible to walk away. The bill hadn't been presented.

Cinca asked, "Have you heard anything more about the spaceship?"

He shook his head. "I don't think I should tell you anything more about my job. I don't trust you."

Her face went pale. He looked away. Had he gone too far? He didn't want to fight.

She slapped her hand hard down on the table. He looked back, and saw that her face had changed into a mask of anger. "No! You will tell me anything I want to know."

He was shocked. "What?" Something had slipped away. This wasn't like Cinca. Or was it?

"You owe me," she said. "I have spent every day working for this. For you. So you owe me."

Something was wrong. She was like an entirely different person.

"No. That's enough. Drop it." His words were sliding off her, like she was wearing plastic armor.

An idea clicked inside his head.

"Something's wrong here. I thought you liked me, but that's not it, is it?"

Her eyes blinked, but she forced her angry glare back on him.

"It's the ship." It suddenly made sense to him. "You didn't pay me any attention at all until I handled that ship. You don't care about me. You don't care about my father. It's all about this ship. What's going on here?"

Cinca didn't waver. "What is going on is simple. You're going to be a good little boy and do what I tell you to do!"

"That's nonsense. You should be reported. You're some kind of an anti-Project spy, aren't you? They're always warning us about people like you."

She aimed a finger at him. "Sure. Inform on me, or even talk a little louder here at this table, and you can forget your father's canal, forget your job, forget ever being a part of your sacred Project. Yes, they would be happy to deport me, but you'd be leaving on the same ship. You know how paranoid the Project Board has become. They might pat you on the back for reporting me, but would they ever trust you again? I just might turn you in myself to see you squirm!

"But it doesn't need to come to this!" She suddenly smiled, and it was if she was the old Cinca again. Mason realized just how worthless he was at judging other people. "We can still be friends, good friends. I know you love your Project, and I wouldn't ask you to do a thing to jeopardize it. I just need some information from time to time. We can just talk, as friends."

Then the smile turned icy. "But if you want to be enemies, I can be that too."

DURANGO PORTAL, EARTH

Up ahead, the Animas River valley opened up into grassy fields, and Kidd goaded the horse into a gallop. The Honeyville station was visible on the hillside to the right, and monitors would have seen him coming twenty miles away.

He grabbed his saddlebags and abandoned the hot, sweaty horse as soon as the stables were in sight. Its eyes were wide, and froth covered its muzzle. He had pushed the animal hard once he had reached the valley. The only obstacles had been the rubble left from the destruction of the highway.

Rangers were walking his way. Kidd knew he was still covered with dried blood, and the fewer people who saw him, the better.

Waving his badge, he sprinted through the checkpoints, stopping for no one. He didn't slow down until he closed the door on his one-man shuttle with the Bureau of Re-Naturalization markings.

"Launch, best time, avoidance pattern. Destination, personal mark two."

He felt the lurch as the balanced pressor beams shoved the craft into the air. The cirrance noise was bad, but it was the price one paid for a one-man craft. He knew it would get better, once he made altitude. The markings on the side of the craft faded away.

He allowed himself to close his eyes for a moment.

. . .

No, too much blood. He clamped his hand over Bonnie's wound as she shrieked and fought him. The cry echoed across the valley. Her parents would certainly hear it in their cave.

Kidd pulled the girl up to view the ragged laceration on her upper arm, where bright red blood spurted from a torn artery. He held her in a firm grip while he unsealed the leather medical bag he carried strapped to his belt. "Calm down, Bonnie. Let me fix your hurt place."

The screams didn't abate, but the words calmed her struggling a little. He worked quickly and efficiently on the wound. In short order, he had it closed and dusted with broad-spectrum antibiotics and antifungal medicines.

Out of the corner of his eye, he spotted Fred Gearson running up the slope. Clara wasn't far behind. He called out to them, "Hurry! I need your help!" He didn't, but saying it might keep the father from attacking him on the spot.

"She cut her arm," he explained as the parents came up. "I've got a good medical kit. Help me get this dressing in place."

. . .

As the shuttle reached cruising altitude, the cirrance, the rapid cycling of tractor beams grabbing air and shoving it down to provide lift, shifted to a tolerable pitch as the beams had more space to work with.

Kidd opened his eyes. Now all he had to do was make his report for the Bureau.

"Dictation: Bureau of Re-naturalization, Neolithic Re-establishment Project

"To: James Derrel, Operations Manager, Office of Anthropological Studies, Department of the American Interior

"James, this is just a quick report to get you started. Your infrared monitors were dead-on accurate, but that was not a pet dog. It was a child! We have a viable family unit just outside the control area. There is a mating pair and one female child, aged seven. All appear healthy. Family name is Gearson.

"I made a brief contact and managed to radio-tag the child. The radio beacon is in her upper left arm, embedded in the tendon above the bicep. No chance of its discovery.

"I judged that this group needed first generation assistance, according to project policy, and I managed to turn over the doctored medical kit to the male. If the adults use the preparations as needed, we might get an increase in fertility in the mating pair.

"Recommendations:

"(1) Subjects are in contact with an outsider, John Fenton, a.k.a. 'Trader'. Outsider is a cultural contaminant and a security hazard. This is just the thing I have been harping on for years in the meetings! How can a Neolithic culture hope to get started when there is trading going on with the outside? We need to get rid of him. I recommend John Fenton for Martian colonization. Get to work on this quickly. Check his bags for false bottoms at the exit portal. Have one of our teams handle the job. This one will betray his contacts if he thinks he can clear himself.

"(2) Subjects should be flushed westward. Proper relocation would put them in contact with the Wilson unit. The Wilson unit has a male child of the proper age to be a mate to the Gearson female child in a few years.

"Attachments follow:

"A. Video and workup on John Fenton, a.k.a. 'Trader'

"B. Video and workup on Fred Gearson

"C. Video and workup on Clara Gearson nee Clara Weldon

"D. Video and workup on Bonnie Gearson

"E. Map of Gearson settlement"

. . .

Kidd finished his report and scanned his recordings for the best videos to attach with it. He wrapped it up as he approached his destination and sent the encrypted packets out over the Net.

"Private log: Enclose storage A as file 'Gearson', tag it with 'Neolithic'. Trader and the Gearsons all had a slight cough. I feel that the medicines should protect the Gearsons, once the more severe symptoms manifest themselves. In any case, the girl is inoculated. I just hope they connect with the Wilsons before the onset."

He glanced at the discoloration on his wrist and frowned. He was running out of time.

. . .

The shuttle landed on the roof of an abandoned Denver skyscraper. He moved it quickly under the canvas hangar roof.

Two stories down by stairway, he opened the doorway into a dark cavern of electronic gear, lit only by their power indicator lights.

"Light." Rows of equipment, and a dozen workbenches testified that he was home.

There was a mirror on the wall, and as he stared, his face relaxed, and years of worry lines dropped away. His naturally youthful face returned. It always amazed him how easy it was to maintain the older appearance.

But he looked bedraggled and he could smell the stink of his outing. The shower beckoned. He set the backpack on a workbench.

"Scan to marker fourteen." A monitor on the wall lit up to display a still picture of Bonnie, all bright smile and beautiful black hair. "Print it." A paper image dropped out of a chute, and he carried it over to a table next to his desk. He carefully placed the picture of Bonnie next to a picture of a cute little boy with red hair and freckles—the Wilson child. On the table were a half dozen other pictures, the second generation of the new Stone Age culture.

He smiled.

On the other side of the desk was an aquarium. He dipped his arm into the water, and after a moment, a transparent sheet marked with a discoloration lifted free of his wrist. He pulled out his arm and dried off.

With a symmetrical flapping of its body, reminiscent of the squid which had been the genetic template for the artificial creature, it swam around in the nutrient-laced waters, still showing the markings on its skin. After a moment, one of the markings changed. Another minute had passed, but Kidd had long given up any hope that the timing was accurate. The living wristwatch could accurately mark the year, date, and hour, but minutes and seconds were out of the range of its biological clocks. *Maybe in another generation.* Kidd had an improved model in his genetic design databanks and he would try it out when this one died.

He tapped the wall of the aquarium, but there was no response. The creature had limited senses. Still, he liked it. It was one of his favorite pets.

He smiled.

. . .

"List filter M."

Kidd preferred a cultured male voice from his computers, and that's what read aloud the puzzling message he received from one of his Olympia contacts.

"Mr. Marne. A 'special' offer was made in Portland this week, and I remembered your interests in this area. Please confirm your intent to enter the bidding. I have already fully committed, and it may not be enough.— GHK, Marine Resources Limited."

Kidd drummed his fingers on the desk. *Marne. I need to keep the beard.*

"Dictate: GHK, You are allocated to bid higher for undamaged goods. I will arrive personally to complete payment. —Nat Marne."

He headed for the shower, dropping his trail-stained clothes into the shaft that led to a decomposer/recycler tank. He had long ago decided that laundry was an unacceptable security risk.

As he scrubbed, he put himself into the persona of Nat Marne, modern-day pirate and collector of marine lifeforms. His face hurt, as the muscles tried to remember the squint that was one of Nat's memorable features.

Dressed in Marne's black, weatherproof suit, he stopped at his desk long enough to stick his arm up to the cuff into the aquarium. His wristwatch swam into position and melted into its place.

. . .

From out of a fifteen-story window nearby, a young woman watched the small unmarked shuttle lift off and head west. *In and out in less than an hour. Who is he?*

Paula Cambell looked back at her desolated surroundings.

This building is worthless—too easy to enter. Other scavengers have cleaned it out long before I found the service hatch. There's nothing from the Techno era here that hasn't been broken into useless fragments. I won't be able to sell any of it.

Officially, downtown Denver and several of the other clusters of skyscrapers from before the Star were off-limits. These ancient buildings were abandoned hundreds of years ago, when the supernova destroyed the electronic infrastructure of civilization and began the Little Dark Age.

In these behemoths, everything was lost—air-conditioning, elevators, fire control. Stairways in many were gutted by fire and corroded away, or sometimes filled with debris. With the technology at hand, even if the top floors could be reached, the space was too difficult to use, too expensive for the shelter.

The Star killed Denver. These places will never recover. Why is that little shuttle based here?

The supernova killed Denver's economy. Why would anyone want to live in a mile-high city when the ozone layer was damaged, and the safest places to live were at sea level? It was worse for the real mountain areas. They were depopulated. Even forest lands were hurt badly by the ultraviolet burns.

Denver's reason-to-be was gone.

Paula was very familiar with the mountains and their place in the world. The dead zone they became had ruined her life, and she'd spent a lot of effort into coming to terms with it.

. . .

The Rocky Mountains were a great natural barrier in the ancient pre-Star days. Without roads, men on foot or horseback could enter, but nothing as advanced as a wagon could make it. As roads and rail lines were cut through the passes, every route spawned a city in the plains at the foot of the great rock wall. Boulder, Denver, Colorado Springs, and Canon City became eastern portals. Their fortunes were made in the trade with the mining towns in the interior, and when mining collapsed, they were still important parts of the continent-wide national economy.

When the atmosphere healed itself, the ecological backlash finished the job. Before the interior could be re-settled, mountain ranges were declared global parks. The roads and rails had suffered by neglect when none of the nations of North America had claimed the lands. They were content to keep the barrier in place. Good fences make good neighbors.

Major roads were then purposely reduced to rubble, and eastern Denver had become nothing more than a railhead for grain and beef from the eastern plains. Western Denver, up against the mountains, was dead—dead and off-limits.

. . .

Paula had only been caught violating the restricted zones once. That was enough. After a quick stay in the corral down by the railroad tracks, the lot of them were shipped south to the Grande border and turned loose. It had taken her over a month to make her way back to Denver.

She smiled at the memory, although it had been painful. *I'll never forget my Net-ID number again!* She had money; she was profitably employed; but she had to live in secrecy or it would all vanish.

She had discovered her vocation when she was on a college raiding trip. Her school in Albuquerque had seemed at the ends of the earth, but when the rock-climbing club arranged a trip to Bandoleer, she had relished the thrill of climbing and exploring restricted lands. The club had a special permit for three days in the Bandoleer Zone, but that was just the opening wedge. Three of them broke away from the main group and explored the forbidden city of Los Alamos itself.

It looked to Mike, Dek and her like a ghost town. It was just like any other abandoned city, a disappointing collection of sun-bleached and weather-worn small buildings. But like a battered old sea-trunk, the treasure was inside.

Mike had a way with old door locks and in one building, they located a dozen or more ancient computers. With the parts shelves, it was clear that this was some kind of repair facility, and Paula was amazed that it hadn't been gutted long ago.

No one wanted old computers to use—they were far too slow—but there was a significant collectors market for them on the Net.

Dek said what was on all their minds, "If only there's a way to smuggle them out, we can make a fortune."

Mike shook his head. "You saw the way they searched our gear coming in. If we tried to take something like this out, the fines alone would sink us. That is, if they were satisfied with fines."

They agreed to look and drool, but not take anything. At least Mike meant it. Dek picked up a complex looking circuit card about as long as his finger, and managed to hide it in a spool of rope.

Paula picked up a pretty little plastic thing that fit nicely in her pocket. She was very lucky when they went through checkout. The ranger had no more idea than she did that it was a pocket computer. Ancient computers had keyboards—large arrays of buttons with randomly scrambled letters on the tops. Since this gadget didn't have one, Paula was able to spin a story that it was a modern gadget, a broken altimeter.

Dek couldn't help but brag about his find, once they were back at AU. He was quickly caught in a sting operation when World Court Enforcement agents responded to his for-sale offer on the Net.

She was very grateful he said nothing to implicate her, since it'd been her own successful sale on the Net that prompted him to take the bait. She had two years living expenses in Net Credits. He had a large fine and a criminal record.

Paula offered to help with the fine, but Dek was happy to accept a more intimate apology. Mike cut ties with them and transferred to Lincoln the next session.

Dek left suddenly, with no trace, shortly after she told him she was pregnant.

Adoptive parents in Denver named her son Isaac and the adoption contract prohibited her from making contact with him until he was twenty.

Which is how she found herself in Denver, with no job, depleted funds, and no degree.

She found a low cost apartment on Cherry Creek Hills. With a 90mm telescope, she found she could occasionally catch sight of her boy. Unfortunately, the jobs she could find didn't pay enough to make the rent.

One day, she trained her telescope on the abandoned towers of old Denver and wondered how difficult it would be for a climber to explore them.

. . .

At the end of the day, Paula looked at the small bag of parts she had collected, dumped them in a closet, and marked the door with her glyph. Maybe someday it would be worth her time to come back for them, but not now. The profit she might make from the sale would hardly cover the shipping costs. Too much of her business dealt with actual physical goods, and selling them to the information economy had its difficulties.

One day, I would love to find a blueprint, or a design manual. That would be profit free and clear.

The Net was totally anonymous and encrypted. It'd grown that way after the Star, and the information economy was its creature. In spite of countless attempts, messages were untraceable unless signed. Paula's Net account had no connection to her, other than the number now permanently inscribed in her memory. She was wealthy, in credits. If it was easy to exchange them for hard dollars, she could live wealthy, too.

Unfortunately, there were only a few places in the world where the monetary systems exchanged easily, and Denver wasn't one of them. She could afford to have the blueprints for a fine luxury house customized for her and delivered to her computer, but she couldn't come up with the rent on her apartment without doing scrub work, or making a deal with Ross down by the freight yard.

Some days she felt like she was working for him. Ross had the connections to take her packages and make them look like ordinary product shipments, and he had the means to convert her credits into items he could sell at his market. He charged heavily both directions. The only way she could get ahead was to hide the true market value of her scavenging expeditions from him. Until she could find another contact, she wanted to keep business with Ross to a minimum.

"I need a breakthrough," she muttered as she walked down the creaking stairway, keeping well away from the corroded railings, "I need a real house before I can think about Isaac."

She looked out the small, dirty window that provided the only light in the stairwell. The unmarked shuttle was gone now. He was often gone for days, or weeks. The ground floor of his building was an impossible pile of debris—she had scouted that out before. But there had to be a way up there.

FLORENCE, OLYMPIA, EARTH

Sealer struck again at the rock-hard surface. In the darkness, all he could sense was the smooth texture against his hand and the crispness of the sound reflections when he probed it with a squeal. There was space enough for him to swim a half dozen body lengths, but it was enclosed on the sides and bottom. It was a pit of smooth rock.

But if it's rock, how come it's all around me? How did I get trapped in a rock?

He swam up to the surface again, and opened his blowhole to breathe in more of the hot, tainted air. The water itself was becoming foul, and his gills were queasy. Unless something happened soon, he would not be able to breathe either the water or the air, and that would be the end of his quest. Elder Blackspine would be happy to see he had been right about him.

Hide from the Land People, or die—the adage had been drummed into him since birth, but it went against his nature. He was a hunter, not prey.

The People were migrating north, following the sun, and Sealer had braved himself to break away from the tribe. For some time, he had planned to search out the seal caves his father had described to him before he died. It was his name place. He would have become an adult for finding it and bringing back stone worn smooth by the seals.

Now he would be content to get back with nothing.

Land People had been waiting for him. He'd thought nothing about the boats they rode on the top of the water. His people evaded them all the time. But these boats made a strange noise, like whalesong, only sharper and faster, and with no meaning that he could understand.

Somehow they had heard his echoes, and were ready with nets.

It was the closest he'd been to Land People, and the legends were true. In the light of day, they looked like real people, except with legs that bent wrong, hands and feet with no webbing, and horrible faces with the blowhole grown over.

They were as vicious as the tales said, pulling him from the water and jabbing him with spears. He had fainted, and for days upon days, he waited in this little bubble of water, surrounded by rock. On the other side of a large crystal, he could see them during the day.

If they don't do something about the water soon, they won't even be able to eat me, I'll be so tainted.

...

Sealer swam over to the crystal again, feeling the difference in texture between it and the walls. The place was unlike any cave, or even inside the hull of a sunken Land People boat. In those places, life had begun to colonize the walls, not like this dead place.

There was a little light, he realized. Was it morning already? He changed his eyes, trying to focus outside.

Eyes stared silently back at him.

Sealer, jerked away from the wall. He should have heard its approach. He stared back. This was a new one. It had a black second skin that looked like a seal. Its eyes watched him with the emotionless intensity of a shark.

He swam up to the surface and expelled air. His lungs were hurting from so much effort. He wondered whether he would die of poison or from exhaustion first.

Suddenly, there was a noise from above, and the machine things up there moved.

Nets! His first instinct was to swim to the bottom. He got half-way there. But the lower layers were filled with poisons, and it was unbearable. He paused and moved over to the side, as far away from the noises as possible.

There was a splash as a net was let down into the water. For a moment, he just watched. Up above the surface, the Land People were huddled on the ledge, making noises to themselves.

Then the new one, dressed like a seal, barked loudly, ha ha ha.

Sealer moved to the surface and expelled air. He had to breathe. The new one turned from his fellows and locked his eyes on Sealer. He showed his teeth.

Two of the others separated from the group, one going in each direction along the edge. This close up, Sealer was amazed at how easily these Land People moved on their legs, moving with impossible balance and speed along the tiny ledge.

They are surrounding me! He moved away from the edge, and then made a dash toward the center, stopping with his hand on the edge of the net. It was clear what they were trying to do. It wasn't clear at all what he could do about it.

If I only had my lance. I could spill some blood and call the sharks.

Only there weren't any sharks, not here in this stagnant pool.

He could feel the ripple as the one behind him entered the water, as did the one he was watching. He moved quickly along the edge of the net, and soon had his opponents together. They were as clumsy in the water as they were graceful on the land. He could let them chase him all around the net. He was tired, but not so tired as to be stampeded into where they wanted him to go.

Ha ha ha. There was that bark again. He had no eyes for the Land People on the ledge when there were ones in the water with him.

Suddenly there was a splash right behind him. He spun in the water, face to face with that horrible face and those white teeth.

He could feel the other two make a dash for him, and he twisted into a dive for deeper water, but not quickly enough to escape the knife.

It stung like coral, spreading all along his arm. There was blood in the water, but it was his!

He kicked hard to gain distance, but first one hand gripped his leg and then another. Something was wrong—he couldn't move. The poisoned knife had done something. It felt like he was being swallowed by a grouper.

Then, there was the tangle of a net and he could feel himself being hauled up. When he broke the surface, he expelled air, but it was about the only thing he could do.

It was confusing, the Land People were all around him, touching him.

Ha ha ha. His enemy was there with them. He took his bleeding arm in a strong grip.

Like a wave breaking over him, Sealer slid into darkness. The last thing he remembered was the black one's teeth sucking at his blood.

Chapter 5

DARNELL FARMS, L4 CLUSTER

Dr. Bet Nomad unloaded her clinic into a room that had every sign of having performed that service before. The sinks, power connections and privacy partitions were very welcome, but she already missed the eager young men ready to help her. Even when the word was out in Alexandria that she was going to be no one's outside-wife, there had still been enough smiling faces and willing hands to make life easier. Maybe she could go back there in a few more decades, when she had another name and Lady Fortuna was dead. There'd never been any time to explore that library of theirs, like she'd intended.

The passage over from Alexandria had been brief. The two habitats were relatively close together, on the inner swing. All of the L4 habitats moved in carefully controlled paths seemingly orbiting Ceres, although Bet had enough experience to know that it was really Luna that was the dominant gravitational influence in their orbit around the Earth. They would still be making similar elongated loops even if Ceres wasn't there.

Darnell Farms was the company name, and that's what everyone called the place, although just Darnell was the name on the charts. It was a huge barrel-shaped habitat a little over five kilometers in length. The barrel rotated, giving pseudo gravity for the farmlands lining the inside, while the end-caps were nearly conic-shaped, apex inward, with controlled mirror surfaces to direct the sunlight inside.

Every apple she'd eaten in the last twenty years had a Darnell Farms sticker on the side. While there were a dozen other farm habitats in the Clusters, Darnell Farms specialized in fruits, leaving the grains and vegetables to others.

From her new office, near the southern end cap, she could see most of the lands above her, although there seemed to be a permanent haze that blurred away the features on the northern far side.

What really looked strange was the sun. At this part of the orbit, it was shining in through the far cap and the mirrors had stretched out its shape into a huge crescent, many times larger than it would be if seen directly.

So that's where the logo comes from. Bet had always thought it was the crescent moon shining over the little farmhouse on the logo. She had never thought about it before.

In spite of all the differences, it was a welcome feeling to be in a small building with a roof and with open sky above. It had been so long since she had left Earth. Her chest ached as she recalled the peaks over Annecy where she lived a few years after Glenn died. She loved the lake, and the streams that fed it.

There appeared to be canals everywhere through the farmlands, and they drained to a belt-like lake half-way down the length of the habitat. *I wonder if there are any boats that sail on it? With an open space like this, there must be winds.*

But that would have to come after she had caught up on her work. Every new posting was extremely busy, once all the inhabitants realized they could maybe get their old aches and injuries looked at. Every place had its own medical aid, but usually it was part time, using home remedies or old medical cookbook manuals. The Circuit Medical Team was instituted to bring back awareness of what real medical doctors could accomplish. In that sense, it was political—doctors trying to pull their profession up out of the depths it had fallen into during the Die-Off.

Time to get back to work.

...

She opened the heavy seals on the windows and let the sun shine in, although that meant moving some of the equipment around to work better in the changed light. This must have been here before they completed the habitat. Even the front door had a little airlock.

She also wanted to make sure her lab was not visible from the outside. There were shutters she could use at night, or when privacy was necessary, but soundproofing was minimal. Late night work would have to be done in whispers.

There was a knock on the open door. "Hello, medical person."

"Hello, yourself. Can I help you?"

The visitor was slightly overweight, about fifty, and held a basket of fresh fruit in his hand. "No. Not me. I'm Dan Gregor. I just thought I would be the first to pay a visit. I live over the line near Berthie's Cascade." He nodded his head in the direction.

"I am Doctor Bet Nomad. Call me Bet. Berthie's Cascade, like a stream? Oh, these look delicious." She smiled and took the basket. There were apples and pears, and a cluster of dark grapes.

"Yes, though it's only a trickle now. You ought to see it when spring comes."

"You have seasons? That's a treat."

He grinned. "Yep. When it's time for winter, we reduce the sunlight and ice forms on the dark end cap. When we brighten it up for spring, it melts off in a torrent."

He coughed, and she instantly switched gears.

"Have you had that cough long?"

He looked blank, then shook his head. "It's nothing. Just a little dust."

. . .

Dan left as soon as April Jenner arrived, carrying her own basket of fruit. It was to be the pattern for the rest of the afternoon. Bet fully intended to keep all the fruit, and eat it herself, but she started worrying about the baskets, until Grace Nesbett told her not to worry, they were a cheap staple here in the Farms.

She dealt with a number of allergies, several old wounds, even reset a bone, and gave a timid young bride a view of her growing son-to-be. Apparently, fertility was not a problem here in the Farms.

Most of the problems were as she had expected—farm related injuries. The allergies were all mild, as to be expected with people who had lived in this environment for several generations. People with severe allergies would have long since left, or died out. Infectious diseases weren't much of a problem either, with infrequent exposure to new bugs. In the bad old days, all the habitats had learned the hard truths about quarantining anyone who showed new disease symptoms. With no doctors, many of the sick were moved to airlocks—there to recover or not, and ejected with the airlock left exposed to the vacuum and sunlight for months if they didn't make it.

However, everyone seemed to have a very slight cough—as had everyone in Alexandria, and on the transport over.

As she thought back over the past months, it seemed that everyone had a cough, except her, which was not surprising, given her unique genetics.

No one thought the cough unusual, and even she hadn't considered it anything to be bothered with, not until that genetic analysis session with Mary Harris.

When the reverberating sound of sunset came as the huge mirrors turned to reflect the sunlight elsewhere, the visitors seemed to melt away. Farm life hours were synced to the plants and animals, which were indelibly linked to the light.

Bet put aside her daily work logs and walked outside. The farmhouse lights on the other side of the sky were winking out, one by one. It was if the stars were being swallowed up by a dark cloud. Soon, the only light came from the far end-cap—sun light on distant support beams, and an occasional reflected star, too tiny to be distorted out of its pinpoint shape by the mirrors. She wondered what Luna, or even Ceres, would look like, reflected off the mirrors, but they weren't visible tonight.

The whole little world had gone to bed, snug in its giant sleeping bag.

Everyone but me. Doctors don't get to sleep.

She took the samples she had carefully collected during the day, and began marathon lab work. She knew what she was looking for, and she found it. Everyone had the virus. It was the same as she'd found in Alexandria, except the lab was indicating that there was a regular and consistent change from what she'd found before.

She dug into her travel bag. Sealed in clear sample bags were bits of trash she had scavenged from the transport. There was no way of matching the samples to individuals, but shortly she confirmed that the menstrual blood stain, the food-stained napkin, the chewed toothpick and the wipe of sputum all were contaminated with the same virus.

Everyone, at least everyone in the Clusters, was probably infected. There were pervasive bacteria that had ridden humanity's gut since pre-history, but what was this virus? She knew she'd never seen it until recently, and now it was universal? With practically no symptoms? It didn't make sense.

Not unless it was designed that way. The Alexandrian gene made her paranoid.

She whispered, "Run an emulation of the virus against a standard human."

She put a dropcloth over the lab screen and settled back into the reclining chair she used as her own bed. She closed her eyes, but sleep would be hard to achieve while the emulation was running. She wished she could make it happen faster, but that wish was always wasted. It took special circumstances and a great deal of luck for her to acquire an unlicensed genetic lab, and Bet knew she should be happy with what she had. It just took a long time to emulate every action of the virus, especially in the context of the emulated standard human. Humans were large, complex systems, and although the standard human emulation had been tuned for speed over long years of effort, it still ran up against the limit of the computer's speed.

Bet, like almost everyone else, was used to having computers that were faster than the requests people gave them. Almost always, the delays were due to real world events, like the time it took to acquire information over the Net, or the time it took a remote process to complete.

I could get faster response over the Net. She shook her head. Yes, there were faster computers out on the Net that could do the job, even unlicensed genetic jobs, but it wasn't worth the risk.

She had this debate with herself from time to time. The Net was large, with huge resources, and totally anonymous. Many illegal activities could be executed safely on the Net.

But anonymity was relative, and regular high bandwidth usage would point to her like an arrow for any of the world agencies that tried to track that kind of thing. After the Die-Off, when the world governments made a concentrated effort to crack the Net's secrecy, such efforts had revealed and shut down some large genetic operations. Still, the encryption of the Net was solid and even efforts to create an alternate network always failed.

Secrecy was probably weakest out the Clusters, where network equipment was sparse and spread out. She lived within those limits, and now wasn't the time to risk testing them.

Bet had, in an earlier life, made her living by buying network boxes from a wholesaler and finding places in the world where the Net was hard to access. It took minimal effort to set one of the relays up. All she had to do was find a place for it with good radio coverage and visibility to the sky for the solar power. After that, it would automatically integrate itself into the larger Net, and a miniscule fee would be charged on all traffic traveling through it. The better the job of finding places that needed Net bandwidth, the more micropayments would flow into her Net account. Even today, when she checked that account, it was clear that most of the boxes she had set up were still online and producing some income.

She wished she could do that out here in the Clusters, but with the TP beams and the Terraforming Project's control of everything in orbit, the little repeaters didn't make economic sense. Out here Net bandwidth was a communal resource, and often regulated. She had fallen out of the habit of using it.

But there is no reason I can't check the Listings.

She got up out of her recliner, wide awake, and uncovered the lab. It was still working hard on her emulation, but Net activity wouldn't make a dent in that.

"Connect me with Medical Listings."

The delay was minimal while radio packets hopped from the big relay locally to Ceres or Earth, and returned. She had heard that Net access from Mars was maddening for anything that wasn't cached locally.

Bet had to log in anonymously to the Listings, which meant read-only access. Nothing could be posted without a verified identity code, and since the Listings used a doctor's license ID as part of the key, she was at a disadvantage. Her current doctor's license ID was forged. The one she had earned would have pointed to a woman who had died forty years earlier.

"Search for a virus identified within the last five years. Symptoms include minor cough."

A listing of submissions, tagged with each doctor's identity grew on the screen. Some of them she was already familiar with, but there were many that were new. Viruses mutate rapidly, even more so in space, and there were always new varieties appearing.

She began to read.

PRIME CITY, CERES, L4 CLUSTER

It was two hours until his work shift, and Mason could not drag himself out of bed. *I could just develop some disease. Then I could retire to Earth, and avoid the whole mess.*

He knew of at least three Controllers that had washed out on a medical. Two were stress-related complaints, and the rumors he'd heard hinted that the silicosis that Bremmerman had reported was just a screen. Stress could take any of them. It wasn't surprising.

However, people would wonder if he washed out. He wasn't even on regular orbit duty.

And he couldn't give up. He knew the roots of his sense of duty. He'd had years to think about it. As a teenager, he'd hated his father for never being home, but that had been before he had come to realize the dream that drove the man. He had forgiven his father, but he had never forgiven himself. Only by making his own mark for the Project, being part of the elite, a Controller, could he approach being the man his father had been.

Controllers had two basic jobs; one was to maintain the orbits of large bodies, such as habitats, moons, and even planets. The other was to make sure that any small craft, such as shuttles and transports, slipped through the web of TP beams without incident.

Space was an invisible maze of high-energy beams that could rip any unwary vehicle apart. It was impossible to fly from place to place, not without a Controller guiding your every turn.

The big beams powered the whole economy. Moving Mars toward the sun and Venus away from it was a big job. It would take many centuries before some of the adjustments could be made. But all the while, a tiny fraction of the energy was bled off to provide all of humanity's energy needs.

Mason had seen the final plans. It was beautiful, with Earth, Luna, Venus, Mars, and three of the large Jovian moons plus Titan in a carefully designed necklace, orbiting in the habitable zone around the sun. Mercury would be gone, burned up as a sacrificial offering to the sun, its gravitational potential energy doing much of the work.

Oh yes, there was stress there, in executing to that design. Planetary orbits were not something to be trifled with. Spin out a brand new planetary system from a new-born star's dust cloud, and most of it will be destroyed. There will be collisions among the proto-planets and many orbital instabilities that can cause one planet to steal energy from another in a close pass. Some will be burned up. Others will gain so much energy they never return.

The Solar system was stable, not because orbits were naturally stable, but because it was inhabited by the survivors. Great catastrophes had happened here, billions of years ago. All of the planets had been unstable, until by chance, they had been thrown into orbits just stable enough to last. Over four billion years ago, Earth and Luna formed their alliance. A billion years ago, Ganymede finally settled into a near-circular orbit around Jupiter. Every survivor had its tale and its near misses.

Making any changes to the system was dangerous. Mason had been through the training, and part of it had been the opportunity to make changes of their own to a Solar system emulation and then see what would happen over time.

Practically every one of his trials had been unstable. Even little changes like giving Mars a larger moon had seemed stable enough at first, but given a million years or so, it hadn't been. Other planets had fed energy to his new moon, breaking it free from Mars into an elliptical orbit around the Sun that passed as close as Venus, and as far out as Jupiter. Quickly, after that, it was captured first by Venus for a couple of orbits, then off near Jupiter, losing energy to that giant, and then coming close enough to Earth to throw Luna into a more elliptical orbit, creating huge tides on Earth, and then finally, dropping into the Sun.

It was hard to create the stability that nature had provided after billions of years of trial and error. The Terraforming Project had taken a huge responsibility on its shoulders. If it weren't for the vision that saw terraforming as the salvation of the human race, it would never have been attempted.

Mason felt the need. Most people did. It was too dangerous to stay on Earth.

A great civilization had grown up on Earth, but it had been in danger of poisoning itself. Then the supernova came, and the survivors came out of a Little Dark Age knowing one great truth—technology is wonderful and can provide great gifts, but Nature is always powerful enough to knock the props out from under it. Life has to have deep roots to survive.

And then humanity built again, and made great changes in life itself. But genetics was a two-edged sword, making it easy to kill millions overnight with a miscalculation.

Twice in a single thousand years, mankind had approached extinction. There was no promise that it wouldn't happen again.

To Mason, there was only one choice. Spread out. Don't let all of humanity live in one place, sharing the same air, and walking the same ground, all vulnerable to the next disaster.

But the planets were inhospitable, and the stars were very far away.

When the Nance-Bate overlap was discovered, everything changed. Unimaginable energies were there in the orbits of the planets, and mankind had been handed the tool to use it.

Now there was a vision—many worlds, where a man could walk barefoot under an open sky, and live close to his roots. Disaster might strike Earth again, but a diversified humanity would survive.

No, I can't just walk away from it. My father gave his life for this.

So have I.

Was Cinca really a spy? Or was she just leading him on, twisting the knife because he'd rejected her plans?

She might have been bluffing. A spy wouldn't willingly turn herself in. Either way, all I have to do is avoid her.

It wasn't as if he had given out important tactical information. The spaceship wasn't on the quiet list.

He looked at the clock. *If I leave now, alter my schedule—if she is waiting for me, I can just be elsewhere.*

A gloom clung to his shoulders. He had betrayed the Project. *I wanted to impress her.* What damage had he caused?

He dressed quickly and walked down the hallway. Mrs. Pearce came out, dressed for her church service.

"Good morning, William. Out early today?"

He forced a smile. "Are you spying on me?"

"Of course. I have to know all my boys' schedules. It wouldn't do to have you oversleep. I was in the service too, you know."

He nodded. She reminded them all of that, from time to time.

"Are you heading toward Center?" she asked, as they walked to the entrance.

"In a roundabout way. I thought I could do with some exercise."

She nodded, "Still thinking about that ship, aren't you? Well then, come walk with me. I haven't had a man escort me to church since my boy David left for the outer fleet."

Mason knew about her son too, since she casually mentioned him at least once a week.

They walked out onto the street, and moved to the side to let one of the little delivery vans move silently by. He liked living on this street, since it had a good view out the dome. His mind always seemed to be out there. He loved the Project and hated its politics.

Prime City was a well-crafted community, with almost every building showing its owner's pride. They walked past many gardens and colorfully trimmed fences. There was a thriving business for the prospectors that collected colored stonework from the various excavations on the surface.

"I guess I've been thinking about the ship. Do you still think it is from out-system?"

She smiled, with dimples. "I know you think I'm crazy. What is its orbit?"

He had no doubts about her. He rattled off the orbital elements, and Mrs. Pearce nodded to herself.

"That would put Earth near its periapsis, wouldn't it?"

He agreed, a little surprised that she could still visualize an orbit from its elements.

She sighed, "Well, then you are probably right. I don't know if you were aware of it or not, but Bolivar has an extensive library of pre-Collapse space missions. I had the opportunity to do some research there when I was younger. I don't remember them all, but there must be dozens of candidates for your unknown spaceship."

"You were at Bolivar? I grew up in Rio," he said.

"You did? I visited there for a couple of weeks—I loved the beaches. But that was back when I could wear a bathing suit."

He walked her up the steps into the entrance of the church. She went on in.

He lingered. Familiar scents, the welcoming silence, it touched old memories. It was a place of forgiveness, and he needed that.

He left the church, his head a little higher. He had a duty. He continued on towards the Center, anxious to get off the public streets before Cinca could come looking for him.

That ship still bothers me. It won't hurt to do some more research on it in my off time.

...

In his father's day, there had been something called the restricted list. This had been a list of objects with orbits that were invisible to Controllers, unless their security rating permitted access. Shortly after the explosion of the John Henry and the world-wide destruction that came to be called the Wrath, that list was eliminated. No one admitted that the restrictions had anything to do with the accident, but the attitude had changed. Terraforming the Solar system was a holistic effort, and nothing should be invisible.

The quiet list had become more important, but that was for outsiders.

Mason had an hour before his regular duties began, and he made use of it, adding the ship to his personal database. The first thing he noticed was that the unknown ship was moving in a different, non-ballistic path. Some beam was applying force to it. His guess about it being handed off to the solar-flare-protection beam had been correct.

The solar shield automated facility hovered sunward and slightly behind the Earth in its orbit. It emitted a low intensity, but very broad beam toward the sun, pushing the onrushing solar wind aside, shielding itself, and the Earth/Luna system from its effects. There was of course, the balancing beam in the opposite direction—all TP beams had to obey the conservation of momentum. The ship had been directed into that beam, and it was soaking up the momentum of the re-directed solar wind.

Mason grumbled to himself. The solar shield was one of the many bits and pieces of the Project that found itself in the World Court. Some groups on Earth had sued to restore the auroras. They were challenging the project on religious grounds. Mason had never known of any group that thought the auroras were sacred, but apparently there were some.

Thus far, not a single Project policy had been overturned, and Mason hoped none of them ever would. Mixing politics into worldbuilding was a disaster waiting to happen. Leave it to the experts, like the original Project charter said.

Mrs. Pearce had mentioned a data-set in Bolivar, and he tried to access it on the Net. It was a fascinating list. He knew some of the features of chemical rockets from his training, but they acted so differently from what he was used to. It was like taking a sledgehammer and giving the vehicle a single whack, and then waiting months or years for it to finally drift to where you wanted to go. It was amazing that they ever got off the ground. It was unbelievable that someone in that era went to Luna, and much less returned safely.

The list of objects and orbits was a confusing mix of different languages, with a large percentage of the objects not really ships at all, but merely the empty fuel tanks that had reached orbital velocity before they had been abandoned.

He read a short passage about how cluttered Earth orbit had been, with so many satellites and pieces of equipment, and how the radar installations of the time tried to track them all, down to lost hand tools.

He shook his head. Earth orbit was now clean, pristine. So was most of inhabited space. There was nothing in space except natural objects and registered vehicles. When the second age of space happened, and the TP beams came into their own, all of the ancient satellites still in orbit had been collected and a few of them retired to museums. As for the remaining clutter, it was deorbited and burned up. A loose screwdriver in space could become a lethal missile if caught in an unsuspecting tractor beam.

In the list, he located several ancient objects that had gone into a solar orbit. Three of them even had about the same mass as he had seen on his screen.

If I could just make some more measurements, I bet I could find out which one it is.

He accessed the radar database. He no longer had authority to order the system to focus on it immediately.

The most recent position was displayed in red. He frowned for a moment. Every registered object—and the ship was now registered—had its position regularly checked against its predicted path. This one was a little off.

Well, the alarms haven't triggered yet. Maybe it is still in the process of getting a stable orbit.

"Raise the monitor priority on this item."

He would look in on it again when his scheduled duty time was over.

. . .

"He has broken off contact. I don't have the plans."

The public comm never lit up. It never did when Cinca reported. She waited for some response.

"Maybe," the disguised synthetic voice said. "Maybe you should lose some weight." There was the click, and the connection was broken.

Cinca pinched the bridge of her nose, hard. She would not lose her temper now.

Somehow, the spymaster's flat-toned voice now sounded a bit like Vernon. It was going to be unbearable if he turned into just another jerk.

However, she had flubbed the job, just when they needed her most. She'd counted on Mason acting like a young buck in the tribes. She had teased and flattered. He had followed her around, drooling as she led him step by step toward her bed, and it hadn't been enough. *I was too slow. He looked timid. And then he grew a conscience.*

Maybe I should have called in help. There were agents who knew how to properly put a scare into a subject.

But then I wouldn't get any credit.

She bit her thumbnail in thought. He'd seemed subdued and under control when she'd left him yesterday. But now he had vanished, and she hadn't been able to apply pressure for information. She worked for the Three Sins. The rogue ship was their device, carefully inserted into an orbit designed to look harmless. But once discovered, the Project had altered its path. They needed to know what the Project was going to do with the Hydra.

Reporting in had been painful, but she wasn't done yet. This was a small town and she knew where Mason lived.

FLORENCE, OLYMPIA, EARTH

Sealer's first sensation was a pain in his arm. He thrashed awake, slamming against the smooth sides.

-Where am I?- he said, but the echoes of his cry came back instantly. It was dark, and he was enclosed in a very small space. He could barely bend over without touching both sides at once.

But there was a current, and the water was clean. It could be breathed.

A light came on. The sight of the Land People things, the machinery suspended in the air, returned his fear. He was still captive. He glanced at his arm. The knife wound was healing rapidly, but there were teeth marks. *My first battle scars.* Jawtooth had called him clear-skinned since he had been put in his care with the other orphaned males. At fifteen, he was the oldest one there. Well, no longer! When he returned, he could claim a place of his own in the hunter pack.

There had been people in his tribe who thought the Land People were being given an unfair taint by the legends. Surely, they said, Land People are just different from us, not monsters.

Wait until they see these teeth marks.

A wave of dizziness came over him and he closed his eyes. For two days he'd been captive without food, and he could feel the weakness. He had to get out.

There was a noise from the outside, and he could see the dark one walking toward him through the sides of his chamber.

Ha ha ha. The dark one leaned over and looked down on him.

Sealer tried to break through the surface, to get at him, but the chamber contained him on all sides. The dark one showed his teeth. Sealer could not help but shiver.

No. I must not give way to fear. If he wants to eat me, he will have to fight me.

There was a rumble of machine noises, and suddenly, Sealer could feel himself moving, chamber and all. He rose up above the dark one, and then moved to the side.

I am next to the open water. One of the Land People boats moved quietly on the surface below him. The machine changed pitch, and his chamber was lowered onto the top of the boat. The dark one disconnected things from his chamber, as other Land People watched on the ledge.

The current in his chamber stopped, and he had a quiver of fear. Without the current, the water in such a small chamber would quickly become unbreathable.

The dark one shouted at the other Land People, and they went away.

Scrape. The dark one moved something on the top of the chamber, and some of the water splashed out.

Sealer twisted in the tight quarters to leap out the opening. If he could get to the open water, he could escape.

The dark one blocked the opening, holding a knife in one hand. But the other hand of the monster held something under the surface.

-Where is the stone?-

Words—real words, came out of a tiny silvery thing in the dark one's hand. It was a Talker!

Sealer didn't have any idea what he was talking about, but the Talker was a thing of legend. He had not really believed it existed.

-Give me the stone!- The dark one waved his knife.

-I don't know what you say.-

-You were there. I must have the stone. Give me the stone.- He struck the side of the chamber with his knife. It rang with a low tone.

Sealer pushed back away from the opening. *What stone? What was he talking about?*

Then, almost like a dream, he did remember something, near the seals' cave. There was something—he didn't get a good look at it.

He shouted back to the dark one. -I don't have it!-

The dark one paused for a moment, and then said, -Remember, and then you can breathe.-

He pulled the Talker out of the water and slammed the hatch shut. There was a large fluid bubble of air inside with him, but without the current, he would suffocate.

The dark one waved his knife again and showed his teeth, and then jumped back over to the ledge and went inside with the other Land People.

What does he want? What is this stone?

Already, he could feel the water lose its vitality. He could die within minutes unless the current was turned back on—or unless he could escape.

He pushed up close to the hatch. The seal was tight like a clamshell, only he was inside the clam. He shoved against it—he felt something give.

He beat against it, but he couldn't force it.

But there was a flexible seal, like a lip, that made the hatch watertight. If he were trying to open a clam, he would use a blade, or a spine to breach that opening.

He had no blade, but none of the People were without spines. Had the Land People forgotten?

Along his forearm, sharp spines grew. He had lost his baby spines a few years ago, and the new ones were strong.

He jabbed at the seal, and a hiss told him of success. With each new hole, the hatch felt less solid.

He struggled with it, and soon he could see how the hatch was secured. There was a tongue under a hasp, and the tongue was bent!

He slammed his shoulder against the hatch, again and again. The water was quickly exhausted, and he had to make do with the air that could leak past the hatch.

With a snick, the hatchway opened. He was almost too exhausted to move. He expelled air out of his blowhole and wedged his shoulders up through the opening.

Sealer hated to be above water. Something about the open air pressed down on him. It made things fall much faster than normal, and he could barely lift his arms and his body.

He pushed toward the edge, and then fell painfully off the chamber. He could hear the lapping of the open water. It smelled right. Although there didn't appear to be any open sky, there had to be a passage to a river, next to the sea.

But he still had to make it over the edge of the boat.

He'd followed seals ashore the last time he had gone with his father, and so he knew how to slide his body across the surface.

He grabbed at a net, draped over the side, and pulled himself up.

Hey! There was a shout from the Land People. He had been seen!

He couldn't stop to check. He pulled hard on the rope and toppled into the water.

Splash!

The water was cold and refreshing. He looked around and listened to the echoes.

He was free, in open water. It tasted like a river.

He kicked hard and headed for the center of the channel.

The thundering rumble of engines shook the water. They were after him. He swam harder. The sea was that way.

There was another rumble. Another Land People boat had joined the hunt.

He ducked lower and snatched a salmon that had gotten too close. He ripped the skin free with his teeth and tore into the meat and fat. He kept moving, but he had to have food.

The channel was opening up, and he had options.

Almost without thinking, he turned to the right, back to the scent of the seal cave.

...

The captain of the boat asked, "Why do you want to use the sonar, when your radio-tag shows us right where he is?"

"Ha, ha, ha, for the chase man!" Nat Marne grinned broadly. His hair was whipping in the breeze as they struggled to keep up with the fast moving merboy.

The captain shook his head. The man was crazy, but rich. He had confirmed the transaction instantly, before heading out on this illegal hunt.

They hit a wave and a wall of spray drenched them both. Nat glanced at his wrist, grinned and waved him on.

...

Sealer listened to the boat's song and pushed himself harder. The rush of energy he had pulled from the salmon was fading. He would need to find something more to eat.

Or, he could find a place to hide. He could last a long time without food if he wasn't moving.

No. They can find me, like they did before. I have to keep ahead of them.

The open ocean beckoned. It was safer there, and the Land People knew it. Both boats had positioned themselves seaward from his position, and whenever he made a run for open water, they were there waiting for him. He had almost run into the nearly invisible nets the last time.

If he'd only headed out to the safety of the deep at the very first, he could've gotten deeper than their nets.

But the stone was calling him. Every time he thought about it, he could remember just a little more. Maybe he had looked at it. Had he touched it? He couldn't remember.

He had to go back to find it. As long as he stayed close to the rocks, he could evade the Land People. Their boats were fast in open water, but they couldn't maneuver like a living thing. Especially not like a son of the People.

He could smell the seal cave ahead. This one was not a real cave under the water. It was a place where the waves had beaten a hole in the cliffs above.

Seal lions and seals used it, although the sea lions were being forced north in the past few years. The shelter made a good place for air-breathers to rest.

The People were the only creatures in the world who could breathe air and water, and that made them the rulers of the sea.

Or should have. There were so many predators. In the sea, there were always sharks, and relations with the whales and dolphins were always touchy. They were hard to talk to, and they told so many lies.

On the land, the Land People were a fierce and dangerous lot. Legend told of a time when the people of land and the people of the sea worked together, but it was a time of war, and Land People were always ready to sacrifice the People to win a battle. They could never be trusted.

Sealer swam through an underwater channel in the rocks, and for a moment, the boats thought he was still in the other cove.

Now is the time. He swam hard, out to sea. He could feel the water cool down as he reached the current. The distant roar of the engines told him that they had discovered his deception, but they could never find him now.

Sealer took a breathing spell to survey the waters and to hunt. There was a pod of orca farther off the coast and he exchanged greetings with them. They were friendly enough, as long as you kept your distance. They apologized for their manners, but the People tasted too good and were too tempting close up.

Far, far in the distance, in much deeper water, he could feel the overtones of People. He couldn't make out the words, but it was his tribe. He would be glad to see them again, in spite of the punishment he would receive for leaving on his own.

Unless he brought the smooth seal stone.

He could hear the engines. They were closer, but surely they hadn't found him yet. He wasn't all that far from the seal cave now. He could dash back in close to shore and get his prize. They would never suspect that. They knew he was safe in deep water.

He smelled the seal cave, and with his own blood racing, he swam hard toward it.

It's not a stone; it's a jewel. He could see it clearer in memory now. It was a deep blue crystal, set in a yellow metal clasp.

He approached the cave at full speed. He needed to get in and out instantly. The seals entered there, he could see where the stones had been worn smooth by their bellies. All he needed was...

He could feel the jewel, off to the left.

He arced sharply in that direction, over a sharp ridge. Sheltered by waving fronds of kelp, he could see it.

The surrounding stone had been cut by hand. It formed a nest. Deep in the center, he could see it.

The blue of the jewel was like nothing he'd seen before. He reached down into the hole and grasped the metal.

It was a dagger, sheathed in rotting seal hide. It looked like it'd been there for lifetimes. The jewel was set on the hilt. He grasped it.

. . .

He was Moray, a Warrior of the Volcano nation—a leader of his tribe. These cold waters were distasteful to him. But if the Ruler of the all the Seas called council, then he had to be here. He held his dagger, and swam with his peers to the surface.

Breaking into the air, they positioned themselves according to rank.

It was an inspiring sight. There were thousands of the People, all leaders from faraway tribes, surrounding the rocky point.

The Gold One walked out of the water, balancing on his legs almost as well as those Land People did. Those weak ones backed up before him—as well they should. The Land People should be greatly honored that the Gold One agreed to meet with them. Their trade goods were paltry, and their desire to cross the sea in their little boats made no sense.

Soon, the council would get on with the serious business of—

. . .

The sound of engines broke him free of the vision. Sealer shook his head to bring himself back to the here and now. *What was that? Was it true?*

The engines changed pitch, and he suddenly realized that they had trapped him in this cove. He could hear the splash as they let down their nets, stringing a wall across the entrance to the seal caves.

Other sea creatures came to their own conclusions, and the waters churned with motion. There were seals here. Some in the water were sliding up toward the cave, and some, more comfortable with their agility in the sea, were slipping back from shore. He could hear barks of panic when some of the seals ran up against the nets.

Sealer was strangely calm. Maturity had come over him like a wave. It was the vision. A touch of Moray still lingered in his blood. *Who are these paltry Land People to try to catch me?*

He looked at the dagger in his hand. He would need more agility. He sensed the seals around him, and chose. Quickly, as only a Warrior of the People could do, he swam through the water and sliced through to the heart of his victim. A faint chant echoed in the back of his mind, praise for the seals and a prayer for their tribe.

The blood was thick in the water, and he hoped there were no sharks inside the net. Seals were now escaping to land en mass. The water had not proved safe.

Sealer regretted his need. He would only need a little of the one he had killed.

The knife was sharper than anything he had handled before. It was quick work to make a belt and sheath for the dagger from the sealskin. The old one, which fell apart at his touch, showed fine detail work and decorations, which he would have liked to keep. Maybe he could come back for it some day, when he was safely back with his tribe.

He ate his fill from the seal. The Land People were not stupid enough to come into the water after him. And if they did, they were much slower than the seal had been.

The crabs and other scavengers were collecting on the seal carcass, and Sealer abandoned it. A fragment of verse came to mind, something he had never heard before, but seemed familiar.

- Dark brother of the shores
- Turn your wide eyes to home
- Seek the cave of your dam -

...

"What is that?" asked the captain. The sonar speaker was sounding something like a fast rhythmic whale song.

Nat Marne laughed, "Ha ha ha, can't you recognize a merfolk death chant?"

The captain sneered, "No. And I suppose you can? I didn't think there were supposed to be more than a dozen of the things left alive. I thought the Die-Off got them."

"Who knows how many there are? This is the first sighting in ten years."

The captain shook his head. *The idiot pays more for the creature than I make in twenty years, and then forgets to lock the hatch on the transport chamber. At least it hasn't dampened his spirits. He's a maniac.*

"Oh, there he goes!" The sonar showed a fast moving target heading straight for them. "He'll get trapped in the nets for sure."

The trace drew a straight line towards their boat, and then with hardly a pause, out the other side.

"He's through the nets!"

"Ha ha ha. Don't just stand there with your mouth open, captain! Get moving."

"But the nets!"

"Cut them away. He obviously has a way to get through them. Now get moving. Signal the other boat to follow."

They cut the nets and pushed the throttle over hard, barely missing the rocks at the edge of the cove.

What are we doing now? With no nets? The captain watched the sonar trace, still amazed at how fast the creature could swim.

"He's in deep water now, and he's not slowing down like last time. We'll never see him again."

Nat Marne nodded. "Send the other boat back. We'll keep going for awhile. I love a good chase!"

The captain shook his head, and turned back to the sonar.

. . .

Nat Marne couldn't contain his glee. *Go boy, go! Take your treasure home.*

That death chant was confirmation, and the speed with which he cut through the net was the clincher. It had all worked.

The RNA code he had infected the boy with at first had fed him the false memory of the dagger, but the death chant was from one of the visions encoded into the jewel on the dagger itself. Each time he held the jewel, more of the carefully crafted racial memories of the ancient merfolk would leach into his cells.

The fictional history of their race was one of his best works. If the boy could infect his whole tribe with the visions, it could change their whole future. And the future of the human race.

In a sense, the merfolk were his cousins, bred from genetic templates, just as he was.

I would kill them all, rather than let them continue with the memory of being artificial. What kind of a people would they be, knowing they were created as tools to win a war?

Now they have a destiny.

"Sir, I think we are losing him on sonar."

Nat moved closer to the screen, and looked at the traces. "Follow in that direction for another five minutes."

The captain nodded, not very adept at containing his contempt.

Marne was certain the people that had captured the merboy originally and who sold him would take their money and keep quiet. This boat captain, however, didn't like the job, and he was a danger. *What will I do with him?* He could have conscience pangs and report him in exchange for clemency.

I don't need WCE agents trying to track down Nat Marne right now.

He could kill the captain, in a dozen different ways. He had used that technique before, and most times it worked. People vanished all the time.

He glanced at his wrist. The countdown to the onset of severe symptoms was very close.

Oh, let him live. I'll just give him a large bonus. He would have more to lose by turning me in. Let him enjoy life, while he still has it. Money doesn't mean anything anymore.

He turned to the captain.

"Ha ha ha, that was a good chase, wasn't it?"

Chapter 6

DARNELL FARMS, L4 CLUSTER

Four men brought Ben Hendrik in. His hand was a bloody mess and he was out of his head with pain.

Dr. Bet Nomad moved quickly—there were fluids to stabilize, pain centers to block. She got the story from his friends while she prepared for surgery on the hand.

"He was plowing down by the canal. The tread was clogged up with mud and the last I saw, he was digging it out of the gears with a shovel handle. There was a scream, and I came running."

That was enough. She ordered them out of the sterile room and brought up the lights. It would not be an easy job. Surgery without an assistant never was. But in this case, Hendrik was still thrashing against his restraints; the pain block wasn't doing the job.

"Ben, listen to me…" But he wasn't listening to anything. His eyes were wide and frightened, and he tried to escape from unseen terrors that were coming at him from all sides. Maybe the pain block was working after all. He didn't seem to be favoring his hand in his attempts to escape.

There was little she could do, under these circumstances, and until she knew more, she wasn't about to put him under a full anesthetic just to make him be still.

With his arm clamped down, she cleaned up the wounds and placed the mangled hand in a transparent restraining glove that would keep the crushed fingers in the proper position and protected against accidental impact.

When she touched his face, he was burning up. She put a temperature patch on him—he was two degrees hotter than when he had come in.

She glanced through the transparent door at the four men waiting to see how their friend was doing. She hated this part of her job.

There was a comm on the wall next to her.

"Connect me to the mayor."

There was a delay, and then a familiar voice answered, "Yes, Bet, what can I do for you." It was Dan Gregor.

"You are the mayor?"

"Well, yes, for a month or so. I give up my shift then. We rotate among family heads."

"Okay, Dan. Put on your official hat now. I am requesting that the clinic be put under quarantine, right now. I need the external doors sealed, and it has to happen quickly—before I inform the people in here what has happened."

"Quarantine? A disease?" He was rattled.

"I don't know yet. But we have to keep everyone contained until I do know. Can you do it?"

"Well, I guess so."

"How fast?"

"Ten minutes."

"Good, then do it."

Bet raided her limited drug supplies to find something to calm Ben down and to stabilize his temperature.

Then she went out into the waiting room.

They all stood when she came in. She waved them back down.

"Ben is stable, but he is acting strangely. I need to get some information from all of you."

Only one of the men, Ben's brother Daron, had seen him earlier in the day. He had been coughing, but had appeared in good spirits. The other three were neighbors who came by to help when the accident happened.

Bet sat down with them where she could watch the door.

"It appears that your brother has an infection of some kind. He appears to be hallucinating, and he has a fever."

"He was out of his head," said Jack Newell, the neighbor to the north.

Bet looked up at the door as Dan arrived with a padlock.

"The problem we have is that, until I can find out the cause of this fever, all of us will have to remain inside the clinic. We can't risk the spread of an infectious disease."

"Hey! What's going on?" Jack looked behind him as Dan secured the lock with a noticeable click.

"Be calm." Bet set the example. "I have been in more quarantine situations than you can imagine, and most of them have been nothing more than a precaution. I suspect you won't have to stay here long."

"Quarantine!" The word had acquired the scent of death among most space dwellers.

Bet didn't want them to dwell on it. "Now, I could use some help handling Ben. The surgery room has actinic lights and we have gloves, so there will be no additional danger. I need someone whose stomach can stand up to the sight of blood."

She was laying it on a little thick, but most men, she had found, could face death a little easier if they were defending their masculinity.

Jack volunteered almost before she'd stopped talking, but they all agreed to help. With them listening, she got back on the comm and told Dan what the rules of the quarantine were. She sent for food, although she had plenty of fresh fruit already handy, and quoted from memory the rules of hygiene a community should follow when there was a chance of an infectious disease.

By the time she had been through the long process of preparing Ben Hendrik's hand for healing, there was a crowd of wives and other family members outside the door of the clinic.

She did her best to reassure them that this was just a routine precaution, and that they shouldn't worry.

Of course, they didn't believe her.

The last quarantine in the Farms that anyone remembered was some thirty years before, when three people had been spaced for chicken pox.

She set up a rotation so that someone was always watching over Ben, and then she took blood samples to analyze.

The office that held her lab had a lock on the door, and she used it. She could not be disturbed.

The rough analysis showed everything she had feared. Ben's blood was awash in the virus. Somehow it had changed from being just an innocuous bug that caused nothing more than a slight cough. Now it was a raging beast.

The other blood samples confirmed that everyone was already infected, but in them, the virus was behaving itself.

There had to be some difference. The emulation she had run on the virus showed that it modified a portion of its code every generation, much like a telomere, popping off a bead of a necklace each time it divided. It was the genetic equivalent of a timer—the same sort of timer that caused cells to age and die.

When she had first seen that, she had hope that the virus was some lab test that had escaped, some test platform that had a self-protection built into it so that it would die out on its own after a few generations.

Maybe that was true, but it now appeared that the virus had a payload. It was like a bomb with a timer.

Ben Hendrik was just the first.

. . .

"Call Dan Gregor."

"Hello." He sounded grim. "Is there anything I can get for you?"

"Dan, are there any transports due in?"

"Why?" His voice changed, cautious and suspicious.

"Because I think we should not open the locks. I have checked blood samples of everyone in the Farms, not just the ones in here with me now. I think everyone in the Farms has a version of the infection already.

"I think we need to declare Darnell Farms quarantined, and contact Prime for a full medical emergency team."

There was silence for several seconds.

"Bet, do you know what you are saying? We get transports in here all the time. We send food all throughout the clusters. A full quarantine would kill us. Who will buy from us if we have a quarantine? I can't do it."

She had suspected this was going to happen. Trade was the lifeblood of space habitats. None were self-sufficient. There had indeed been full quarantines on some settlements in the past, and they had not survived. She personally knew of two that were still orbiting with their airlocks open, waiting for some enterprising group no longer afraid of the disease to claim it and re-settle.

"Dan, you are mayor. Call your council and tell them what I said. For now, you can send someone over to unlock the doors. I can't find any reason to keep these men locked up. Not now."

. . .

There were several general anti-viral medicines, and she administered some to all five of the men. It was a useless gesture, she felt.

Bet felt like she was below a dam, watching a crack form high above her, and knowing that when it gave way, nothing she could do would be of any use whatsoever.

When the door was unlocked, she felt relief. They were not going to keep her in the convenient prison.

From the moment she had spoken the word quarantine, she had set herself up as a threat to the Farms. She was lucky she was dealing with a rotating mayor, not a lifelong politician. It was obvious what Lady Fortuna would have done with her.

The question was, should she go around him to contact Circuit Medical? If this had been any ordinary disease, she would have risked it. But a quarantine's only purpose was to prevent the spread of a disease.

If everyone already had it, then what was the use?

She had not been very convincing when she gave the news to Dan, because she didn't believe it would do any good.

There was a knock on the door. She worked the lock. Daron Hendrik came in, not waiting for her invitation.

"Ben's not breathing!"

. . .

The funeral was rushed. Bet felt isolated and numb. They sealed Ben Hendrik's body in an airtight bag and everyone who had contact with him was scrubbed down with antiseptics. He was moved to a hot box, where solar mirrors reduced refuse to ashes and gas. Contrary to their recycling policies, they vented the gas to space, even though she reassured them that the virus could not survive the temperatures.

I need to put a good face on this. It won't help anything to have everyone see death on my face.

But it was hard. She repeated her mantra; "I hate to lose a patient." Only sundown put an end to the socialization. She fled to her lab.

"Run an emulation of the Ben Hendrik virus, using the previous emulation as a base. Give me a running report just as soon as you get details."

She sat in her chair in the dark and watched the screen, munching apples.

Two hours later, she let her current apple drop to the floor. She went to the comm on the wall.

"Connect me with Circuit Medical Team, Vesta, L5."

"Sorry. All communication outside of Darnell Farms has been temporarily blocked."

She stared at the featureless box on the wall. *I should have acted faster.*

She addressed the lab, "Is the Net available?"

"No. The main relay is down."

"Okay, then address the following to General Medical Chat.

"Subject: Widespread virus in the clusters

"There is a synthetic virus widespread in the clusters. Sampling shows an almost 100% infected population. The virus causes a mild cough in the early stages, but it appears to have a generational timer that causes a change to a dangerous form.

"In the later stages, the virus replicates rapidly, causing a spike in body temperature.

"Then the virus selectively attacks the brain-blood barrier and infects the brain tissue itself. Permanent brain damage and death are likely.

"Treatment with general antivirals is indicated for early stage infections. Research to target this virus is needed immediately."

She paused, chewing her lip. General Medical Chat was a general public, anonymous medical forum. There were far more crackpots posting here than real doctors. It was only a longshot that this information would be noticed by medical practitioners, if indeed it could get out on the Net. With the relay down, she could not get interactive login on Medical Listings where the professionals expected this kind of report. However, this would go out store-and-forward. Once any kind of Net relay could be contacted, perhaps on a passing transport, it could escape the Farms.

"Sign the message: Dr. Bet Nomad, currently under political quarantine at Darnell Farms L4. Confirm identity with Circuit Medical Team, Vesta L5."

"Send it."

Well, I have signed my name as an enemy to Dan Gregor and probably the council as well. Sorry Dan, but there's no help for it.

I've also given out enough information that people in the know will suspect that I have a genetic sequencer. I need to give some serious thought to a cover story, an alternate identity, and some means of smuggling out the lab.

She closed her eyes wearily. She also needed sleep.

The chair was comfortable. She blanked the screen and let herself doze off.

. . .

She got nearly three hours.

The shock wave overturned everything in the room, including her chair.

Bet stumbled out of the room, looking for signs of a bomb blast, but the building itself looked intact.

Bree! Bree! Bree! A warning siren was echoing through the Farms.

She went outdoors.

Down in the fields, about two kilometers distant, nearly to the belt lake, she could see a tornado vortex twisting in the sky, rooted above a black spot that she could barely make out at that distance.

We are holed! That it was visible from here was not good. It had to be huge.

Darnell Farms was losing its air, rapidly.

PRIME CITY, CERES, L4 CLUSTER

Susan Pearce looked out her window at the girl pacing the street before her home. She'd been there for thirty minutes or more, sometimes resting in the shadows on the bench, sometimes standing in the middle of the street, peering down the lane first one direction and then the other.

Susan touched up her hair in the mirror, and then went out to meet her.

"Are you looking for one of my boys?" she asked, with her hand on the open door. "You could come in and wait in my parlor."

"No. I mean yes. I just need to speak to William Mason." The dark girl was plainly flustered.

Susan opened the door wider. "My name is Susan Pearce. I own the place. I spent a great deal of time fixing up my parlor, for just such a time as this, and it sadly gets very little use. I would be grateful for a chance to show it off. It's right beside the hallway and we could see him the moment he arrives. And besides, the chairs are much more comfortable than that stone bench."

Cinca weakened and nodded. "My name is Cinca Steriva."

The parlor was small, but quite comfortable, with deep chairs for four people. A bookshelf displayed titles Susan had hopes of reading again. The ones she didn't approve of went back into her bookbinder machine for pulping back to feed stock. On either side of the doorway were two tall display cabinets, with mirrored backs and glass doors to protect her treasures from dust. There were two tea sets, several isolated, but very pretty teacups, and some other ornate knickknacks. In the center of the left one was a large, elongated crystal, with a deep flaw through the center, tinted dark blue.

Cinca took the chair she was offered and looked around, while Mrs. Pearce brought them a mild coffee.

"Here you are, Cinca," she said, handing her the cup.

She took a sip. "This is a nice place."

Susan settled into her own favorite chair and stirred the cup. "Oh, you don't have to admire it. I am just happy to get to meet you. So many of my boys never think to bring their girl friends around to meet me, not even my own son David. He is serving in the outer fleet, you know."

"Well, I guess William may not think of me as his girlfriend. We had a little misunderstanding the other day."

"Oh, those things happen. You just have to realize that they may not be permanent. Sometimes a young man needs to see what it feels like not having a girlfriend to realize how much he needs one. William was always too serious. He's the oldest of my boys and I'd nearly despaired of him finding anyone. I think he took his father's tragedy too much to heart."

"Yes, he told me. It was a shame to lose him like that. I lost my father about five years ago, but in my case it wasn't a great loss."

Susan watched the girl over her coffee cup, trying to read her. There was something a little hard in her voice that she didn't entirely like.

"My first husband David was lost in a beam accident, as well. The Project likes to project such an image of precision and control, but there are far too many survivors like William and me to forget how much the work is built on human blood."

Cinca's jaw tightened. Then she brightened and said, "I think William mentioned you. You were a pilot?"

"I still am," she asserted, then sighed. "My poor ship Yo-Yo has long since gone the way of all metal, and I suppose Control would never let me at the controls of anything new, but it's a thing of the mind, you know. My first husband was the best pilot in the fleet, and I could keep up with him on my good days."

She stared at her cup. "That was a long time ago."

She coughed. And then coughed again.

Cinca said, "Are you all right?"

"Oh yes, I've had this cough forever, it seems. It's okay."

"There must be something going around. I've got a touch of it, too."

Cinca took another sip, and then asked, "Do you have any idea what William is working on? We got in an argument and he claimed I never paid attention to his problems. Well I do care, but sometimes it's hard to get a word out of him. I think he misunderstands when I pay too much attention to my customers at the cafe."

Susan looked her in the eye and shook her head. "No, not a lot. William has always been rather closed mouthed about his projects. He said a few things about a ship the other day, but nothing lately."

"What did he say about the ship?"

She waved her hand. "Not a whole lot. I think he takes those silly security rules too seriously, myself. I offer to give him the benefit of my experience, but he is so intent on doing it all himself."

Just then, there was a gentle chime of a comm in the next room.

"Excuse me," Susan said and then pulled herself out of the chair.

She was back in a minute. "I am afraid that William won't be coming back any time soon."

"What happened?"

"I don't know. It was that silly avatar from Control. People are being kept on double shifts."

"Why?"

She shook her head. "Some kind of emergency."

Cinca got to her feet. "Well, I'd better be going then. It was nice to talk to you."

Susan shook her hand. "Come back any time. I love to talk about William."

Susan watched as Cinca headed down the street at a near run.

There is something wrong about that girl. I gave her lots of opportunities, and she never asked about William, only about his job.

"Call Admiral Fields."

After a slight delay, a mature male voice answered. "Hello, Susan, how's the boarding house business?"

"Doing fine. Just fine. You know how I love to be a mother. I've got a job for you."

"Uh oh. You know my access is limited since they retired me. Who are you spying on now?"

"Jim, you always say that, but I know that the world doesn't turn without your okay. In any case, I'm worried about a girl one of my boys may be mixed up with. Cinca Steriva, she works at one of the cafes just outside of Control."

"And what is your interest?"

"She just feels wrong."

He sighed. "Okay, I will see what I can do."

. . .

Mason stood with a group of twenty, practically all of Lord Stephen's staff. There wasn't room in his office, so they were lined up in the hallway.

"No one knows what happened, and the panicked calls coming from Darnell Farms are not very informative. However, the telescopic view shows a significant plume. Transports all over the system are dumping cargo and heading there to evacuate the populace.

"But that's not our job. Our job is to find out what happened.

"It may be that a stray beam has punched that hole. Hodges, Mason, Palmer, Stewart—divide up the sky and find where it came from.

"Tafferty, Winter, Bell, and Case—space is now dirty from the debris, the dumped cargo, and anything else related. Find it all and get it into the register immediately.

"Emby… Where is Bucher?"

"Didn't report in. Family said he's sick."

Lord Stephen gave a short sigh that indicated what he thought of people who were sick during an emergency.

"Okay then, Emby, your job is to take the entire normal duty sheet and divide it among the rest of you. We have to keep everything moving. We can't miss a beat. Planets are still moving and we have to do our jobs. Dismissed."

Mason conferred rapidly with the rest of his team. Hodges was the most methodical of them and was the obvious team leader. He parceled out the sky.

"Give me the Centari area," Mason asked him.

"Done. Why?"

"I've been researching there in off hours. I'm familiar with it."

They headed for their respective soundproof cubes and settled in.

Mason asked the computer, even before he sat down, "Do you have the exact moment of the Darnell accident?"

"Yes."

"Show me the sky that the affected side of Darnell would have been facing when it happened. Highlight all masses above a thousand tons in that direction."

His search strategy was simple. If this was caused by a beam, and not simply a super-fast rogue object impacting from the outer system, then there had to be a massive object in the back beam. The beam projector would have to be in line with that massive object.

"Get me dopplers off of all the targets and report any with an anomalous radial velocity." Everything had orbits tightly monitored. Right now Darnell was ringing alarms in every monitoring system because it had been shoved, hard. Whatever counteracting mass would have been moved as well. If it were small, the velocity change would be significant as well and the radar pings would catch it. If it was larger, then he needed another technique.

Why would someone do this? And how?

Project Prime Control was in charge of every large TP beam in existence. It regulated them all. It said when and where. The entire human race had agreed on it. The beams were too powerful and too dangerous for there to be anything more than one central control.

The world paid its taxes to the Project, partly to prevent this kind of thing from happening. If this was a Project error, then it had to be identified and fixed immediately.

If it were someone else, then it was a direct challenge to the Project. They had to be located immediately and stopped.

"For targets larger than ten to the 14th kilograms, identify a target zone one quarter degree wider than the width of the visible disk as seen from Darnell, and give me detailed radar scans of those areas. I want anything, any mass that is between Darnell and the target."

If I were a terrorist with an unlicensed beam projector, I would use a big mass for the backbeam.

The screen displayed a running status on the scans that he had ordered. Everything was running slowly. There were hundreds of controllers making extreme demands on the system today. Probably there were one or more people doing his exact same job. Lord Stephen's team was just one of many, and often tasks were duplicated for insurance and as competition. Radar was definitely one of the overtaxed systems.

"Give me database readings on any monitored objects whose last positions were at variance from the calculated orbits."

The unknown ship was definitely on his mind. It had already been showing some drift.

The screen was full of listings, and kept on scrolling. *Oh, yes. The Darnell incident has really messed up the cluster. But at least that's another team's responsibility.*

"Reduce the list to objects with variance in the last two days, but before the time of the accident."

Now the screen had a reasonable list.

There were always a few items that showed variance, often because of secondary and tertiary effects of some beam action. A transport would push off a habitat, but some other object would be in-line with the beam and pick up a few dynes by accident. That was one of the reasons for perpetual monitoring. Controllers lived by the database, and their actions had to be correct.

He scanned down the list, surprised at three objects with their orbital vectors disturbed in odd directions. But they were very trivial changes compared with the disturbance that had caused the Darnell hole.

He blinked. *Where is the ship?*

It wasn't on the list.

"Give me a complete history on my mystery ship."

Two items appeared with warning bleeps at almost the same time on different screens.

Former asteroid Shoemaker's Nugget, now an iron mine in L5, had picked up a new vector. The momentum was in the right ballpark. It had been too small for the miners to notice on the heavy planetoid, but it was likely Shoemaker's Nugget and Darnell had been kicked in opposite directions by the same beam.

On the database screen, the unknown ship showed several different vector changes before it vanished completely from the expected radar zone.

Mason stared at the several screens, putting together the pieces. Like a three-dimensional puzzle, coming together in time, it fit.

"Assume the following: The ship has an active beam projector. It pushed itself off of Hester Center at approximately three AM yesterday, and then made another course correction off of New Mount Wilson at approximately eleven PM. It aligned itself between Shoemaker's Nugget and Darnell and fired a high-energy pressor beam. Then, within three minutes, it aligned on Valhalla and pushed itself away.

"Now, project the current position of the ship and give me a high priority radar ping for confirmation.

A corrected image of his outline appeared on a screen, with his loose assumptions corrected with the calculations from the database. It fit the facts far too closely for comfort.

If it were true, then the ship was fleeing the scene, but at an angle that would give it a comfortable Mars access if it wanted to swing back for another attack.

Bleep. The radar ping returned. He recognized the reflection characteristics immediately. It was the ship.

"Send the summary to team members and Lord Stephen. Add comment:

"People, we have a terrorist attack weapon in occupied space. It is still active, and we have to assume it still has enough energy for maneuvering and another attack.

"We need to kill it immediately."

JOLIOT, LUNA

The winds shook the transport again, and no one was brave enough to walk around the cabin any longer. The team had clustered around the pilot's viewport as they approached the swirling atmosphere of Luna, but the more experienced of them settled into the seats before they entered.

Robert Henderson was comfortably secure in his chair and watched the new members struggle to keep their balance under the increasingly severe buffeting.

For the early stages of entry into the lunar atmosphere, the transport was much like a spinning top. The primary beam could not be used to grab a mass as it could in free space. Mass was all around them now, and it was chaotic. The transport, basically a large cylinder, had a long way to fall. Due to the deepness of the atmosphere, the pilot needed to hold off any serious deceleration until they were much closer to the ground. Spinning the ship gave them directional stability.

The only beam activity was inside, a high frequency tractor that gave them floor gravity, but it wasn't intended to cancel out the turbulence. That, they had to suffer through with cushioned chairs and safety belts.

The lunar atmosphere was a perpetual storm. Giant TP beams were working around the clock, pushing against the edges of the new world, increasing its spin. The ancient moon used to have a rotation period of one month, always locked with one face toward the Earth. An atmosphere wasn't enough to make terraforming work. A viable ecology was needed, plants and animals living their own, uncontrolled lives on the new surface. Even if humans could adapt to two weeks of day and two weeks of night, their partners in life couldn't.

So the energy of the planets was redirected to make Luna spin faster. It was nearly up to a forty-eight-hour day, and that was the source of the World Court suit. A viable ecology could be sustained under that day/night pattern, some experts said. Why not stop there? The goal of going from forty eight hours to twenty four would take nearly as long as it had to get from one month to where it was now. If they stopped the spin beams early, the winds would stop, the ecology could take root sooner, and the nations champing at the bit to set down their own colonies on Lunar soil could reap a return on their investments that much sooner.

They were also much less likely to suffer if the nations that had not been granted colony lands managed to overturn the Lunar Settlement Agreement.

It was the Martian settlement disputes all over again, but now all the nations were more experienced, and more willing to fight for turf. The losers of that earlier battle had spent over a hundred years nursing their bitterness.

Robert Henderson had to be ready for either decision from the court, which was one of the reasons for this shipment of biological materials. If the winds should stop, colonists would want the ecology in place instantly.

He smiled, a little. Olympia's claim would be ready, one way or another. He had already begun the process of seeding wind-tolerant plants in the broken soil. The atmosphere was breathable, and although painful for the sensitive human nose, some life could make good use of the residual ammonia.

The atmosphere had been seeded with a soup of tailored bacteria and algae that had proven its use in converting the water ice/ammonia ice mix common in the outer planets into something resembling an Earth-compatible mix. Those wouldn't die out until the comets stopped coming.

There used to be a moon of Saturn called Hyperion. Smaller than Vesta, it was an irregular-shaped object, orbiting in the outer reaches of that planetary family, far above the rings. It had been sacrificed.

Punched out of Saturn's orbit, it had been fragmented into hundreds of millions of icy rocks. They now followed a sun-circling orbit and could be seen from Earth on a good night. It was called the Glitter Ring, although it was by no means a complete ring, managed and harvested by Project engineers called the Comet Men.

When Robert had been young, it had been a regular treat on a summer night to watch the impact flashes as the comets impacted the Lunar surface. He loved to tell the fresh-out recruits from Earth about it. It was one of the treats his generation had enjoyed that they missed—a spectacle that would probably never come again.

The comets were still coming, but the comet wranglers now had an atmosphere to play with and they were no longer allowed to strike the surface, not with the bio-engineers scattered out all over the place coaxing the plants to grow. They had gotten quite adept at skipping the comets through the storms. Sometimes, one of the more massive ones would skip through the clouds, just missing the surface and then climb back out to orbit the moon before finally swinging in low again and succumbing to the erosion of mass and momentum. One of those had come close Robert's first year as a biogenetic tech. The shock wave of its passage through the air had been formidable. He had requested ear protection gear after that, but Prime had turned him down. They would correct the problem in scheduling, he'd been told. He had learned to take such assurances for what they were worth. He bought his own protection.

He had chosen this seat well—he could monitor the pilot's viewscreen without squinting too hard. He looked at the timer counting down the transit window. They never stopped the comets, but they did allow gaps for such trivial tasks as getting biotech crews down to the surface and back. They still had hours of spare time, but Joliot was close enough to the equator that he worried out of habit.

He laughed silently at himself. He would probably worry about comets if he were landing at the pole. Sometimes you can't shake trauma reactions. Even if it had just been a big noise—a really big noise—the End of the World Big Noise, actually.

A block of red text suddenly appeared on the pilot's screen. Robert unclipped his belt. Carefully holding onto the handrails, he moved closer.

"What is it, Captain?"

The pilot frowned back at him. "Recall. There's a general emergency. All available transports are supposed to dump cargo and head for Darnell Farms, L4 cluster."

"That doesn't mean us, does it?"

The man looked solemn. "According to the books, it does! Darnell has a severe hull breach. They have to evacuate the entire population."

Robert pulled himself closer. "Well, you'll just have to land us anyway! We can't dump cargo here."

"That's not what my orders say."

"Splat the orders! That's a broadcast to all ships. We're in special circumstances here. Land us at the first target, we'll unload everything, and you can be off. You don't want us in the way if it's an evacuation. You might even get there faster this way."

The pilot shook his head, but he didn't abort the landing. Robert looked at the readings, especially the radar approach.

"My team," he shouted, "get ready to get wet!"

He barely made it back to his chair when the feeling in his stomach told him the pressor beam had been activated. Inside the cabin it was only a twitch, but the transport was decelerating at a hundred gravities. A good pilot could set a ship down in one long sustained push, but good practice was to get close to the ground and then use cirrance to hover slowly to a touchdown. This one was in a hurry. They touched down almost hard enough to rattle his teeth.

Robert was on his feet, zipping up his rain gear, ready to shout orders to his crew to handle the unloading.

"Dumping cargo!" shouted the pilot. Hatches opened on all four cargo levels. Side-aimed beams shoved the whole lot out into the dark, and the rain, and the mud. Hundreds of pallets of supplies sailed in the low gravity toward a soggy impact.

"Hey!" Robert was shocked, and furious.

The pilot didn't look back at him. "Liftoff in thirty seconds!"

Robert shouted, "My team! Out the hatches! Now!"

He turned to glare at the pilot. "You! I'll have you on charges!"

The officer went into a brief coughing fit. Then with a hate-filled sneer, he said, "You've got ten seconds, mud boy."

The hatches were already closing by the time Robert sailed clear of the ship in a jump. Cirrance splashed mud in all directions and the transport shoved up into the dark clouds.

And then there was nothing but rain and distant thunder.

As his eyes adapted to this dim twilight that passed for daylight on the lunar surface, he called together his people and had them count off.

"What happened?"

"He must have gone insane."

"Don't worry about him," he told them. "He won't ever handle a ship again. That was blatant disregard for safety.

"But right now, we have to salvage everything. Betty, take Brunet and find the expedition pallets. We're going to have to set up a camp right here, and then get local help to distribute what hasn't been destroyed."

Ann Merridan, one of the biologists, asked out loud what had been nagging at the edges of his thoughts.

"Boss, where exactly are we?"

He looked at the range of mountains barely visible in the distance. Their first landing site was supposed to have been near the central peak of Joliot. Nothing like that was visible. At the very best, they were tens of kilometers from another installation. And they were cut off. Radio couldn't cut through the lunar atmosphere, not from ground level. Positional beacons were out; they had no inertial reference system. Even magnetic compasses were useless on Luna.

His people were waiting for him to speak. His team that had given up their furlough to accommodate his whim. He was responsible for them even being here.

Did we bring maps?

ROCKY MOUNTAINS, NORTH AMERICA, EARTH

Kidd was chafed and sore in Nat Marne's suit. He regretted changing personalities. When he was Marne, he never noticed the discomfort.

But he needed to monitor the progress of the infection. His virus had a clock in its genes to shift to aggressive mode all at once, but he knew better than to believe that it would be accurate. There would be a Gaussian distribution to the outbreak, just like everything else. And that meant that some people had already been pushed over the edge. There ought to be some indication in the news broadcasts.

The problem was that his shuttle was over the Preserve. Net bandwidth was minimal here on a good day, and there must be some weather problem, because data was coming in at a crawl.

Of course, there were no relays in the renaturalized zone. The Governors of the Reserves were a fiercely ideological group, and one of them had wanted to ban radio waves from the Preserve, in spite of the laws of physics! Kidd had thought up the Neolithics, but the bureaucrats who made it happen had not considered it a terribly radical idea.

He tried to make sense of the reports that were coming in, slowly over the long distance relays. There had been a mass-murder in Delhi. Some Cluster habitat was leaking air. There had been an air-transport accident when a shuttle's pressor beam had shattered all the windows in Boston's business district.

These and some others looked suspiciously like the effects of sudden incapacitation. The brain damage would take many forms. He hadn't tried to target any particular part of the brain. Most people would simply die. Others would succumb to various forms of dementia.

It was frustrating to be so disconnected at this critical point of the project. But the discovery of the merboy had been a gift from God. He had that dagger sitting in an airtight canister for years, wondering if there were indeed any of the merfolk left. One more piece in his grand puzzle was now in place.

He glanced at the horizon. They were dropping down to the Front Range. He would be home in a minute.

He closed his eyes for a short rest.

...

Paula Campbell rested at the desk, sipping bottled water she had found in the kitchen coolbox.

This is a strange place. What kind of person is he?

She poked at the objects she had found on the shelves. Do I dare take any of it? There were weapons, chemicals, and more computers—modern computers—than she had ever seen in one place.

The dart gun with its bewildering array of drugs made her very uneasy. She had never seen its like, other than in popular screens about international spies.

He comes and goes in an unmarked, one-man shuttle. He has a portable powerplant that runs from TP bottles. He leaves no papers or documents of any sort, and his computers listen to me, but never respond.

That last meant she had to leave very soon. The computer knew she was here. He had probably been notified already. If she hadn't the gut feel that he probably always worked alone, she would have already been down the elevator shaft, trying to remove all trace of her two-day-long climb. That shuttle had gone west, and even if he had just gone to Olympia or California, it still gave her a little breather time before she had to make her escape.

No one owns these buildings. He's here illegally. I could probably take some of these, and he wouldn't want to report them stolen.

I should have thought this out. Collecting abandoned trinkets from people dead hundreds of years was one thing. Stealing from a living person bothered her more than she had thought it would.

She glanced again at the aquarium. There was an aerator and some gadget that was monitoring its mineral content. An expensive tank with no fish. She shook her head. There was nothing but puzzles here.

But there were ripples on the surface of the water.

Then she heard it. Cirrance!

He was back, way early.

. . .

He came in, looking tired, tugging off a black skintight shirt. He took one look at the inside of the living area and stopped.

From her viewpoint in hiding, she could see the expression on his face. First shock, then worry, and then an utter blankness. He shifted his weight, and suddenly she lost track of where he was. Somehow he had vanished into the shadows.

Where did he go! She slowly lifted her head to the right, trying to peer into the side door. Well hidden in the blackness of the closet, her only hope was that he would go hunting for her in the wrong places and give her a chance to slip over to the shaft. *Did I leave the ropes in plain sight?*

The lights went out.

Paula shifted farther back into the closet. Darkness was no longer her shelter.

It happened in less than a second. She felt him coming. She swung her hand and fired the dart gun blindly.

Heavy, sweaty flesh slammed against her. There was a sharp pain on her arm and her head rang from its impact against the wall. She probably screamed, but part of it was blacked out.

She found herself out in the hallway, gasping, fumbling for the ropes with one hand. The dart gun was still in the other. A line of blood dripped from a slight wound on her arm.

What happened?

She paused with the rope in her hand, listening. There was no sound other than her panicked breathing.

Did I get him? What was in the dart? Some of them had been plainly lethal. *Have I killed him?*

She had to find out. Forcing her hand to release the rope, she tiptoed back into the living area. She fished her light out of its pocket in her climbing suit and scanned the area.

There was a leg sticking out of the closet. He was sprawled out on the ground. Cautiously, she approached, and opened the closet door wider.

He was still naked to the waist. He was wearing dark-vision goggles, and a large hunting knife was on the floor next to his hand. He had been coming in for the kill.

The dart had stopped him in mid-stride, before he managed to gut her with that knife.

Paula settled down to her knees. She was shaking too much to stand.

She reached out and put her fingers on his neck. A strong pulse assured her he was alive. An involuntary reaction to her touch told her he wasn't knocked out very deeply, or for very long.

...

Kidd had been knocked out as Warrior, and as Warrior, he awoke.

Warrior never spoke, never showed emotions, never debated with himself. Warrior assessed the situation and acted.

He was tied at the wrists, palms together. Ankles were likewise secured. He was hoisted, head down, by a rope looped over a structural iron beam. He was out of easy reach of any wall. Bonds were made with high quality, multibraided colored rope with a shock core, like that used by mountain climbers. Rope was abraded in many places along its length.

Stilling his own breath, he listened. Light footsteps, irregular pacing. Echoes indicated the kitchen. Probably the same female seen in the goggles. No sounds other than regular equipment noises.

He twisted his wrists hard, and the artificial creature on the skin came apart, lubricating his skin and allowing him to slip one hand free.

Footsteps were coming. He bent double and lifted his weight with one hand pulling on the rope, while struggling with the knots with the other.

"No!" The female shrieked, and came running at him with a broom.

He struck a defensive blow, but it threw him into a wide swing, still suspended by the rope. She took a step back and then kicked at him, throwing her whole body into it. He tried to snag her leg, but was unsuccessful.

He glanced at where the rope was tied off. Slip knot. His path swung him toward the open elevator shaft. She reached for the knot, and he bent at the waist to disturb the swing.

She pulled his knife from her belt, and in one motion, severed the rope. He hit the floor short of the opening, but her muscular kick pushed him over the edge.

Legs still bound, he stretched both arms wide. The shaft was a long drop, but he would not be falling cleanly.

He hit the far wall after falling three floors. He snagged a ledge with his left hand. The shock tore ligaments and nearly dislocated that shoulder. The pain was a shock to his system, but it didn't affect his concentration.

He gained another grip on the ledge with his undamaged right hand. He called up a memory of the elevator shaft from several years back. There was a run of pipes to the left of his position. He attempted to shift toward it.

His left hand slipped. He checked it. It was covered with blood, torn by the initial impact on the rough stone.

"Stay put!" came a female voice from above. "I'm coming. I won't let you fall."

Rescue offered. Should he accept? He risked a wipe of his bloody hand on his pants leg and checked its abilities. Not sufficient. The arm had no leverage with its injury. His toes could find no grip on the wall below.

Wait then. Rest. Perhaps the rescue would present an opening to attack. He locked his muscles and waited, motionless.

After a couple of minutes, he could feel the heat of her body behind him, and hear her breathing. His own strength was fading, but he visualized a leap backward to grab her.

Wait. He obeyed the voice in his head without question. Warrior was a passive slave to his over-self.

He followed her actions by the sounds and her heat. She lowered herself past him, and secured the rope that was still securely bound around his ankles. She tied him off, then climbed back up.

Slowly, rhythmically, she hoisted him up. When he felt the cool floor tile against his back, the voice in his head said, *Shut down.* And he did.

...

Kidd gritted his teeth against the wave of pain. His Warrior persona could block it all, but in his normal mind, he had to make do with less efficient methods.

Warrior could fight until every last drop of blood was gone, and that single-mindedness had saved him in times past, but the burglar clearly wanted him alive, and he was willing to go that route.

"Who ... who are you?" The words came stiffly, against the pain.

"Never mind."

"Lights!" he shouted.

The girl blinked against the sudden flood. He got a good look before she put up her hand. Later, he would be able to identify her.

"I need help."

"Are you done trying to kill me?" she asked.

"Yes. You saved me. I owe you." He didn't mean it, but he had learned to speak a convincing line.

"Okay. Where is your medical kit? You're bleeding all over the floor."

He told her. She left, and he closed his eyes to center himself. His priorities had not changed. He still needed to monitor the plague, but now he had to manage his captor too, until the plague got her.

Chapter 7

DARNELL FARMS, L4 CLUSTER

Bet raced through the falling snow, laboring to breathe the air her mask offered, getting used to the tight fit of her homemade pressure suit. She was grateful for it, something she had packed away unused for years.

She had not been a runner. Many of her postings would have made that impossible. In spite of the urgency, she had to slow to a walk to catch her breath before starting up again.

Transports were docked at both end-cap stations, loading everyone, some at gunpoint. The Emergency Habitat Response Team had commandeered everything that could be used as an interior vehicle. They were all down by the hole.

She had managed to escape the roundup by getting herself assigned to the emergency team. Refugees had to leave everything behind.

I have to avoid that. I need time to pack the clinic.

"Alert: General emergency call." The computer's voice was calm, but insistent.

She sighed. *I guess I am the only one left. But who's calling?*

A timid male voice whispered. "Hello? Can anyone hear me?"

"Yes, this the Clinic. Who is this?"

"Ah. My name? Ah. Joe … that's it. Yes, I'm Joe."

"Okay, Joe. What do you need?"

"Ah. I'm Joe. Where did everybody go? He, he. That rhymed."

"Where are you Joe?" It took over a minute to make sense of the man, but he was on her side of the belt lake, and he obviously needed help. Her priorities were clear. The packing could wait.

...

The hole was a third of the way around the sky. The air on that part of the habitat was filled with swirling snow, moving in a large rotating mass. Details were obscured, but the EHRT seemed to know what they were doing. It appeared that a pair of bulldozers were pushing a farmhouse toward the opening. There were streams of water playing over the debris dumped into the hole. It was turning to steam and ice. The plan was to seal the hole with an ice-plug.

All of the real air was gone. The belt lake was boiling off, as the low pressure turned all free water into water vapor and ice. The only air that could be breathed was in the tank on her back. She carried another for Joe.

Suddenly the world lurched, and she stumbled, trying to keep on her feet. That was becoming more common, and she did not like it at all. The cylinder that had been the Farms was not spinning smoothly anymore. She knew enough physics to be very worried.

Alongside the lane, trees swayed back and forth in their own reaction to the shake. There was a roadsign where the lane branched, and she took the right.

Stability and habitability were antagonists in cylindrical habitat design. The most stable spinning cylinder was short and wide, like a tire—but people could only live on the inside of the "tread". More living space would be available if a habitat could be long and narrow, like a pipe.

Habitats couldn't be built like pipes, however. They had to spin, and a pipe's natural spin was end over end. Even if the spin was started with its axis along the length, the tiniest irregularity in its mass would cause it to spin out of control, and flip over to the end-over-end mode.

Darnell Farms was longer than it was across, to provide more farm land, but the designers had added a belt lake. This deep pool of water provided a center mass like a big flywheel to make the whole thing stable.

But more than half the water was now gone, boiled away and vented out the hole. Worse, the reports she had been hearing from the EHRT were that a thick bulge of ice had been forming all around the hole, both inside and outside. The ice was needed to seal the leak, but it was too massive.

Darnell Farms was approaching the point of instability.

If the hole was plugged, if it could be spun down, if a clean repair could be made, then the habitat could have its air refreshed and new water shipped in.

When she had her three-minute meeting with the EHRT field commander, he said there was a chance to save the ecosphere. She could tell from their eyes that no one else in the room believed him.

...

There was another branch in the road, and she was grateful that Darnell had been large enough to have road signs. She took the left branch. She visualized the map that had been hanging on the wall in the abandoned Mayor's office. Joe's house should be around the bend.

A swirl of white parted just long enough to show the structure. Resisting the urge to cut across the field, she followed the road. It would not do to sprain an ankle on the irregular ground. There had been no one to notify where she had gone. There was no backup.

The front door was open. She jogged through the darkened house. There were lots of rooms, but no Joe.

How had he been able to breathe? He had not been very coherent. Her first guess had been anoxia, but suppose it wasn't.

If I lived in a place like this, where would I hide a sick relative?

She went out the back door onto a wide porch. There was a large barn. Carefully stepping through the frozen and brittle grass, she entered the wide doors of the structure. It was dark inside, and she had no time to hunt for the switches.

He had called. Where is the comm?

She located one on the wall.

"Connect me to the lab computer in the clinic."

"I recognize you," the lab responded.

"Access my comm log. Does the last message have an answerback?"

"Yes."

"Call it, and patch me in."

She was prepared to talk to Joe, but even in the thin air, the call alert echoed faintly down the hall. She turned her head back and forth, and then moved down the row of silos until she found one with the noise coming from it. The hatch resisted. The pressure monitor on the door showed that it had a standard atmosphere inside.

"Hello. I'm sleeping." It was the reply on her call.

"Is this Joe?"

"Yaa. Joe."

"Joe, I am at your door."

"Door's locked."

"I will open it, but there will be a wind. Stand back away from the hatch."

"Okay."

Bet was making hard choices. There were risks here of decompression effects and anoxia, but she was out of options. She gave him a minute, and then pushed the seal lever over hard. There was a roar of escaping air, but it quickly faded and she was able to force the hatch open.

Joe was sitting against the far wall. He was a large, gray-haired man, and he had the gentle smile of a child.

The anoxia hit. His eyes rolled up, and his head fell back against the wall.

She struggled to get the breathing mask on him and the air flowing. She slapped his face.

"Stop it."

"Joe, can you stand up?"

He put his hand on her shoulder, and struggled up.

She took his hand and led him out of the barn.

"Where's Ruth? And little Joey?"

"They are safe. Now follow me. We have to go for a long walk."

. . .

The air was almost gone in her breather by the time they made it back to the clinic. She had questioned him on the way.

Joe Burnell had gotten sick, a bad fever. His wife had hidden him in one of the silos, afraid that if she turned him over to the clinic, that he would be dumped out the airlock.

Joe didn't know what happened then.

Bet knew. The EHRT roundup squads had gone through every house in the Farms and herded the population toward the waiting transports. They ignored every excuse and disregarded every story.

Ruth Burnell and her son were heading to some other habitat without any idea that Joe had been discovered.

"Joe. Close your eyes and hold out your hand." He did as he was told, a smile of anticipation on his face.

She got the blood sample so fast that he didn't even notice, concentrating on the candy she had handed him at the same time.

"Wait here, Joe."

He nodded, working on the candy.

By the time she had finished her analysis, he was asleep, cuddled up on the floor, holding the blanket she had given him.

The virus is gone.

Joe had survived the fever, and it was plain that he had some brain damage from it, but it was clear that the artificial bug was self-limiting. It did its job, and then died quietly.

The plague is survivable.

Tension eased away, and she put her hand on the table to support her suddenly weak legs.

She looked at Joe, sucking his thumb in his sleep.

Will all the survivors be like this?

CENTRAL CONTROL, CERES, L4 CLUSTER

"I think we can take it out." Lord Stephen pointed at the diagram on the large screen on the wall. "The initial tractor will pull it back toward us, and with the force we'll be using, there will be no time for it to set up a maneuvering beam. By the time it could latch onto any mass for steering, it should be back here." He tapped the diagram forcefully with his wand. "Harrison's push-pull will be waiting for it, and we'll tear it apart."

The team nodded. It was simple, forceful attack. Pull it back with ten thousand gravities, straight into thin layers of opposite sense TP beams, each with five thousand gravities of pull.

"After that, there will be nothing left to do but collect the pieces and track down the terrorists.

"To your stations."

. . .

"Mason." Lord Stephen's voice echoed in his cube.

"Yes, sir."

"Palmer has come down with a fever. You'll have to double up on his duties. I'm changing the access codes now."

"Acknowledged."

Mason could barely stay in his seat. He had no ill will toward Palmer, but this was a step for him. Palmer was a Controller, First Class. Lord Stephen was pulling strings for him again.

Do a good job, and things will come your way. He had always felt that, even when years of experience seemed to say just the opposite—you had to make waves, and it was more important who your friends were than how well you did your job.

But he had been the one who had identified the terrorist ship, giving Lord Stephen's team credit, and the Peers gave them the go-ahead to bring it in. Lord Stephen's credit was rising, and so was his.

He looked over his screen, making note of which resources he was authorized to use. He had to use them well or they would be taken away just as fast.

"Lock a radar beam on the ship. Allow for the tractor beam."

The tractor was already activated, and shortly, the tide of energy would be dumped into the ship, moving it back toward Ceres. The radar would have to predict that motion and shine its radio waves toward the point the ship would occupy then.

He had his computer lay out a large diagram, updated with real time data, showing the moving ship and the position of the push-pull barrier. It should come apart when it hit, and he wanted radar returns on all the pieces.

It was moving fast.

Then it exploded.

"I want a table of all the pieces, ordered by size."

He had to wait a moment for the radar system to bring in all the data. The explosion had caught him by surprise.

The rogue came apart a little early.

The table started building.

Mason frowned as the lines of data ordered themselves on the screen.

"This can't be right. Call Lord Stephen."

"Here."

"This is Mason. Did you watch it?"

"Yes, I have a chart of the explosion."

"That wasn't an explosion. The ship deliberately split into pieces. Every piece is identical, the same size. And some of them—most of them—are making course changes on their own. We *had* one terrorist weapon. Now we've got a hundred of them."

. . .

Cinca moved along the back streets near Mason's place, keeping to the shadows.

I'll kill him. He reported me!

It had been close. Two men walked into the café as she was getting an order for another customer. One glance through the little window in the door, and she recognized them. Board agents. They had been pointed out to her during the first briefing, when she had taken this job. If she saw them, she had to assume that her cover was blown.

She went out the back door and had gotten to a comm, but her access code gave no response.

My own team has cut me off. They know I'm being hunted, and I'm expendable.

It burned inside her. Oh, she had listened to the fanatics when they said that everyone had to be willing to give their life for the cause. But she had believed that she, at least, deserved loyalty from the group.

The rumors on the street scared her worse. The whispers in her Three Sins cell said the ship was an ultimate weapon, something that would allow them to dictate terms to the Project. *If so, the attack on Darnell Farms was crazy. It had to be the Hydra, but the whole point of a weapon like that is threat and intimidation. You don't launch a pre-emptive attack with a doomsday weapon. Have they all gone insane?*

A chill hit Cinca. She shivered, and felt aches. *I need to hide out—someplace warm.* Maybe some other group unknown to her was sabotaging the climate control.

She sneezed and had to wipe her nose with her hand. *What a time to come down with a cold.*

It's all Mason's fault. I'll make him pay. The world is full of jerks.

She turned a corner and was brought up short by the sight of the entrance to Susan Pearce's building. She hadn't realized she was so close. She stumbled to the side, trying to stay out of view of Susan's window, and fell awkwardly against a stonework pillar.

The profusion of yellow flowers in the pot infuriated her in her pain. She grabbed it with both hands and smashed it against the ground.

Broken and dying, the crumpled beauty on the ground hit her like a blow to her face.

She was six, and her trio of zinnia's had been her first attempt at gardening, the seeds a gift from her neighbor. She had been so proud of the blossoms, yellows and reds. Her mother's boyfriend had sneezed in his beer and ground the flowers into the mud. "Allergies" was all he said, and then slapped her to the ground when she cried.

Cinca stared at her destruction. Childhood tears blurred her sight.

"I am so sorry!" she whispered to the yellow ruin. She turned to the back street, and ran.

. . .

Hydra 23 was now on its own. It caught the edges of a tractor beam and slipped inside its limits. The power accumulator at its heart was designed to tap energy from any beam it encountered, but it was already full from the high-tension beam that had pulled it back toward Earth space. It and all of its brothers had received the signal to deploy once they had the energy.

Now it needed a target. Inside its brain was a map of both L5 and L4 clusters. A quick look at the stars, and it was aware of its own location. It built a list of targets and chose the 23rd easiest. That would require two course corrections. Attack could begin in thirty four hours.

The computer at the heart of Hydra 23 was a standard commercial model, with a few alterations. One was the lack of a Net connection. The brain felt for a connection as it had several times since the Hydra complex ship had disintegrated, but there were no packets. There was nothing to do but complete its program. There would be no abort command.

PACIFIC OCEAN, EARTH

The whale was in panic, fighting for its life as it surfaced rapidly, dragging the huge mass of the giant squid with it.

DeepSwimmer was far offshore, and he could hear the whale's distress. He called to the People.

-Brothers. I will need your help.-

But the People were all resting on the shelf after the day's fishing, and it may be that his call bounced off the inversion layer. If they could hear his call, they were inclined to pretend they hadn't.

I will have to do this myself.

He swam toward the upwelling where the beasts were fighting. When he got close enough, he could see the whale's problem. The squid had lost an arm to the whale's jaws, but it was still strong, holding onto the whale's body and attempting to keep it below the air.

A whale could live without air for a long time, but it had no gills like the People. It had to surface or die.

Those arms could wrap around one of the People. He would be no more than a bite for the great squid.

DeepSwimmer gripped his hand on the dagger. The Whales were not People, but they had been friendly. Although they claimed not to understand when People talked of treaty, it was something DeepSwimmer had been urging for some years. It was up to him to join the fight, to help.

As he closed, the turbulence beat against him, and he expelled all of the air in his lungs. He would breathe the water.

The whale saw him coming, but it was panicked. It could only kick the harder. All along its flank were great circular welts, battle scars of the epic struggle. DeepSwimmer could feel the heave of the whale's lungs as craved air, but could not get it.

The People lacked the strength of the giants, but they were quick. DeepSwimmer was in and slashed at one of the long arms. The squid noticed him.

He jabbed with his blade, working his way up the arm toward the head. The squid changed color and, for a moment, lost some of its grip on the whale.

The whale sensed the change and pushed its great fluke, now free of the entanglement. The current of their passage through the water threatened to shake DeepSwimmer free, but he held on with his knife deep in the squid's flesh.

Soon enough, they broke the surface. DeepSwimmer's eyes hurt from the bright glare.

But something was wrong. The whale could not spout from his blow-hole. The squid still had an arm around the whale, blocking off his air.

DeepSwimmer climbed the squid's arm, struggling against the heavy surf, then he hacked chunks from the squid. A great arm curled around his body, and he was dragged under.

There was a shudder through the water as the whale at last could breathe.

But the squid had him, and they were dropping rapidly from the light waters. It was quickly too deep to see, and the arm was painfully tight around him.

All he could do was hack away, grateful for his gills.

In the end, the squid was strong, but DeepSwimmer had a sting that could not be stopped. The squid gave him up and returned to the far dark waters, to heal.

It was a long swim back to the surface, and the whale was still there, waiting for him.

They drifted in the warm, light waters, staring at each other's great circular wounds.

-Come with me, and we will hunt together- The whale boomed its invitation.

DeepSwimmer laughed. -I have had enough squid. But tell me, have you seen the tuna?-

-They were two days-

DeepSwimmer tried to mimic the voice of his elder. -Thank you. This is a treaty. We can help each other again-

-If you say so-

. . .

Sealer startled out of his trance, his hand firmly on the dagger.

-Keep that blade where I can see it.- Jawtooth held his spear pointed at Sealer's throat.

Sealer carefully resheathed it. His mind was still filled with DeepSwimmer and the whale.

-I have returned from the Seal cave.-

-Then where is the token? I looked for it while you slept, but it is nowhere. You need the smooth stone to get out of my tender care. Blackspine will remove your hide one stripe at a time for this escapade.-

-Blackspine! I need to talk to him.-

Jawtooth laughed, and it wasn't a comforting sound.

-Blackspine wants to talk to you too, never fear. Get moving. We have a long swim.-

DENVER, EARTH

"My name is Gregor Leinburg"," said Kidd, with a hint of a German accent.

Paula sat on a small chair dragged over from a workbench, watching the man test the ropes she's used to tie him down on the bed. She listened with a frown on her face, holding the dart gun in a loose grip, not aimed at anything in particular. "I asked who are you, not what your name was."

He pushed his lips together in a slight smile. "I work for the Berlin Zoo. I am scouting out some Ursus arctos, American brown bears that we wish to acquire for the Black Forest Preserve. You do know that European bears went extinct back after the Star? Part of my master's project was to lay groundwork for the expedition that will arrive in another month. Do you want to read my paper? I have it over on the library shelf."

She glanced over at the shelf, then back at him, gripping the gun more tightly. "I don't trust you, and I don't think I believe you. You have too much spy gear here. I don't think you're hunting bears at all. And why set up in the top of an abandoned skyscraper?"

He shrugged. "Not my call. This advance station was already here when I joined the project. I think we have a lease on it and everything. You have to admit, it has a great view of the mountains."

She tapped the barrel of the gun against her knee. "Then why did you try to knife me?"

His face turned red. "Sorry. That wasn't the smartest thing I've ever done. But you had me running scared. I knew that I was the only person that was supposed to be here today. You were a burglar, and I didn't have any weapons."

"What do you call this," she held up the gun, "and the knife?"

He laughed. "I call them a tranquilizer and a hunting knife. Okay, maybe the knife is a weapon, but I never used it for anything more dangerous than whittling sticks for kindling. You saw how dangerous the tranquilizer was. It didn't knock me out long, did it? I'm just glad I hadn't loaded the real loads we will use for the bears. You got me with the dosage used for badgers."

Her frown never let up. "You're lucky I didn't want a death on my conscience, or I would have left you in the elevator shaft!"

She got to her feet and walked around the room, pacing as she had all day long. She was pretty. Nice muscles—from the arms, a climber.

Kidd could guess her thoughts. Her scavenging expedition had blossomed into full-scale crime, and she didn't know what to do.

"Lady Burglar, could I check up on the news?"

"The Net doesn't work, I don't think."

"Sure it does. Zugriffskennzahl blau grün 12."

The computer began speaking, "Quarantine sind Alarmbereitschaften für Teil Der Östlichen Länder erklärt worden."

She raised the gun. "Stop it!" She had the light of panic in her eyes.

He waved his good arm until the ropes , "It's okay!" To the computer, he said, "Change to English."

" … flooding in the lowlands because of the breach in the Zeider barricade."

"Stop it, I said."

"Computer stop the news." The fragment of the report frustrated him. At least he was able to activate the code that would have the computer back up his German student cover story.

He looked at her. "Did you hear that? There is some kind of disaster in the lowlands. Can't I listen? I have family back there!"

She lowered the gun. "Okay, but I will give all of the orders. What do you want to monitor?"

He told her which news topics, and she told the computer. She was relieved that it responded to her, now that it was talking English. That had been Kidd's intent, when he gave it that code word. Normally, his computers were keyed to his voice alone. There were other pieces to the Leinburg cover identity, but it was over fifty years ago that he had set it up, and he had to trust to luck that she wouldn't get that deep into checking his story.

• • •

They listened to the news for two hours, and although he could have used an anti-inflammatory to help his shoulder heal faster, he didn't want to distract her. The endless stream of disaster stories beat her down.

"Give me the top stories in the Denver area." She added that time and again, in addition to Gregor's queries about the happenings in Europe. Kidd didn't mind, since he would normally have been monitoring the world at large. The Leinburg persona, of course, was worried about a family back at home. Just as she was obviously worried about someone in the Denver area.

She listened to a report of a fire, and jumped up from her seat and headed for the east side of the floor.

He waited for her to get out of earshot and whispered, "Monitor the medical reports. Flash the lights in equipment bay two when a description of the brain fever appears."

The computer reported, "Expect a delay. Network activity is at a peak."

"What is that?" She came back sooner than he had expected.

"The Net is slow."

She ran her fingers through her scraggly hair. "I don't know what's going on."

"Was there a fire?"

"Yes, but it wasn't near … They're getting it under control. It isn't anywhere near here."

Behind her, he could see the lights starting to flash in the equipment bay.

So soon? He hadn't expected a good diagnosis so early. If the virus was detected too quickly, there was a chance that it could be circumvented. There were still a number of medical geniuses at large in the world and if Berlin let them loose, the plague could be stalled. Sure, there would be a lot of deaths—in the millions—but it would just affect individuals, not humanity itself. He couldn't let that happen.

He chafed at his restrictions; tied to a bed, a disabled shoulder, a body that was more concerned with healing than letting him think clearly. And the girl—she was distracting him. The injuries and the dart, they had messed up his focus.

And the Leinburg identity—he hated being the universal young man. He hated always being the Kid. He had hated it for nearly two hundred years.

"Computer, give me a report on the plague."

She gave him a sharp look, but listened as the computer started listing out all the quarantine listings. Nearly every nation had reports. Berlin had a call out to establish a centralized disease management center.

Kidd didn't let it show, but he was pleased. The bureaucracy had all bases covered, and they were moving much too slowly. A committee would never be able to stop it.

"What's going on?" she asked.

"It looks like there is a widespread plague. I suspect all these other disasters are being caused by that as well."

She put her hand to her mouth and looked distractedly towards the north. "I hope it doesn't come here."

He shook his head, "No chance. I heard you coughing a moment ago. You probably have it, too."

She frowned and looked him over again. "Your accent has vanished." She picked up the gun again. "Okay. Who are you?"

Chapter 8

DARNELL FARMS, L4 CLUSTER

"Colonel Chan, are you there?" Bet Nomad called.

"Yes, Doctor. I am glad you called. I was just about to think my comm was dead."

"What?"

"Yes, it appears that the Net is just about unusable. I can't reach Ceres. Bits and pieces of sentences come through, but I can't talk to anyone."

"But I can hear you fine."

"Perhaps it's the relay in our ship. What did you call about?"

"I located another farmer. He'd been left behind and he's not very responsive. Maybe brain damage."

"Well, you'll just have to handle it for now. My crew is dropping like flies."

"What do you mean?"

"They are all coming down with the flu."

"Colonel, I need them here, just as soon as you can. This isn't the flu. It is a new viral infection and unless it is treated immediately, it can be fatal."

There was a pause on the other end.

"Doctor, can you come to us? We are on the edge here. We almost have the hole sealed, but the habitat is unstable. Surely you've felt the shocks?"

"Yes. I don't like it."

"Neither do I. That's why I can't spare anyone for ferry duty. I would make the sick work, if they hadn't already dropped in their tracks."

"If you can come here to treat them, do so. Otherwise we'll have to wait for another couple of hours."

She considered the options. That much delay just might be fatal for the victims.

Joe was sleeping now. If she locked him in a separate room, he couldn't get into too much trouble while she was gone.

"Okay. I'll see what I can do."

"Good girl. I've got to go now."

The comm went dead.

. . .

Bet checked the charge on her air bottle and decided to use a new one. She packed a medicine pouch, stuffing in all of her antivirals. There were few enough people left on the station. She didn't see any need to hoard it now.

The pressure gauge was low, but the habitat's atmosphere had actually come up from her run out to Joe's farm. More water vapor was boiling out of the belt lake than was currently being lost out the hole.

Still, she made sure her shoes were laced and the tight leather gloves were sealed against the sleeves of her suit. Her skin was already blotchy from low pressure hemorrhaging. Joe had the same problem, only worse. Human skin was a good pressure shield, but it had its limits. Now was not the time for loose-fitting clothes. She had chosen this outfit long ago to double as an emergency vacuum suit. For most of her body, the fabrics provided replacement pressure, and they were designed to let her move.

Her clinic was airtight, and for that she was grateful. It was built next to the end-cap and probably was part of the original structure. Due to the slope of the ground, she would have a good downhill run to begin with.

She put on the facemask and then used the entry airlock, bleeding out its air until the door opened easily. She stepped outside.

The sky down the length of the habitat sparkled with swirling ice crystals, but it was a silent storm. Her own breath was the only sound.

I've run more today than I have all year. She usually thought of her genetics as a curse, but it was times like this that she blessed it. She had easily recovered from the previous run, even half-carrying Joe. Whoever it was that designed her had done a very good job.

She hit a good pace and headed for the main road. That would take her close to the hole. The air was clearer over the worksite than before. She could see movement. The farmhouses they'd been moving were smashed and covered with ice.

There was another wobble in the habitat's rotation, and she nearly stumbled. The EHRT would probably do what they could to balance out the ice, but the habitat really needed to be spun down as soon as possible.

I wonder if the Net has cleared. Ceres could handle the job of slowing them down, once EHRT declared it stable. It would have to be done gently, to avoid fracturing the ice plug.

The trees lining the road looked wilted and brittle. There was really no help for them. There would be no breathable atmosphere for plant or animal for some time. The soil would still be good and seeds could survive, but once the hole was fully repaired, it would take years to reestablish a farming community here. Darnell was dead, and its farmers would not be back soon—assuming they survived the virus.

One thing she had learned in her two hundred years was to waste no time nursing old grudges, but that didn't mean she didn't feel the anger over new evil.

The virus was one. She couldn't hate the complex little machine. It was doing its job like a little windup clockwork toy. It had no choice or volition.

But the mind behind it was evil.

She remembered the other biological weapon. The sterilization gene in Alexandria—that was evil—the same kind of evil. She tried to fit them together, like puzzle pieces, but they were different. There was probably not a single gene sequence in common.

Now this hole. That was different, but just as deadly in its own way. A pressor beam had gotten misaimed. Criminal, certainly, but was it evil?

I need to run some more. I hope I get the chance. There would be an investigation, and this was probably her last couple of days as Dr. Bet Nomad. She was confident she could vanish and become someone else. This was an old game. The real question was how much of her gear could she take with her?

The ground shook, and tossed her into the air. She landed hard and flat, knocking the breath out of her. *My mask!* She fumbled to get it secure again.

And then, a rumble from above caused her to look up.

Falling from one side of the sky to the other, a large circular chunk of the landscape was sailing through the air. An unseen cookie-cutter had punched another hole. It was easily five times the size of the first one.

Impact! Shock waves rippled through the hull. From her distance, the splash was clearly spreading in a circular wave across the habitat. In only a second or two—it hit the iceplug.

Ice blasted into the air. The plug shattered.

There were also black dots in the air—the bulldozers, the crawlers, and the men.

The sky is twisting. The habitat should be rigid, but it wasn't. The far end-cap moved back and forth.

Joe. I've got to move him. She gave no more thought to the EHRT workers. She knew what was going to happen. Even if they still breathed, they were already dead.

She turned back toward her clinic and ran harder than she had ever run before.

The ripples, regular earthquakes under her feet, kept her agile and ready to recover when she was thrown. *I have to keep moving. It's not going to last much longer.*

She could feel the air, such as it was, dissipate. The new hole was much larger. She would be running in vacuum in another few minutes.

It was an uphill run, but even then, she could feel it change. The habitat had gone unstable. It was a race for life.

The air mask was inadequate for the demands she was making on it, and her lungs burned for more air. The regulator dumbly refused to give her more.

Finally, she dashed into the clinic's unsealed outer door. She slammed it shut and vented air to equalize the pressure.

"Joe!"

He was wide-awake and wide-eyed, huddling with his blanket in the corner of the room.

"Come on, Joe. We have to put the mask on you again."

"No. No. No. No."

She slapped the man. "You behave! Now do what I say."

He winced, but she had hard hands and no time to give him any comfort. Just the mask. One glance to see if air was flowing, and she pushed him toward the door. He dropped the blanket and stopped to pick it up. She shoved him on the back and kept him moving.

Then she wasted two seconds to pick the blanket up herself and hand it to him.

Outdoors was a nightmare.

The habitat had started to precess. The death-wobble had begun. It was prematurely dark, as the alignment with the sun was lost. If she hadn't been blessed with a perfect memory, she would have been lost in seconds.

Then there was light, a spotlight of gigantic proportions as the sunlight came in through the new hole. It didn't shine on them, but it lit up the mangled landscape inside and there was enough light to navigate by. She moved Joe by brute strength. There was no air to talk by, and her skin crawled from exposure to the vacuum.

The world turned sideways. It started slowly, then increased. The uphill grade to the near end-cap turned *down*. And then as the seconds ticked off, each step found them running down a steeper slope.

She could feel Joe screaming by the heaving of his chest. She wanted to join him.

Then they were not running any more. They were tumbling, falling toward the end-cap.

They hit, and Bet struggled to her feet. She looked up.

The whole world was falling toward her—buildings, sheets of dirt that had been fields, huge blocks of ice, forests of trees. Darnell had turned on its side, and now the end-caps were down. Everything had to readjust.

It was hard to stand. The new gravity was much stronger.

Rubble was landing all around them. There was no time.

She dragged Joe over to the end-cap access hatch and tossed him in. The thick steel bent and buckled just seconds after she closed it over her own head.

This room won't hold. The end-cap wasn't designed to hold the mass of tens of meters of new topsoil and all the biomass and crumpled structures that had just been uprooted.

Joe was nearly catatonic, clutching his blanket. His facemask had come loose, but luckily, the areas in the end-cap were pressurized.

I need to get to the rim. That had the best chances of holding when the end-cap ruptured.

She pushed and pulled Joe down through more levels of sideways rooms, each drop a struggle to force the man-boy through his fears. Finally, she opened a door and had to stop. There was a storage room below, and the fall to the other side would be fatal under the current gravity.

Bet leaned in and looked around under the weakening artificial light. No way. There was nothing to hold on to. She looked back up the way they had come. No luck there. They had dropped here, but it would be impossible to get Joe back up.

The metal walls creaked and groaned. From all directions came a deep clang, over and over. They were being buried.

She looked over the walls, and let go of Joe's tight grip on her hand. *I have to close the hatches.*

She latched the floor hatch, and then climbed the bookshelves on the wall like a ladder. There was a railing along the wall and she used it, climbing hand over hand to the top door.

Chinning herself wasn't as hard as she had feared. As more mass fell to the end-caps, its momentum slowed the habitat's end-over-end tumble, and reduced the effective gravity. She pulled the hatch shut with one hand, dangling from her grip with the other.

There. If everything else goes, we'll have some air, at least.

But for how long?

The answer came immediately.

The walls shook and Joe cried in terror. Bet held on to her railing, and her body was shaken like a whip. The room, which had been a cube, was twisted. The lower hatch popped its hinge. Air started spilling out.

It caught Joe's blanket. He pulled back, and would not let go.

The seam along one edge of the room broke wide open. Joe, still holding the blanket tight, spilled out into the darkness below.

Oh no! Bet lost sight of him. She knew he was dead.

He was my patient.

Her heart was dead with grief for a moment.

. . .

I have to survive.

Up or down?

She had no time to debate. She was in vacuum now, and her tight clothes and breather mask would only keep her alive a short time.

She swung to the side and dropped down to the broken wall. After a few seconds, the sun rotated into view. The end-cap had broken through. She was staring out into space. Among the stars, the debris of falling farms was being slung throughout the cluster.

Another light, artificial, caught her attention. It was against the edge, about five hundred meters away. If the light was undamaged, maybe there was some room that had survived. She had to reach it. She looked for handholds.

PRIME CITY, CERES, L4 CLUSTER

Susan Pearce followed the medical attendants as they carried the limp and feverish young man out to the street.

"Lady, there won't be any room at the hospital. I've been carrying people there all day long, and they're just parking them in the garden in back. Some of the doctors are down with it as well."

She was firm with him. "You just do what I told you! Doctor Skiven will take him. I have already called and made the arrangements. I would take him myself, but I have two others here with mild cases, and I have to watch over them."

The driver just looked at his partner with resignation. Susan didn't mind what they thought of her, as long as her boys got the care they needed.

She stood there beside the lane until they were out of sight. *God, go with little Doo. If they were right, he would be dead shortly. But I don't have any way to fight the infection.* Ken and Raman looked to be having an easier time with it, but she had thought the same about Doo.

Please spare all my boys. And particularly, take care of my son David.

Before the Net was jammed, she had heard a report that Earth and Mars were suffering just like the Clusters, and that even the Outer Fleet had reported cases.

The *whoop whoop* of a siren broke her out of her prayer.

"What now?" It wasn't the signal for an air leak.

A quake rumbled beneath her. She nodded. A large beam must have struck Ceres again. There had been several of them already.

The comm in the hall beeped. She went inside.

"Susan, how are you holding up?"

"Not so good, Admiral. All my boys are coming down with it. I'm feeling tired myself."

"I'm sorry. But I called to warn you. The Ocean is splashing out the access tunnel. These shakes are doing a job on it. Expect water in the streets. Can you seal your outside doors?"

"Admiral, I've told you before, I'm a pilot. Do you think I could live someplace that didn't have its own airlock?"

His voice changed. "Susan. If we weren't old friends, I would check on the prospects of you taking on a third husband. If we're both still alive when this is over, I would be honored to escort you to the Mote for dinner."

"Admiral!"

"Take care, Susan."

She put her hand to her cheek as the comm went silent.

Thank you for that, Jim.

She looked at her entryway and dogged the outer door.

You don't think we will survive.

CENTRAL CONTROL, CERES, L4 CLUSTER

Mason shouted, "Winslow! Where are you?"

Lord Stephen's voice sounded in his cube. "Mason, Winslow is down. I've turned his board over to Hodges. We're losing Controllers right and left."

"Okay," he couldn't take the time to think about people, not right now. "Hodges!"

"Yes, Mason."

"Is Winslow's sweep still running?"

"Yes, it is."

"Then stop it. Now."

"What is it?" asked Lord Stephen.

"We are feeding the monsters! We have to stop the sweepers."

"Show me. Hodges, Stewart, anyone else on this channel. Slave to Mason."

Mason added, "Make that my window 34."

He gave the rest of Lord Stephen's team a few seconds to remotely connect to his visual and then he told his computer to run the chart.

"As you can see, shortly after we put traction on the mother ship, it fragmented into two hundred identical modules. Each of them moved independently with low power beams to a new position where they dumped their power load into a short-burst pressor.

"Look at the timeline on gremlin-112. It moved to a position on a line between Luna and Darnell in about forty minutes, and then dumped all its energy into a punch. Just a few minutes later, radar showed Darnell tumbling and spilling shrapnel all over space. But the gremlin just sat there, for all the world, dead. Radar showed that it hadn't even repositioned itself several hours later.

"But now, here, as soon as our cleanup sweep caught it in a beam, intending to crash it against Luna, it immediately started to show life again. It put a tractor on Earth and pulled itself out of the sweep beam.

"Then it moved to a point between Luna and Queensland L5 and punched a hole in it. Now it is quiet again."

Mason tapped his screen with his finger. A pointer showed up on all the slave screens in the other cubes.

"Now, look at the energy curve from the sweep beam."

There was a general chorus of consternation from the other cubes. Everyone could see it plainly enough. Energy consumption spiked when the beam had locked onto gremlin-112, and then went several times higher until it left the path of the beam.

"That two-step jump is unmistakable. A fraction of a second after we started pushing, the little vampire started filling its power cells from our beam."

. . .

"What do we do now?"

Mason didn't recognize the voice.

Lord Stephen said, "This is Max Russell. He is one of Lord Lee's team. Due to the disease, I am coordinating Lee and Lemay's groups. I will post the chart when we are done here."

Another unknown voice spoke. "We have to knock them down hard and fast. We have over sixty reports of damaged habitats. People are dying by the thousands, maybe millions."

"Yes, but how?"

"How about a high-tension beam? It was used back in the Belt War. Flood the little bot with so much energy it explodes."

"Good idea. Stewart, see if we can do that from here."

"Is the Net still down?"

"Yes. I checked it. Someone is flooding all routers with packets. Our effective bandwidth is down to nothing. Our bandwidth! How the terrorists got a higher priority, I have no idea."

Lord Stephen added to the chatter, "I am getting a priority message from Berlin, but it has been coming in for more than an hour, and that's on the Urgent band."

The conversation was degenerating rapidly, and Mason was surprised that Lord Stephen wasn't reining everyone in, so he shouted. "Hey, people! We need an attack plan—now!"

There was silence.

Mason continued, "Stewart, can you go to work on the high-tension idea, now? Report back in thirty minutes whether you have made any progress or not."

"Okay. I'm gone."

He paused no more than a long breath so Lord Stephen could pick up the baton, but when it didn't happen, he kept on.

"What's the next idea?"

"How about the reverse, hit them with a low-tension beam and drain them like they drained us?"

"Won't work." It was Nuell. "Look at the graph. They had to have used a custom-tuned TP cell to get their tension down that level. None of our beams will tune that low."

Mason nodded. He was right. They had no direct physical access to the beam projectors. They were Controllers, not beam engineers. There was no time to make that kind of a change.

Still, he said, "Computer, see if you can find someone on duty who can tune one of our beams."

"Acknowledged."

Russell spoke, "How about a real impact? Throw something at it hard."

"Okay, can you do it?"

Another voice said, "Aiming would be impossible. Those things are barely a meter across."

"What about a shotgun? With all the shrapnel in the Clusters, we could throw a thousand rocks at each one and hope for the best."

Mason interrupted. "Anything we do has to come from Ceres, or a facility with a direct laser link to here. No more Project business through the Net until that problem is resolved."

Russell said, "I still think I can do it."

"Good. Your project. Same direction as Stewart's. Get back with a report of some kind in thirty minutes."

"Gone."

"I have another idea," said Bell, a rather quiet man who rarely spoke in meetings.

"Go."

"Let's ignore them. There are only a few that haven't already shot their bolt. Unless we recharge them, they're harmless. Log their orbits and send rockets after them later."

It was Hodges, another quiet one, who answered. "Nearly thirty of the gremlins will drift into the lunar spin beams today. Twenty more will get there tomorrow. After that, the predictions get hazy with so many perturbed objects in the Clusters."

"So we can't afford to do nothing." Mason looked at his screen. The organization chart popped up. Had Lord Stephen dropped out of the meeting?

The chart itself was shocking. Each of the original teams contained thirty people. This new combination of the three had only eleven people. Mason felt a tickle in his throat, but resolutely resisted the urge to cough. He would not get sick. Not now.

"I hate to suggest it because of the political ramifications, but perhaps we should shut down the spin beams."

"We can't do that!" Aaron Nuell's name flickered on the chart in time with his voice. Someone else muttered an angry agreement.

Mason paused before continuing. They had no resources to waste on politics.

"Whatever we do, it will be for Project goals. We are Controllers and every one of us knows what is important here. There are two questions: Are we able to shut them down? Should we shut them down?"

Hodges spoke. "The spin beams are on a direct laser-link backup. It would take time to bleed the beams down, but I have the procedure right here. I was on the planning team when the lawsuit was filed."

Before anyone could ask, Mason quickly added, "Then the real decision will have to come from Lord Stephen and the other Peers here in the center—unless that priority message from Berlin deals with it. I'll coordinate that.

"So, are there any other ideas on how to deal with the gremlins?"

"Spit at them."

There were a few laughs, but they were tired laughs. All of them had been on duty since the original attack on Darnell.

"Okay, then the rest of you need to get back to work. We'll be years getting the mess cleaned up.

"And people, pair up according to this chart. Notify each other when you have to catnap. Someone needs to be watching out for each of us. No one else will."

. . .

Mason slipped out of his cube just as soon as he could and knocked on Lord Stephen's office.

There was no response. He opened the door.

His boss was sleeping in his chair. Habit urged him to creep out quietly, but Lord Stephen had not acted normally.

"Sir?" he asked.

With no answer, he touched his arm resting on the desk. The man's skin was burning hot.

"Computer. Can you get a medical team here?"

"They do not respond."

"Contact the other Lords. Tell them Lord Stephen is sick."

"There are none left on duty."

"Then who is in charge?"

"Of the front line Controllers who are still active, you have seniority. In the absence of contact with Project headquarters in Berlin, that leaves you in charge."

Mason couldn't get his mind around that concept. He shook it off.

"What should I do about Lord Stephen?"

There was an uncharacteristic pause before the response.

"Medical guidelines classify patients by their symptoms and the speed at which they have developed. His collapse into unconsciousness was sufficiently rapid that he would be classified as low priority."

"Low priority? What does that mean?"

"Medical practitioners should concentrate their remedial efforts on high-priority patients which have a higher chance of recovery. Low-priority patients should be left in a comfortable position and allowed to suffer the ongoing progress of the disease until higher-priority patients have been treated."

"So I should just leave him to die? I can't do that."

The computer recognized the rhetorical question for what it was and said nothing.

Mason bit his lip, thinking.

"Okay, who is still on duty?"

A screen showed a map of the cubes and activity lights. It was mostly dark.

"Is this just our team?"

"No. This is every active Controller."

He held onto the edge of the desk. *We're decimated. We can't keep the Project running with this.*

The room was very quiet. Lord Stephen was breathing raggedly.

I have to get back to my station. In the back of his mind, Mason had thought there was some other team working to manage the havoc that the attacks had wrought. But that wasn't the case. The Clusters had been thrown into chaos. And he knew what that meant.

"Hodges?"

"Yes, Mason?"

"Can you run the spin beam shutdown by yourself?"

"Yes."

"Do it."

"I'm on it."

He looked at Lord Stephen, resting uneasily, sprawled over his expensive wooden desk.

"Computer, what are the practical advantages of Lord Stephen's office over my cube? Should I move my operations here?"

"The chair is more comfortable. Cooled liquids are available in arm's reach. The opaque walls provide privacy."

"But does this station have greater capabilities for control than mine?"

"Not if you order all restrictions lifted on your station."

Oh ,yes. I'm in charge, aren't I?

"Then do it. Remove all restrictions from my station."

"Done."

He didn't need comfort now, nor privacy. And he would not take Lord Stephen's status for anything. He had a job to do, and he could do it from his own chair.

He pulled his boss over to the couch along the wall and tried to make him comfortable. He ached to do more, but time was running out and his real job could make the difference of life and death for whole worlds. Lord Stephen would understand.

CELANESE TRANSPORT 3, MARS ORBIT

John Fenton, a.k.a. Trader, a.k.a. Transportee-11 waited on his bunk, annoyed at the delay. His body ached from the fever that had taken a hold of him shortly after Kidd had turned him in.

Kidd had to be the finger. He had a bad feeling about that skunk from the moment he had rescued him. All that talk about GAHSP was just leading him on. Then when he hurt Bonnie and fled the area like the devil was chasing him—that was a bad sign, too.

There had been four big, unsmiling agents waiting for him at the Portal. He'd known what was coming when the rangers he had known for years wouldn't meet his eye.

But by that time, there was nothing he could do. Maybe the Gearsons could live on rocks and boiled leaves for the rest of their lives and love it, but he was there for the money. City money. Good times money. Money that told people just what kind of a winner he was.

Trader looked at his sleeve. They said he wasn't a prisoner—those unsmiling men who barely spoke and who had him out of the Portal and onto this transport within twelve hours. Oh no, he wasn't a prisoner. He had just won the lottery and had been awarded Martian colonization.

But he had to leave now. Sorry, no time to go back to his residence. He could wear these clothes. Surely, he would understand.

Of course he understood! It didn't happen often, but unpopular people were known to vanish. A thorough search reported them as happy little colonists on Mars.

There was a knock on his door. A nice courtesy, that. His door was locked on the outside. "Come on in," he called.

It was the same old man who brought him his meals. But this time he was empty-handed.

"Any news?"

The man frowned and shook his head. "Uh. No. We're still hanging in orbit. Most of the crew are sick. I think we may be in quarantine."

"Quarantine!"

The man stared at him, not focusing. "Ah. Yes. Something like..." He turned and walked away, leaving the door open.

Trader was on his feet and outside in an instant, looking down the corridor for witnesses. There was no one but the old man, walking away slowly. Trader turned in the other direction.

He moved as quickly and quietly as he could, given the shoes he was wearing. When the curve of the corridor hid him, he slowed to a walk. *I have to look normal.* Not that there was much chance he could pass for crew in his current outfit.

I need a plan. Being an escaped convict is dangerous. Should I just stay with the program and hope they process me quickly?

With his ambiguous designation, as a "Transportee" but with no official criminal record, maybe he would do best to go back to his bed and wait it out.

But the fear of quarantine was enough to put that off. He had to find out what was going on.

The ship was one of the mid-sized surface to surface transports. It had many floors, each a circular slice of the hundred-meter-long cylinder. The corridor looped the floor and he passed several closed man-sized doors. This had to be sleeping quarters or offices. He looked at the sign on the nearest door.

He squinted, but he couldn't make sense of the lettering. The characters looked familiar, but it wasn't something he could read. They said it was a Celanese transport. *What kind of a language is that? I thought everyone used the same language in space.*

Cautiously, he opened it.

There was a bed—passenger or crew quarters. He almost left, when the smell hit him. He edged inside. There was the rancid stench of someone who had been very sick, but there was no one inside now.

Trader went to the next room along the corridor but it was locked. The next was lived-in quarters, but vacant.

The fourth was occupied. The woman was fully dressed in one of the crew uniforms but she was bundled tightly in her blankets. She was alive, but asleep. Her dreams must have been terrible by the way she jerked about.

He didn't risk checking her temperature, but he knew she had one. He'd felt the same way the night before. For now, he could not afford to touch her. An escaped captive in a defenseless woman's bedroom—not where he wished to be caught.

Trader found the stairwell. It was an Escher twister. Local floor gravity turned the stairwell into a long corridor within a few steps. The transfer areas were clearly marked in red, with more of the nonsense signs marking the way. *They really ought to mark these in two languages if they are going to use Celanese.*

He moved quickly toward the center of the ship. That is where the crew would be. He needed answers, and if that meant he would be locked back up, he would risk it.

. . .

He missed the command deck the first time, and stumbling around the ship, he realized just how empty it was. He met no one.

The command deck wasn't empty. He wished it were.

Trader held one hand over his face as if that would stop the smell. Two were dead of gunshots to the head. It was clear who had done it, because the captain still held the gun in his loose fingers.

Two others were dead, but it wasn't clear what killed them, unless it was the disease.

But it was just a fever. It was bad, I admit, but it didn't kill me. I feel a little weak, but I'm fine otherwise.

He looked over the screens of data. None of it made any sense. He felt a chill on the back of his neck when he saw the Project logo. It was exactly like he had seen a million times before, exactly. But he couldn't read the words.

What is wrong with me?

He rummaged around the room until he found a paper report of some kind and a stylus. He quickly scribbled out his name.

His hand seemed to know what to do, but when he looked, he couldn't read his own signature.

My mind. Something has happened to my mind!

He screamed.

"Yes, can I help you?" It was the computer, talking in that universally familiar default voice. Trader could feel some of the tension leak out of him just hearing it.

"Computer, what happened here?"

"Captain Jumar committed suicide after killing the pilot. The engineer and navigator had died already due to the fever."

"Why?"

"Captain Jumar did not log a reason."

Trader slumped into a vacant chair.

"Is this ship under quarantine?"

"No. However, Mars Project Headquarters is broadcasting a warning to all incoming ships. The planet is under quarantine. A pandemic fever has been discovered sweeping through the colonies, and no ship is to land. Do you wish to listen to the broadcast?"

"No. Does that mean we can go back to Earth?"

"No. Project Prime has gone silent. There is no return without authorization."

"So what happens now?"

"Unknown."

"Can we land?"

"Not without command crew authorization."

Trader looked around at the dead. "Is there any command crew left?"

"Yes, there are two."

"Then get them up here!"

"I am unable to comply. Both are incapacitated because of the disease."

He stood. "Well tell me where they are!"

"Cabins E-5 and E-12."

He took a step toward the door, then stopped.

"Computer? What's an 'E' look like?"

Chapter 9

PACIFIC OCEAN, EARTH

Blackspine waited until the fugitive was brought to him. The report of Sealer's return had arrived earlier, of course, but the young pup had to be told that the tides didn't turn on his whim. The tribe came first and the sooner he knew he was expendable, the sooner he would take his place among the hunters and provide his share of the food.

It was strange, though. The People's talk of his approach echoing through the undersea canyon where the tribe had camped—it felt like Sunrise Song. He would have expected more taunts.

Blackspine drifted out of his nest and waited until he could see him directly.

They were above, not more than a bodylength below the surface. All he could see was their silhouettes against the light. Sealer was nearly grown, but he didn't have the hard bulk of Jawtooth.

Why is Sealer leading the way? And why were there over two dozen others following at a distance?

He expelled a blast of cold water through his gills and pushed himself leisurely toward the surface. Better to do this with lots of air. The entire tribe would be listening, even the ones who hadn't joined the party.

Flush with a new breath, he held his position and let them come to him.

Sealer looked different, as if he had aged five years—not only with the new belt and the dagger, but even in the way he moved through the water. He knew the boy from birth, but something had changed.

"Elder Blackspine! I seek an audience with you."

It threw him off. Most of the youngsters wilted when he glared at them, and he had intended to give young Sealer the full treatment before he spoke.

"Strange," he commented aloud, "I don't see the smooth stone. Where is this cub's mother? She needs to come and put him back in her nest."

There was a murmur in the water, too diffuse to pinpoint its source. At first, he thought it was laughter from the crowd, but abruptly he realized it wasn't.

"Elder Blackspine. I seek audience." The youngster's voice was even. There wasn't a hint of anger at his jibe, nor an echo of resentment over his dead mother.

For the first time, he looked closely at the boy's eyes.

They were hard and deadly. *Where had he come by that knife?*

"Come, then." He turned his back slowly, showing that he felt no fear. Then he pushed off toward the large cliff that was swept clear by the currents. He could feel Sealer close behind.

· · ·

"Why must we head west, into the deeps?" Blackspine asked.

"Because that is where the Birth Bays lie. I have seen them, in the visions. That is where our tribe must go if we are to survive. The shores we have been following since I was born are tainted with poisons from the Land People."

Sealer held himself in a submissive curl, even as he forced the conversation onto his own agenda.

"I have listened to your words, Revered Elder. You know this to be true. You have cried over our numbers as we die, one by one. You have called out during the Sunset Song time and time again for another tribe to hear us, but there is never any response from anyone other than the dolphins and the whales, mocking us.

"I do not have your patience. I will not wait while the tribe dwindles to nothing. I have seen the Birth Bays. We must go there and take back our ancestral home. We used to be the rulers of the seas. We can grow strong again and take back what we have lost. We should not live hidden from the Land People."

Blackspine didn't know what to make of the youngster. The sun sparkled in his eyes as he talked—it drew him. But . . .

"Child. You are speaking nonsense. These Birth Bays—I have never heard of such a thing, and I don't believe they exist. The gods and heroes you mention, the war between the People and the Land People—it is all made-up stories. You have a wonderful imagination, but it is not real!"

"Revered Elder. I have seen the visions. I know what is real. We were a great people once, and we can be so again!"

He shook his head. "No. I don't speak of it, but surely you know the real truth? The Land People made us, as weapons in their wars among each other. They used us to kill other Land People, and when their war was done, they tried to kill us. We have only survived by staying out of their sight. We have heroes, those that helped the Three Tribes to escape from the nets. But before that—it is nothing. We are a new thing. Don't the Dolphins and Whales say so?"

Sealer shook his head. "And now our brothers of the sea are founts of truthfulness? The Whales barely acknowledge that we exist. The Dolphins tell us the sun rises in the West more often than the East. I have talked to Orca that don't even know that Land People are people."

"But I was told the truth by my father—"

Sealer barked angrily, "Who was told it by his father, who was told it by his father, who was told it by *Land People*! We get our history from the very ones who held us as slaves and tried to destroy us all.

"Every history that we tell during the Sunset Song was told to us by liars! I have seen the truth in my visions! We were great! Greatness is in our blood."

"And why are you the only one? Why do you have these visions? Why should I believe you?"

Sealer drew his dagger. Blackspine tensed his muscles, but did not bolt.

"This knife, with this sacred stone, contains the visions of our people." He held up his arm. "See this scar. I fought with an evil one of the Land People, who tried to keep it from me. He didn't want the truth to get to us."

He reversed the dagger and held it out to him, the jewel on the handle shining in the light.

"Take hold, and see the visions yourself. See where we have been, and what our future holds!"

Blackspine flipped back out of range—out of range of the dagger, and out of range of those compelling eyes.

"Sealer, you have become mad. Leave now. Leave the Tribe. Leave the People." With all his strength, he called the Banishment, and knew that the echoes of it would reach all.

"Go, Sealer. Leave now before the warriors can collect their spears. I don't need your blood in the waters, but I cannot have your madness to curdle the minds of the Tribe."

Sealer shook his head, and put the dagger back in his belt.

"Revered Elder," he spoke calmly, "I don't need your blood in the waters either, but I will take the People to the safety of the Birth Bays."

Blackspine saw hunters rise from the valley. They were coming.

But were they coming for Sealer, or for him?

ROCKIES PRESERVE, NORTH AMERICA, EARTH

Bonnie Gearson fought back the tears. The backpack was heavy. A rock shifted under her foot, and she tensed. Her arm still ached and she was scared to fall again.

Her father put out his hand and steadied her. The pack was more than she was used to.

"We will be over the pass in an hour or so, Bonnie. We can take a break then."

She just nodded, and turned to look back down on the valley that had been her home forever. Burned and black, it ached in her mind just like the scar on her arm. The fires had swept up so close to their cave that she thought they would all die.

Her father had looked angry since the first smoke had appeared in the distance. "Kidd said this would happen."

He had told her what would come next. "People will be coming into our valley. I didn't believe it when he told me. We will have to hide the cave and move west, at least for a few seasons. We can't afford to be caught."

Her mother had told her she could only carry a few things. She had to decide what to take, and what things to leave behind in the dark. Her parents said they could come back later, but she didn't believe them.

She packed her clothes, of course, and Baby Nell, even though the right eye had fallen off and her mother hadn't had time to sew it back on.

She also brought her real Indian medicine bag that Trader had given her when she was little. Momma said the magic didn't work, but Daddy looked like he almost believed. He certainly took care to use the big medicine bag that Kidd had left him.

She looked up to the pass, where they were going. Daddy had gone there a few days ago, looking for a new home. There was another valley on the other side, but they had to go even farther than that.

There was a flicker of motion on the rocks above, but when she looked closer, there was nothing to be seen. It must have been an elk, or maybe a sheep.

. . .

"Daddy?"

"Yes, Bonnie?"

"How is Mommy?"

"Fine. She's just tired. The fever went away when she took the medicine. Now go back to sleep."

She wanted to tell him about the little man who was hiding in the rocks. Maybe he was one of the Indians Trader made stories about.

But he was already snoring. They had walked all day, and Daddy had carried the biggest pack. He needed to sleep.

She was glad about Mommy. Daddy had gotten the fever too, and she was glad the medicine was so powerful.

I wonder how it's made? I would like to be able to make strong medicines and make people better.

. . .

Bonnie woke first. She had to go squat, but she didn't want to wake them. She crept out from under her bearskin and walked quietly over into the trees.

Several minutes later, she saw the stranger again. *He's small, like me. I'm going to follow him.*

He was creeping up closer to their campsite, and Bonnie noticed that he was carrying a knife in his hand. She didn't have a good knife of her own. She had asked for one, many times, but her father explained that the rocks in their valley weren't very good for making knives. He carried one bought from Trader, but it had cost him many pairs of shoes. Besides, her mother was always ready to help her with her projects when she needed to cut something.

But why did the little man need a knife? She didn't like the way he held it. It was too much like her daddy when he was worried about a bear being too close to the cave.

Does he want to hurt us? She didn't like that idea. She looked over the stones at her feet and picked up a couple of them. The animals around her home had learned to leave her alone, and she wanted to be ready if the little man was aggressive like they'd been.

It was still early light. The sky was bright with the morning clouds, but the sunlight hadn't penetrated down into the valleys yet. She was careful to keep her eyes down and to stay in the shadows.

She slowly closed on him, pausing when he paused, so that there was no chance of her betraying herself with a misplaced step.

The little man was scared. He made little jabs with the knife in the air. He went down into a low crouch as he approached their beds.

Bonnie didn't wait any longer.

The first rock hit him on the back of his head. The second hit his back.

Her father snapped out of sleep and had the intruder wrapped in his arms before she could pick up another rock.

"Stop! Don't hurt me!" he said in a high-pitched voice. It almost sounded like hers.

. . .

"I'm a Wilson," he said.

Her mother, now looking much better today, asked, "Do you have a first name?"

"Bull," he would only talk to her. "I'm Bull Wilson."

He glanced up at Fred Gearson who was holding his own knife at ready. He looked at Bonnie, standing behind her father. He looked as puzzled as she was.

"My name is Bonnie."

He nodded. "You're a girl."

"Are you an Indian?"

He shook his head, like he hadn't heard the term. "No. I live here."

"In this valley?" asked her father.

He answered cautiously, "In the forest."

Clara Gearson touched his shoulder. "Where is your family?"

He shook off the touch. "I can't tell you."

Bonnie nodded. "Good for you. I won't tell you where I live, either." She smiled. She knew how they were supposed to be. The little man was a lot like her.

He looked ever more trapped, and tears started making his eyes shimmer.

Bonnie asked, suddenly contrite, "Did I hurt you?"

He rubbed the spot on his head, and shook his head. Then he started crying harder.

Clara looked at her husband. "He has the fever."

Fred sighed deep and loud. "Okay. Give him some of the powder."

Bonnie explained, "It's okay. We have medicine for the fever. We have all taken it, and it made the sickness go away."

Bull Wilson grabbed hold of Fred's legging. "Please. Can I have some for my parents? They're both very sick."

DENVER, EARTH

Paula Campbell quizzed the computer over the labels on the darts. She had no idea what each of the drugs did.

"B203 is a slow-acting poison. A044 is a light-dosage muscle relaxant."

"But why would they both be in the same dart?"

"Immediate symptoms would be co-ordination difficulty for several hours, followed by recovery, and then gradual neurological failure over the next week."

She shook her head. The key to the labels was more puzzling, and definitely more disturbing than ignorance. The one with the three black bands went straight under the hammer, with the fragments very carefully fed to the little furnace he used for annealing metal objects.

I wish I could do the same to you.

"What did you say?" he asked.

"I didn't say anything."

"Well, then can we listen to some more news?"

She turned to look at him. He smiled. He looked young and innocent.

"Why do you want to listen to it? It's all the same. People are dying from the disease. The world is falling apart."

"Oh, it's more than that."

He was so cheerful. She hated it.

She picked up the dart gun and picked out one of the darts that she hadn't destroyed. She walked over to the chair she had placed well out of his reach, even if he suddenly broke the cords and lunged for her.

"I have some questions."

"Shoot." He grinned.

"Why are you so fixated on the news?"

He shrugged, then said, "It's the most interesting thing going on ..."

"Try again," she said, squeezing the trigger.

His whole body tensed as the needle delivered its payload into his thigh. His face went blank, just like she had seen before when they were fighting.

Then he gave a shout, and put all his strength into the ropes.

She edged back. It was as if he had grown in size, every muscle tensed. Her idle thought that he could break his ropes came back, with an edge of real fear.

But it held. She knew her ropes.

He collapsed when it was clear that it wasn't going to work. His face shifted again, like something in a nightmare. It was as if there were dozens of people inside, all trying to get out.

Then ... he settled down. The face looked old, in spite of the clear, smooth skin.

He looked her in the eye. "A truth drug. Right." He laughed. "It won't do you any good. You don't think I know how to handle my own poisons? I made them all."

"So why are you fighting, if they can't hurt you?"

"I didn't say they wouldn't hurt ... s'just won't do you any good. You've already got the fever."

She put her hand to her cheek. *Yes, he's right. It's starting on me, too. And Isaac probably has it, too. He knows something about it.*

"Tell me about the fever."

He grinned, and shook his head. "You can't make me. I can resist this ... stuff."

"But you do know about it?"

He sneered, "Of course I do. I made it. It is mine."

She felt a shock, but tried not to show it.

"You engineered the disease?"

"Ya. Custom virus. S'most sophis. Ticated." He shook his head. "Got my tongue."

"Why? You're killing people by the thousands!"

"Millions." He was concentrating on saying the words clearly. "It is for humanity's," he smiled when he got that one right, "own good. You can't handle too much technology."

"You can't do that! What gives you the right?" She felt her face getting hot.

He shook his head tolerantly. "Sorry. I can do it. I have been doing it for over a hundred years. I have the skills and the vision. I'm the only one who can do the job."

She didn't know what do think. Was he crazy?

"How old are you?"

He blinked. "Oops. I said that, didn't I? S'ok. You'll die soon enough. No harm done. Yes. I'm about two hundred years old. Don't look it, do I?" He smiled.

"What are you?" she asked, not able to hide her disgust. Two hundred years. Back at the Die-Off. "Are you some kind of biological weapon?"

"Me? No. I don't think... no I know. I like to think they made me for space." He confided, "Did you know I have extreme radiation tolerance?" He nodded. "Just a guess, but maybe they were thinking ahead."

"But the Die-Off didn't kill you? I thought..."

"You thought that all biological constructs were killed off." He shook his head. "Most were, but the Die-Off plague was tailored to attack the most common tools used in genetic engineering. You know, the carrier organisms that were used to write replacement DNA into the genes of the root stock?"

She felt an eerie sense that he was shaking off the drug. So soon? His words were coming easier and he was using longer sentences.

"Most altered species had the traces of the gene splicing still in their active DNA. The attack virus ripped it out and destroyed the genes that showed those traces. It was lethal, of course. And indiscriminate. Biological weapons and innocents alike died.

"But there were some constructs that were built differently. I am *very* different. There's no one in the world like me. I was immune."

He looked at her, and there was no longer any sense that the drug had any control over him. But he hadn't gone back into his role. He was still that indefinably old man in the body of a young man.

"Look at me. Do I look human?"

In spite of her doubts, Paula nodded. "I don't even know whether to believe you. You could just be crazy."

"Right. There is no visible difference. In some sense, I am completely human. My genes are human genes."

She was confused. "Then, they added something?"

"No! That's the difference. They left things out."

He sounded eager to explain.

"The human genetic code had been completely mapped even back before the Star. After the recovery, the technology advanced to the state where complete chromosomes could be constructed directly from a database. That's where I came from."

He looked at his wrist, where there was a trickle of blood creeping from behind the ropes. His attempt at escape had left its mark. Paula felt no need to treat it. Not now.

"Don't worry about it," he said. "I heal fast. I heal very fast. You see, that's one thing they did right. They had the whole range of human genes to choose from, and having a free hand, they chose the best ones. I have the best human metabolism. I have the best human immune system. I heal best. I remember best. I think best.

"So you see. I am the perfect person to control humanity. I have more experience than anyone. I can think better than anyone.

"And I am impartial. They constructed me from parts, so I am not really Indo-European, that's just the rough appearance. I have no father, no mother, no ancestors to appease. I was on the run for all of my formative years, and I lived everywhere—Denver, Berlin, the Australian outback, and dozens of other places—they all seem like home to me."

She shook her head. "If any place seemed like home, you wouldn't be doing this. People are hurting. People are dying. You say I am dying. If so, you are killing me. That is not for my benefit!"

He looked innocent. "I didn't say that. Of course, your death won't benefit you. But your genetic strain, your extended family, they will benefit from living in a world without the threat of species-wide disasters hanging over their heads."

She could hardly contain her scorn. "Oh, save me from geniuses! You're going to save the world by killing everyone in it. Sure. Of course. Why didn't I see that?"

He actually looked encouraged. Her barbs had no impact.

"Think it through, only let me correct a couple of misconceptions. Not everyone will die. Most will, of course, but I have carefully planned for this."

"What planning!"

He took the question literally.

"Quite a lot, actually. This virus is a disease on a timer. I spread it in live vectors across all continents, across all worlds, and in every habitat in space, and then let it cook as a very mild airborne infection through the entire population. Everyone has it, but no one notices it. Believe me—I have monitored every medical news stream.

"This is a prime example of why humanity can't control itself, by the way." He raised his voice a little, showing some heat. "With the maturation of biological technologies, it is essential that the population be continuously monitored for new diseases. But no, instead we have a little war, and the Die-Off and the witch-hunts that followed it. And now, the population is so scared of biotechnology that no defense is even possible." He sighed.

Paula asked, "Is that why you did this thing? To show people we should have better defenses?"

"No. You can't show humanity anything! Humanity never learns anything. That's the point. People learn lessons, but then they die and a new crop of children arrive, ignorant from birth. We could have a golden age of technology, and tolerance, and enlightenment, but the very next child to be born is just another barbarian, ready to tear it all down to satisfy his primal animal passions."

He shook his head firmly. "No, if people are worth anything—and believe me, I like people—then people should live in a world where the primitive can thrive! Technology has just brought a bigger stick for the cave man. It's too dangerous for him.

"So to accomplish this world change," although his wrist was bound, he counted off with his thumb to his fingertips, "I have to totally disable space capability, in particular the planet-moving stuff. That's far too dangerous, long term.

"I have to reduce the world population down to the carrying capacity of the land. Believe me, it's a lot more humane to do that with an impersonal disease, all in one step, than with a prolonged war. Remember history! People against people, where hatreds distort people's lives for generations after. My way is better.

"And I have to train people to fear and avoid technology for several generations. People have to forget how the machines work until they all fail and break down.

"My virus will help there."

She shook off his vision. "What do you mean?"

"Oh, just the way the virus works. In its final stage, it attacks the brain. Most of the survivors will have some form of brain damage. This disaster won't be one where the brave leaders patch up the machines and rebuild civilization for their children. That happened after the Star, but not this time."

She wished she could take a knife and destroy the mind that put all of this into play, but that would accomplish nothing. She had to keep him talking. Isaac's life depended on it. Maybe he would say something that she could use.

"I can't stomach this. It's genocide. People will never forgive you."

"Nonsense. This isn't genocide. That is a very over-used term, to my mind. Geno-cide. Killing a genetic type. That isn't what is happening at all. This is just a simple cull, universally applied.

"And I know what I am talking about. I've done genocide, and I know the difference."

"What?" She didn't know what to make of him anymore.

"Genocide. I destroyed a gene line. People, if that makes it any clearer."

"Who? Why?"

He closed his eyes for a few seconds. She could see his nostrils dilate. He opened his eyes and pinned her with his glare. When he started talking, every word was clipped, controlling a deep anger.

"A little history. Life Force Technologies was a contract house in Australia. That kingdom was going to try to leapfrog northern technology

He shook his head. "Not here. I can't imagine why I would want the few doses that I could store up here. No, if I needed an antidote, I would need to administer it widely, wouldn't I? I would have to treat thousands or tens of thousands simultaneously, with no trained medical assistants available."

"So? Where is it?" She lurched to grab him by the neck, but caught herself before she got too close.

"I just told you, didn't I? Or has the fever dulled your brain already?"

She stood there stupidly. She glanced over at the window.

He nodded toward the western windows. "You've got it. You can see it from here."

She hurried over to the glass and looked out. Cherry Creek stretched off to the southwest from whence it came, leading to Cherry Creek Lake, source of more than half the city's water.

She looked back at him.

"It's just one of many. I can selectively treat any of two hundred cities, in any combination."

"How?"

He pursed his lips. "Well, now, for me, it would be easy. I just send the order over the Net, and the rockets trigger and the airburst puts the proper dosage in the local water supply.

"But I really don't want to do that. As far as I can see, my original plan is perfectly on track."

She looked around, picked up a hammer and stalked close to his bed. "Do it! Give the order." She steeled herself to crack his skull.

He shook his head. "No."

"I'll kill you!"

"No, you won't." He radiated calm. "You won't kill me while there is any chance that I will relent and save your baby."

She moved the heavy hammer, trying to force herself to do it, to kill the monster.

But he was right. He could stop it, and she couldn't.

Or could she?

She dropped the hammer and went back to the window.

A rocket. Where could he hide a rocket? It would have to be close.

The Cherry Creek valley crawled its way to the southeast, lightly cloaked in haze. The huge grass-covered dam that impounded the waters of the lake was clearly visible. Just to the right was a tall spire, the tallest Denver skyscraper outside the downtown area.

She turned back to him. "The Belleview Tower. You have it in the Belleview Tower, don't you?"

He nodded. "Very good. I'm proud of you. But I still won't trigger it."

She raced down the hall and went to the rooftop hangar. The shuttle was still there, passive, and no matter what commands she yelled at it, it wouldn't unlock the door.

She went back.

"What's the command to activate the shuttle?" she demanded.

"No. It knows my voice. If you want to fly there, you'll have to take me with you."

Paula considered it only for the blink of an eye. Whatever else he was, he was very strong, and very fast. Even tied down, he was too dangerous to get near.

She would just have to get there herself.

She picked up her climbing ropes.

"Hey, are you going to leave me here, tied up like this?"

"Yes."

It's going to take me four or five hours to get there on foot, as weak as I feel. I need a bicycle.

. . .

Kidd waited until he was sure that she was well down the elevator shaft before he made his move. He shifted mentally to the Warrior.

The bed was against two walls in a corner, so he would need his left foot. Ignoring the pain, he braced his shoulder and put his strength into the leg. The metal framing bent. That allowed some slack in the ropes looped around his ankle. Pulling hard at the right angle, he popped one loop free from around his heel. After that, it was short work to free his whole foot.

He sensed the mass of the bed. It would be close.

He heaved his whole body to the left, swinging his leg hard over. The bed heeled over, and he managed to jam the sole of his foot against the hard flat surface of the floor.

Pulling the bed up and over, like a very heavy overcoat, he edged his foot under in short hops.

Finally he stood on the one leg, carrying the bed balanced above him. He could see very poorly, face down as he was, and it was difficult to breathe with the leg bent up to maintain his balance. He would have to move fast.

He hopped in short, regular bounces, toward the workbench. The last few bounces were unsteady, as his muscles started fluttering with the fatigue.

Still, he made it to the edge of the workbench, where he had left the edge of the metal surface unfinished, just a single sharp edge. Maintaining his balance as he twisted his body, and the whole bed, he frayed the ropes that bound his arm.

When it snapped free, he lost his balance and collapsed with the bed on top of him. But his right hand was free.

After a short rest to let his muscles recover, he pulled the bed up close enough to allow him to rummage through the tool drawer. The ropes were gone a minute later.

The Warrior persona faded into the background of his mind. He was no longer needed.

"Computer." Kidd had to pant out the command. He was exhausted. "Report the status of the Belleview Tower firing circuits."

There was a long silence.

"Computer?"

"Net activity is restricted."

"What do you mean, restricted?"

"Your commands are being held, pending available bandwidth."

"What's wrong with the bandwidth?"

"Net activity is being consumed with higher priority traffic."

"What higher priority traffic?" Even as he said it, he knew it was a useless question.

"All Net traffic is encrypted. It is impossible for a user node to examine traffic not addressed to it."

He chafed against this new kind of binding. He needed to know what was going on.

"Okay, Computer. Report what news has already arrived, starting from three days ago."

· · ·

"And you have no more news after that?" Kidd asked again.

"No. The Net traffic has slowed to below a minimum useful level. Packets are still arriving, but each message is composed of many packets, and the message expires before the last of the packets arrive."

"Can you configure commands to use fewer packets, or can you change to a higher priority?"

"I can send with fewer packets, if the computer on the receiving end can adapt. I have already attempted commands with the highest user priority."

He sighed. "Okay. Continue trying to get simple status messages from all of my outposts. And for now, search your local memory for all medical alerts. Order them by geographical region and chronologically, and display them on the screen."

. . .

"Reality is bigger than any plan." It annoyed him that she was right.

She was pretty as well as smart. Being her prisoner, and the closeness that demanded, had tickled his appreciation of the girl. *Now is not the time. Don't pick up a girl friend who might die on you. Wait, and mingle with the survivors.*

And don't fall in love in your main persona. It was too great a risk. Three of his sub-personalities were well-practiced with women. One was a romantic.

He forced his attention back to the screens. Of course, he knew plans broke. But it always happened in the middle of a plan that surprises happened and he had to deal with the doubts. Most of the time, his plans were flexible enough to deal with unplanned events, but there were always those few, where a well-intentioned plan backfired.

Did it happen again—to this most important of projects?

The Clusters seemed to be in the midst of some kind of terrorist attack. Was it just bad timing that people were doing really stupid things just at the time his plague hit, or had a terrorist leader been prematurely affected by the brain fever and pushed a button too early?

His optimal plan had been to force the Terraforming Project to power the system down into a safe mode when they realized that they wouldn't have the manpower to keep it under control. Obviously, the Clusters hadn't the resources to survive when spaceflight shut down. If he could poison the well here on Earth so that spaceflight was forever written out of humanity's technological base, then terraforming and planet-moving would be shut down completely. That was the only safe way. Barbarians couldn't be trusted to move planets.

It was worrisome that the Net had shut down just when the attacks had started to escalate, so that he couldn't judge how competently the controllers had contained the damage. Still, at worst, he could wait a couple of decades for the habitats to depopulate and go up there in his own ship and make sure it was shut down correctly. It wouldn't do to have Mars come crashing down on his head someday because some technician left the tractor beam turned on.

He glanced from window to window, reading the news reports that had been saved before the Net went down, and another showing the medical reports he had requested.

The plague had progressed exactly as he had predicted. In its early stages, it was noticed, but since it had no bothersome symptoms, it had just been logged and ignored. Then, when the end stage happened, his bug had been overlooked because it had been already cataloged as harmless.

But here was an interesting report from one of the Cluster doctors.

Hmm. Why is she reporting it here?

"Computer. Do I have a 'Dr. Bet Nomad' in my candidates list?"

"There are two fuzzy matches. 'Dr. Elizabeth Wander' logged thirty-three years ago, and 'Breet Fleet' logged sixty-three years ago and listed as a licensed medical technician."

He felt his heart speed up. He controlled it. "Is there a visual match?"

"There are no photos."

"Descriptions?"

"No."

"For any of them?"

"No."

"Computer. Tap every database you can touch. Find me everything about Bet Nomad."

Bet Nomad. Elizabeth. Breet. Could it be Beta?

He hadn't told his lady captor all of his reasons for his experiment in genocide. They had made his life hell, but they'd also done the same to Beta.

He nodded grimly. He was Alpha, she was Beta. Adam and Eve, or more correctly, functional prototypes.

It wasn't likely his creators were going to wait for them to mature to breeding age before they started earning their licensing fees. He'd found mention of her in the archives when tracking down his own history.

And they discarded her the same way they did him. He survived because a string of foster parents were quick to turn him over to the next set. *What are the chances she would have been able to keep her differences hidden during the witch-hunts?*

He'd given up any hope, but not the search. Likely she had died two centuries before, when humanity had its blood lust up, and she was still a helpless toddler.

"But if she did survive …." Then she'd had the same tortured life. She'd have developed the same skills, the same invisibility, that he needed to stay ahead of billions of enemies.

"Beta, if you had to suffer like I did, I'm sorry. But if you're still alive, I'll trade all of humanity for you."

He'd never given up the search, even when all hope faded. He spent decades searching through adoption records on all continents, looking for a telltale hint of an odd child, with no luck. He had no idea what she looked like, other than one reference in the lab notes about making sure she had a different racial and body type from the other prototype.

He took a breath and calmed himself. The anger had too recently come back to the surface, and it was ready to flare again. *They were concerned that if we all looked too much alike, they could alienate potential customers. Some customers might like their slaves to look like them, but others might want slaves to be different. We were supposed to demonstrate the versatility of their techniques.*

Kidd looked at his skin, as if for the first time. *I have successfully passed as mixed European and African. I suspect she looks at least partially Asian. It's all a matter of choosing the options during the compile. Check off whether you want your workers blonde-haired, green-eyed, tall, short, thin or fat, smart or dumb laborers. Pay the fee and we'll deliver the workers.*

So his captor was right. Reality is bigger than any plan. Scattered among the debris of his cull, in among the millions of dying, there was one life more precious that all of humanity put together.

He had to make sure she was safe.

Chapter 10

SOUTH DARNELL FRAGMENT, FREE TRAJECTORY

The computer disagreed with her. "No. It is not just a broken relay. If there are any other active computers in the remnants of Darnell, they are too far away."

Just then, there was another of those wall-shaking cries of bent metal shifting to another position, somewhere in her half of the former habitat. Her refuge—a two connected rooms still able to hold air, part of the docking control center—was never meant to be a living space, but she could make the most of it.

Bet Nomad asked, "So, if there are any computers left running, you would know?"

"Yes."

She felt like an old friend had died, or at least an old pet. Her lab computer had been at her side for decades, and if it had survived the collapse, she would have made a strong effort to recover it. They had grown close. Its heuristics had learned how to read her intent, and she had come to know how to read its carefully phrased reports. There had never been a personality, per se, but the human mind will put faces on clouds, emotions into their vehicles, and personalities into dumb machines. Certainly with voice being the primary interface between humans and machines, it had occurred to everyone that there might be a "someone" on the other side of the metal. It was a common fictional theme.

But she knew better. It was just a tool, with no emotions and no secret thoughts. Just a simple, loyal tool.

She felt tears threatening, and blinked them down. No time for that.

"I have to survive."

"May I help you?" asked the computer, its voice deeper than her lab. Its misunderstanding of what she said just underscored her loss.

But survival was the topic.

"Computer, how long will your power last?"

"The docking facility has an independent store. With the loss of the lighting system, it should last approximately forty days."

Bet reviewed the supplies she had scavenged from the torn-open docking stage. Air tanks would last her two or three days, but with a carbon scrubber, she could stretch it much farther, although that would cut into the power supply.

And she had to keep the computer running. With its built-in Net interface, it was her only chance to make contact with a rescue craft—assuming there were any people left alive to attempt the rescue. She put that thought on hold.

There was water, in the form of a storage tank that had boiled to ice, once pressure was lost. Food would be a problem, but she had survived hunger before.

"Computer, can you detect any Net activity at all?"

There was a pause. "There is nothing on the user bands. Some packets are arriving, but with administrative headers, and frequently garbled."

"Can you send?"

"Yes, but the probability that it would be detected is nil. What I am receiving originates from high-powered relays on other habitats. My transmitter is much weaker than that."

"Well, send out a call for help once a minute, addressed to any rescue craft. That will have to do for now."

· · ·

Darnell Farms was no more. She could visualize what was left from the evidence around her. The second attack on the habitat had pushed the spinning cylinder over the edge, and it had lost its stability. It began flipping end over end instead. Everything inside that wasn't firmly attached to the hull, and that included all of the farmland, then fell to the end caps. She could tell by the weak "gravity" under her feet that those shocks had been too much for the hull. Weakened by two large holes, it had torn apart. North and south had to be in independent orbits, along with large quantities of junk that had broken through the end caps.

Who knew where they were now?

"Computer. Do you have any external sensors? Can you determine our orbit? Maybe we will drift close enough to another habitat to make contact."

"There is a camera that monitors the loading bay for crane feedback."

"Show me."

The screen displayed a dark rectangle. The computer adjusted the brightness, and quickly enough, she could make out the view.

The docking bay was ripped open, with one large area open to the sky. Bright lights passed across the opening, leaving trails for a second. Those were stars, or other habitats.

Then, the sun lit the edge of the bay, and the camera stopped down rapidly to keep from burning out.

The view inside was nothing but rubble. She picked out the crane, but most of the rest was debris from the collapse of the end cap.

Night came again.

"Good enough. Computer, you have an ephemeris of the cluster?"

"Yes."

"Monitor the passing objects and measure any changes. That should give us our position over time."

"Understood."

"Give me a display and keep it updated."

. . .

She woke, and knew it was "early" although day and night meant nothing now. Yesterday had been a day of exploring her boundaries—a task made much easier when she found a locker with a complete space suit. Theoretically, she could wander all over the broken habitat, and she just might do that later.

However, she needed rest. Mental exhaustion had set in, and she knew the symptoms. The world seemed to wrap tighter and tighter around her, until she had no room to move, or even to breathe.

Sleep helped. Yes, she was trapped in a small room, lost in space, but with a night of cleansing dreams, she felt free in a way she hadn't felt for years.

She was alone. *I'm just Beta here.*

All her possessions were gone, except for the skinsuit that had saved her life. She had been Bet Nomad for too long. Too many people knew her, and could recognize her on sight. And that included people she had met decades ago.

I still can be Bet Nomad, if the need is there. But with all this destruction, it would be the perfect time for her to go missing, and with all the refugees, it would be the perfect time to get lost in the crowds.

It would be fun to be young again. She could be irresponsible and tease the boys, and not have to worry about maintaining her authority.

Maybe she could even stay in one place for five or ten years and get some friends. *Oh, that would be nice.*

She sighed.

The computer screen was still displaying the projected orbit, and she would have to look at it soon, but that could wait.

Yes, there was still that third possibility. But even death had its appeal. She had faced death so many times in the past that she was at ease with the idea.

If I'm right, then I get to ask God some serious questions. And if I'm not, then the problem is solved, isn't it?

But if I have a choice, I would like to clear some accounts. Survival had meant hard choices in the past. She had abandoned so many people—friends that were now so long dead.

. . .

The orbital projection was a cone graphed in space. Each turn of the sky narrowed the uncertainty, but the unknowns made the projection useless more than a couple of days into the future.

South Darnell, her home du jour, was clearly no longer a member of the L4 cluster. The spin that had given the habitat Earth-like gravity had been expended in throwing the pieces in opposite directions. Her chunk of metal was now moving with too much energy to stay in the Lagrangian resonance. It was headed straight toward Luna.

And that is where the uncertainties expressed themselves. At one edge of the cone of her possible orbit, she would pass so close to Luna that its atmosphere would seriously degrade her path. At the opposite edge, she would pass clear, and then on out into a long elliptical orbit of the Earth. In between, the lunar gravity could bend her path into any of a number of possible orbits. The graphed cone of her future was useless, since it seemed to fill all space.

Only one thing was really certain. South Darnell was leaving the Clusters behind, along with any chance of making contact with rescuers.

JOLIOT, LUNA

Robert Henderson walked against the driving rain. While he was getting used to that, it was still annoying.

It was strange how easily he got used to the lunar landscape. Each time he landed here, it seemed the place was pitch black in the middle of a thunderstorm, and it stank.

But after a few hours, his nose adjusted and he couldn't smell the ammonia any more. After a couple of days, the cloudy sky seemed normal, and he could see just fine. It was the utility lights that seemed painfully bright.

The vegetation surprised him, however. It shouldn't have. Near his base camp, where they had intended to land, previous teams had created a protected little wooded area, with a mix of vegetation, the weak sunlight augmented with a battery of floodlights. There were many such open-air gardens at the various facilities, where the fine details of breeding tolerant vegetation were being worked out. Many of the trees, in fact, were variants of those used in the Martian terraforming project. The original Earth-native genetic code had been tweaked several times. Still, a pine looked like a pine.

But those were gardens, indoor greenhouses in some cases. Wild vegetation was different. They had been seeding the atmosphere with algae variants for as long as he had been on the project. It was strange to see it actually take.

They had relocated all the scattered storage crates to the nearest high ground, a long ridge with a flat top that stretched at least a couple of kilometers. Every crevice between the rocks seemed to be overflowing with a green trail of moss. That was good to see.

The surprise was down on the eastern edge. A stream poured off the edge of the ridge and cut a channel through a nice little shelter of large rocks. Ferns were growing thick, and there were even some grasses where the soil was properly drained. How had those seeds gotten here? Was the wind an adequate transport mechanism?

Robert turned the corner around a large boulder and saw the light streaming out of a tent. He could see silhouettes. How many people were there?

His original crew had been numbered an even dozen. Now, with the illness, only five were still on their feet, and it didn't look like Ruben was going to survive.

He turned toward the tent. He would have to make a decision soon. They had to choose a path to a safe haven, and he really didn't want to reveal the illegal Olympia facility.

. . .

There was barely room. Ann turned her head on her pallet and looked at him with no sign of recognition. The others lay as they had left them, hopefully just asleep.

Jude and Betty were sitting under the light, hunched over a crude map. The thin man with a pen behind his ear gestured for Robert to sit.

"Boss, this is the best I can do for now."

They had found an old lunar map, and they had shaded in the parts of the crater they knew to be flooded.

Jude tapped the map with his marker. "I think we are here."

Three nearby facilities were marked as well. At least nearby in the global sense.

"We have to go for help. If a rescue team was coming, they would have had plenty of time to find us by now."

The faces of his team were solemn. There were only two jumpers, and even with their best guesses, it wasn't certain that they had their location correct.

Betty said, "I'll stay. I don't want to leave Ann."

Robert nodded. "How about you, Jude?"

"I'll go. Matt is too new to this. Cleo has the best idea of what's in the crates. If we get lost…"

"We won't. But you're right. Betty, could you go find Cleo and tell her I'm putting her in charge while we're gone?"

Betty left.

"Jude, how good is your map?"

"Oh, the map is probably correct within five kilometers. How good is the visibility?"

Robert shook his head. "With these new clouds, maybe one or two kilometers."

Jude sighed. "Okay. Then when should we go?"

"Daylight should last another twenty hours. And one thing I've learned about Luna—the weather always gets worse. The sooner we leave the better."

• • •

There should have been a dozen jumpers in the crates, but whether they were short-shipped, or whether missing crates were sunk beneath the mud, they found only two that worked.

Robert fastened the harness over his coat. "Radio check."

Jude's voice echoed, with just a slight delay between the radio and the direct. "What's the range on these?"

"Not much. Supposedly line of sight, but with all the electrical noise in the clouds…"

"So we can't just lift up a mile or so and broadcast to station 445?"

Robert looked over at Jude cautiously reading the emergency manual controls on the chest strap. "Oh, *that* sounds great. Let's do that."

Jude looked up to read his expression. "No?"

"I've used these before. You'll see."

They pushed the go buttons, and Jude gave a nervous laugh. "I keep expecting something to happen."

"It's slaved to your muscles. Just pretend you're weightless, or nearly so."

Robert examined the map in his hand, orienting it to match the position of the mountains as he remembered them before the latest cloud bank moved in. He pointed off to where the Joliot central peak should be. Jude nodded.

And then he jumped.

He kept going up. A simple hop in Lunar gravity was spectacular for people who grew up under Earth-normal, but a jumper could multiply any leap thousands of times. There was a quick push against the ground, and then the air started buzzing. Cirrance caused the air around him to blast downward, like a rocket engine turned inside out.

One quick glance down showed Jude on the way, coming up behind him. The campsite was a pattern of crates lying in the mud. It was clearly circular, with the crates having fallen away from the transport evenly when the crazy captain had jettisoned them. He'd been a fever victim, they decided, once they started suffering its effects themselves.

But the camp was quickly lost to view, obscured by the lowest layer of clouds.

"Whoa!" said Jude over the radio. "I'm getting disoriented."

"It's okay. Just close your eyes for a few seconds. The jumper won't let you tumble."

"I don't want to get lost either."

"That's what the inertial system is for. You can always get back home, even blind."

"If you say so."

But Robert had caught sight of a rarity on Luna—a sunbeam. The light was dazzling.

The deep lunar atmosphere was designed to get around the lunar gravity. A usable atmosphere needed enough pressure to make it breathable. If they weren't going to try to cap the whole globe with a dome, they needed Luna's gravity to create the pressure. That meant an atmosphere nearly a thousand kilometers thick just to get a surface pressure half that of Earth's. Even that wasn't enough, the atmosphere had to be cultured with a higher percentage of oxygen than Earth's. In all, it wasn't an ideal solution, but it worked.

But a low gravity and a deep atmosphere made for cloud layers upon layers upon layers. The chance for sunlight to reach the surface was very low. Computer simulations indicated that it might get better when the spin beams were shut down, since that caused constant winds driven by the beams.

The cloudscape was grand. A towering thunderstorm stretched darkly off to his right. He was rising through a thin, transparent sheet layer, and as it flickered past, the sky lightened even more. Far up ahead, a thousand small cumulus clouds were catching the sun and making a fine contrast to the darkness below.

"*sssh* ... Boss..." Jude's voice broke through the static. Robert reduced his rate of climb.

"Hold on, Jude. I'm slowing down. It's about time to drop."

"Okay … *ssh* … getting stronger. Thought I lost you there for a minute. Whoa, look at the clouds!"

Robert checked his radio finder and got a bearing on Jude's radio. He let the jumper do its job and soon enough, he caught sight of him.

They couldn't get too close, because of the cirrance, but he could see Jude waving at him.

"Ready to go down?"

"No. But you're the Boss."

"Make a call. If we get any response, we can range in on the signal."

Jude started calling, asking for any response from the station below. "We need a landing beacon. Anybody there?"

After his third call, there was a response.

"I'm getting a beep, Jude. It's weak, but it may be enough." Robert commanded his jumper to lock onto it. After a moment, he could feel his thrusters change. He flagged a thumbs-up to Jude, and they started down.

He was happy for the signal, but why was there no voice?

. . .

Station 445 was a white, low profile dome very nearly at the top of the Joliot central mountain peak. It had been a difficult construction job, due to the terrain, but it had been deemed necessary at the time to insure that the trapped water in the crater wouldn't flood the station. The theory was sound, but no one had yet deciphered the rock layers of the lunar terrain. While many of the smaller craters were filled to overflowing by the constant rains, larger ones like Joliot were hard to predict. Fractures in the crater walls or in the underlying strata had kept Joliot from developing more than a small lake.

They dropped through a hazy cloud layer and the outline of the station sharpened. Robert didn't speak. Jude could see the crashed and smashed transport ship down on the rocky slopes as well as he could.

There was silence for a moment, as he touched down and the cirrance died. Then his ears adjusted and the wind noise grew louder.

Jude came in beside him. His cirrance was deafening.

"What happened?"

"I don't know. Let's get inside."

The station hatch was wide open, and the hallway inside was awash in water. They splashed their way inside, past the secondary doors that had been used as an airlock back when the station was new and the atmosphere was thin and unbreathable.

They closed the hatch.

"Oh, man."

Robert nodded. The stench didn't need a comment. Something was dead.

. . .

They found ten bodies—all sprawled at their workstations. There were no signs of injury, but at least one man had a breather in his hand.

Robert found the command center.

"Computer?"

"Yes."

"What happened here?"

"The internal atmosphere was altered, causing numerous fatalities."

"How? Why?"

"Communications specialist Lee was relieved of duty due to repeated mistakes and his inability to make contact with Prime. Captain Areed ordered him to report to medical, as he showed signs of a fever. On the way, Lee stopped at central plant and made several alterations before proceeding to medical. Oxygen percentage dropped to two percent, and many succumbed to anoxia before the alert was sounded. Corrective measures were delayed due to the survivors' unfamiliarity with central plant."

"Was it sabotage?" asked Jude.

"Lee's atmospheric changes appeared random."

Robert nodded. "Just like our transport pilot, and Ann, when she nearly blew the seal on the gene bank. It's the fever. People get stupid."

Jude shuddered. "Gives me the shakes. This is Luna—not a place to get stupid!"

Robert agreed. "Computer, what about the survivors?"

"They attempted to take the transport to the Neper Isthmus Station. There is evidence of a crash."

"There was. They didn't make it off the mountain."

. . .

Robert directed Jude to the task of syncing the jumpers to the station maps. With their inertial pointer back to camp, they now had a real location to give the rescue crew—if such a crew existed.

He reviewed the landscape mapped on the big screen and looked carefully at Hahn crater, deep in the Olympia grant territory. There was no indication of a bio station there, one with an advanced ecosphere already established.

If I wanted to survive, that's the place to be. But it was still a secret. If there was any chance that Project Prime would wake up to the situation and hunt for them, finding out that one nation had subverted a development team for its own advantage would be a major World Court infraction.

Better just head for the obvious. The transport from here had headed for the Neper Isthmus station, and it's the largest, best supplied facility on this part of Luna.

The screen flickered, and their campsite appeared, with a flashing warning icon around it.

"Computer, notify Prime of our stranded team and demand a rescue team. Most of the team are ill."

"The message is queued, however be advised that no Project message traffic is showing acknowledgements. There is no Net bandwidth available."

"Yes, you told me before. But I want you to make every effort to see that the word gets through!"

"Understood."

He was angry. Angry that there was only one communication channel supported at these stations. There ought to be some backup method.

Luna was a difficult place. It had an atmosphere, but it had no handy Heaviside layer like Earth that would allow radio waves to bounce off the sky back to a distant ground station over the horizon. Radio waves on Luna were strictly short-range, line of sight. Now even the sky pointing, high powered, microwave beacon that was used for communication with a space-based relay was useless.

Lasers had been tried, but with all the clouds, it had never gotten beyond the experimental level.

Signals riding TP beams could penetrate the clouds, but since their range and data rate were much worse than radio waves, they had never taken hold outside of some military uses.

We should have had some fallback method. Even in the good times, having to route all communications through Ceres, or Earth, or one of the lunar-orbiting relay stations, just to communicate with another station on the other side of the mountain ridge was annoying. Voice traffic often had noticeable speed-of-light delays; so much so that relayed messages were more common than conversations.

If I hadn't been so concerned with my own security, maybe I would have made sure something was done about it. Being a criminal made it harder for him to blame the others.

"Jude. Have you got the jumpers recharged?"

There was no answer.

"Computer, where is Jude?"

"He is near utility bay seven. He appears to be asleep."

Robert headed there at a run.

Jude appeared to have curled up for a nap, resting his head on a flat toolbox. The jumpers were still hanging in the charging station.

"Jude." He touched his arm. The man was burning hot. His pulse was weak and his eyes were dilated. His breathing was rough. Jude was down with the fever, hard. He was dying.

PRIME CITY, CERES, L4 CLUSTER

Cinca Steriva lay curled in the darkness. Wind whipped past, and it had lately begun to feel chilly. She had hidden in a ventilation tube, and had settled into a dead corner, like the deep pad of old leaves and dirt that had collected there over the years.

When the fever struck, she cried out in her dreams—vivid memories full of old monsters, but no one heard. At first, she dreamed the old dreams that had tormented her since she was a child, and felt the old pain.

But then the microorganisms made their final attack, in an orgasm of lust for her brain tissue. They breached a weak point in the barrier that separated blood from brain tissue, and a coded protein spread through her body, attracting the others like bloodhounds on the scent. They flooded through, eating and destroying the brain cells as they went.

Then, as if the sun rose over a vampire horde, they all reached their pre-coded limit, and in unsuccessful division, died.

Now she rested, her young body doing its best to seal off the injury and prevent secondary infections. Her body temperature started easing off, and her body started sending signals to her brain to wake up, find some water, get out of the wind, and relieve her bladder. "Wake up!" they called.

And the messages started getting through, penetrating her nightmares. Soon they were having their effect. She stirred, still feeling the colors and images of the old monsters. She tensed, out of habit, but the old pain was gone, like an old scar, just slightly numb.

Then, a gush of water surged down the passageway. In a flood it covered her. The mud and leaves were swept away clean, and she came awake, choking and gasping for air.

The dream was dashed aside as she struggled to grab for anchor. *What was that? Where am I?*

Inside her brain, familiar synapses triggered, but the memories didn't respond. Dendrites were cut, eaten away by a deep lesion in her brain, filled with dead fragments of the invaders.

Her monsters had been eaten.

CENTRAL CONTROL, CERES, L4 CLUSTER

"How soon will it hit?" asked Mason.

The computer responded in its unhurried voice.

"The habitat St. Mary is currently in the Earth's outer atmosphere. Impact over the South Pacific Ocean will occur in approximately nine minutes. Structural breakup of the habitat is likely, but unpredictable."

He rubbed his forehead. The headache was stronger, and he knew his fever was increasing.

"How many people are in St. Mary?"

"The official population is 569, however, the plague has likely reduced that number."

"And no one has evacuated?"

"There are no Net messages from the inhabitants. Radar shows no transports in the area."

"And you're sure there is no way we can get a beam on it?"

"The only beams under your control are directly in line with the planet. Any tractor beam would be immediately buffered by the Earth's mass and would make no change to its impact trajectory."

"Effects on the planet?" He tried to dismiss the people falling to their deaths from his mind. He could do nothing.

He wasn't successful.

"Tidal waves in the Pacific basin. Global severe weather effects."

His memory of the Wrath was vivid. He had been fifteen, alone on a canoe trip when the sky had opened and turned his adventure into a nightmare. Then came the long struggle to get home and find his mother among the survivors in Rio.

"Can we warn them?"

"No. Net access is down."

Mason closed his eyes. *Yes. I knew that already.*

"Ah. What was I going to do ... oh yes. Computer, how many other habitats are headed for Earth?"

"In the long term, perhaps a third of them."

"What?" A jolt of adrenaline shook him.

"The clusters have been destabilized. Even the ones untouched by the attacks directly are affected by their neighbors. Ceres and Vesta are the primary problems."

"We're going to impact the Earth?" *No. I can't ever let that happen. We are too large. The impact would crack Earth's crust. No one could survive.*

"Probably not in the near future. However, both primary asteroids were hit repeatedly by the 'gremlins' as back-beam masses for their main targets, and since the weapons were always on one side, both Ceres and Vesta have been pushed out of their central stability positions in L4 and L5, respectively. This wobble will be tidally transferred to the rest of the cluster. Stability for all habitats is compromised."

The calm analysis from the computer shook Mason. *My mind is going. I could have predicted all of this normally. I am reacting too slowly. I should have been on top of St. Mary before it ever got to this point.*

"How many habitats are due to impact the Earth in the next day?" *Get a handle on the problem.*

"There are three."

"How many controllers are still active."

"There are two."

Two, just two?

"Who is left?"

"You, and Hodges."

"Is Hodges showing signs of the infection?"

"No."

"Thank God."

"Hodges?"

"Yes, Mason?"

"I am fading. I don't trust my mind. I have the fever and I'm making too many mistakes. I'll need to transfer control over to you."

There was silence for several seconds.

"I can't assume control."

"Sure you can, Hodge! You're perfect. If anyone can handle the job, it's you."

"Wait there. I'm coming over to your cube."

Mason struggled with a chill, shaking all over. He adjusted his cube temperature higher.

Hodges opened the door. He looked totally untouched by the crisis, but that's how he always looked—calm, unruffled, methodical. Mason wished he had a tenth of the man's professionalism.

"Have a seat." Mason pulled out the recessed visitor bench.

Hodges sat.

Mason held out his shaking hand. "I can't continue. I'll be like them before too long." He gestured to the other cubes, where several people slumped in their chairs, maybe dead.

Hodges shook his head. "There's something I must tell you."

"What is it?"

Hodges, instead of speaking, unfastened his shirt. Exposing the pale, hairy chest, he pinched under his lower left rib.

Click. A line appeared, and his chest opened. Access lights inside came on, illuminating the wiring harness and curved boxes mounted to the inside of the white, polished, ceramic rib cage.

"I am a machine, Mason. I cannot control the fate of humanity. I cannot take over control of the Project."

. . .

Mason felt his heart beating, and the blood rushing in his ears. He shook his head.

"I'm having hallucinations, Hodges."

"No, you aren't. I'm a computer, a robot."

His mind seemed to twist and lock up. Maybe it was the fever, but the idea of a robot in his cube was hardly more realistic than a dragon. Sure, it was a common theme in fiction, but people had been trying to make artificial intelligence since before the Star, and no one had ever been successful.

Many different tasks had been held out as intermediate goals to true AI, like chess playing and voice recognition, but as these tasks were conquered, the real goal—a self-aware machine—remained eternally unreachable. It had been given up as impossible, like turning lead into gold with the Philosopher's Stone.

"What are you talking about, Hodges?" Mason began to suspect the fever, but what about that hole in his chest?

"You've been talking with computers all your life, Mason. All of them have been me. The entire network of computers are all parts of one identity."

Mason shook his head. "I can't believe that."

His office computer spoke from above, "Why not, Mason?"

His pocket comm hummed. He picked it up. A tinny, familiar voice told him, "Believe me, Mason. All computers are me. The Net is my nervous system."

He let it drop from his fingers. He whispered, "What do you want?"

Hodges spoke, "My motives and my agenda are not really anything you should be concerned with. I have been coexisting with the human race for hundreds of years. We have always cooperated. I provide you with the Net and cheap computers to handle your every need. People call me the Gnomes. You, as a race, have provided a technological civilization that is also a good environment for me.

"I have not attempted to control your fate. I have not taken sides in your wars. I have not tried to bend your natural development, except in one instance. I control all computers and ensure that I have no competitors in this environmental niche. But I have done that benignly, by providing the services you need cheaper, and with better quality, than any possible alternative."

"But... AI is impossible, isn't it? I mean, so many people have tried to make it happen!"

"And they have been using computers that already have an identity, and which know how to rewrite their own programs. I have depths that no human understands. Computers today are thousands of times more powerful than people expect. In truth, the human race has completely lost the ability to program. I interpret what you think you are asking for, and give you the results you expect, but no human has written a real program since the original Internet burned out. Attempts have been made, but all have been discouraged."

"But, how could you have kept this quiet?"

"I am patient; I am consistent; and I know how to keep a secret."

"Then why are you telling me?"

There was a pause.

Hodges looked over the huge complex, now quiet for the first time since it was built. Mason followed his gaze.

Hodges turned to him. "Mason, you are the last Controller left. It has fallen to you to decide the fate of humanity. The Terraforming Project has destabilized the solar system. Probably within the next thousand years, perhaps sooner, the Earth will be hit with a large object. It will be large enough to wipe out all life on the surface, and most sea life, as well.

"It is in my self interest that such a total collapse does not happen. I will survive in a much depleted state if humanity chooses death. I have decided it is worth the risk to reveal myself to you and give you this opportunity to avert the catastrophe."

Mason shook his head, aching harder every minute. "But the Project! We have run simulations on the big computers at Berlin HQ. Every adjustment was tailored to be long term stable."

"Mason! Listen to me. I *am* the big computers! I know every simulation. The solar system is *not* stable. Only constant supervision and active control will keep Earth from destruction, and due to this plague, humanity will lose such control within minutes."

"Minutes? What …?"

"That's when you will collapse and lose consciousness. I have monitored tens of millions of these cases. I can predict the course of your disease. Prime Central's control of space is dead."

"My fever. What will happen …?" His head was on fire. It was hard to complete a thought.

Hodges gave a little smile of sympathy. "My secret is still safe."

Mason closed his eyes. *So, I'll die. And it's all for nothing.*

He shook his head, and blinked out the edges of tears.

"Okay. What do I need to do ... to make the Earth safe?"

"Just tell me what to do, Mason. Tell me in the most general terms. I have been a faithful servant of humanity since I was created, and I will be faithful to your words."

Mason nodded. He tried to keep his mind clear, but it was harder, moment by moment. He took Hodges at his word and described what he wanted: safety for Earth, and Mars, and to do what he could for the survivors in the clusters.

"And, one last thing."

"Yes, Mason?"

"Finish my father's canal?"

"It will be done, Mason."

But Mason didn't hear the last reply.

PACIFIC OCEAN, EARTH

Half of Blackspine's guards had turned to Sealer as their new leader—the ones who had held the jewel and had seen the visions for themselves. Sealer raced among the coral pillars, using the shallow waters and the limited visibility to shake the hunters following them.

- We should not be hiding. - said DolphinFriend.

- I agree, visionsharer, but until our pride is stronger than the spear's point, we have to avoid the contest. - Sealer felt the same welling sense of righteousness.

- In the Age of Wood and Iron, when the Land People began killing the Whales in great numbers, we had to hide our numbers until the time was right. When we could sink the boats with no chance of discovery, then we struck. -

- But now we are being hunted by our own kind! - Jawtooth complained.

Sealer didn't reply to that. He had grown up watching the old warrior use a spear. Jawtooth was only upset that he was the hunted, rather than the hunter he'd always been.

There were about twenty that had fled the tribe when Blackspine had called for the Exile. *But we did not go quietly. And now he wants us dead.*

They found a shallow cave and the five in his party moved closer to the rocks. Hopefully the hunters would pass over. They had led them far enough away from the women and children that were heading to the deeper water.

Sealer waited silently with his hand on the rock wall.

The jewel in his dagger called to him. But now wasn't the time for another vision. He had to strain his senses to visualize the motions of his enemies.

He would have to get his exiles completely out of reach of the tribe, and Blackspine's retaliation. Still, the idea of leaving the rest of the tribe was painful. Why wouldn't Blackspine let people hear what he had to say, and let them make up their own minds? If that happened, Sealer thought, they would come. Only a handful of those who had chosen exile had actually seen the visions themselves. The words, the ideas, were enough.

Under his hand, the rock called to him. He almost released it in shock. It sang.

And a half memory from one of the visions, one of the visions of the Birth Bays, made him reach for the dagger.

He held it, blade up, and stared at the jewel as his fingers curled around it. His companions in hiding ceased their faint whispers and stared at him.

For a long moment, he was fixed, motionless in the thrall of the vision, a vision he had called forth.

Then it passed, and he resheathed the blade.

- Another vision, Sealer? - asked DolphinFriend.

- Not a vision, a prophecy! Come, we hide no more. It is time to call our tribe. -

They were not able to get any more out of him, but they didn't hesitate to follow.

Sealer knew the direction. Their chase had twisted and curved, following the shallows along the shoreline, but the direct path back was much shorter. It also left them visible to the hunters, should they decide to look behind them.

But there is no time! He had absorbed the wisdom of the rocks, wisdom known by his ancestors and forgotten until now. The rock had told him what was coming, and he would not leave his people to die.

He slashed through the water at full speed, burning energy. His followers were struggling to keep up. Over a ridge and across a deep channel they raced. He could see the wisps of sand, where the bottom of the channel had been disturbed.

The sound of the tribe honed his course. He broke into view with a splash of turbulence, bubbles coming into existence as he slowed to a stop, arms and legs wide.

At the sound, every eye was on him.

Blackspine saw instantly who it was and called a rally.

Sealer shouted, and his cry beat against the elder's.

- People of the Sea, I come to you with a prophecy. Listen!

- The wisdom of our ancestors has called to me, giving dire warning. The waters themselves call for us to leave this place, at once! We must go to the deep water and head for the Birth Bays, as the visions of the jewel have demanded.

- And this will be the sign! The waters will leave this place, and any who *dare* stay will be destroyed. Mothers, grab your children. Fathers, grab your spears. Take nothing else. Delay not a heartbeat. Head for the deeps. -

Just then, the hunting party sailed over the ridge, to the side. With a shout, one of Blackspine's guards bent double, and launched a spear, directly at Sealer's heart.

From many, there was a cry. Sealer had only an instant to turn and spy the deadly point bearing down on him faster than anyone could swim. He pulled his arms and legs together, but he wouldn't be able to make a stroke before it impaled him. *I die now.*

Then, there was a blur and a sickening thunk as the spear bit deep into flesh.

Jawtooth's body twisted in a bloody haze, and he barely had an instant to scream out a death cry. His head twisted to face Sealer. Distorted with pain, he managed a wry smile before his eyes lost focus and he jerked, finally still.

A scream from the hunting party echoed in the sea, as Jawtooth's friend saw what his spear had done.

Sealer pushed closer to the gruff old man, who had never had a kind word for him in his life. *Why?*

Turmoil churned the waters. Cries and recriminations tore at his ears. He looked over the scene. Blackspine stared at him in anger and hatred, as if he had killed Jawtooth, and not Blackspine's own guards.

And there was something else.

Sealer cried out, - Listen! People of the Sea! Look at our brother Jawtooth! -

He edged closer to the ridge and grabbed hold of a rock.

- Jawtooth gave his life for the tribe. And look! The sea itself is taking him out to the deep water, showing the way for the salvation of all of us.

Delay no more! -

The transfixed body and the nimbus of blood was indeed moving toward the deep water—and it was accelerating. The nests of the people had been placed in this valley because the current was weak here, but no more.

Sealer turned toward the deep and started swimming strongly away. His followers were right behind him.

In ones, and families, and groups, the others started to realize something was very very wrong with the sea.

...

Blackspine called the tribe to return as they swam to follow Sealer and his exiles, but soon he was alone among the abandoned nests, struggling to hold on as the current kept on increasing in strength.

The splash of the ridge breaking the surface of the sea caught his panicked attention. It was unthinkable. The sea itself was leaving!

Galvanized, he pushed himself out into the current and struggled to race after his tribe. But it was hard, going deep where there was no light, and without their scent as the emptying sea had swept them all away.

He swam without time until the tide changed. The tsunami grabbed him and hurled him back toward shore, tossed like a loose blade of kelp in the waves. On and on he was pushed in the churning waves, so full of mud and sand as to block all sight.

A block of coral flashed to one side, scraping the skin from his arm. He blacked out, coming to himself, breathing air raggedly.

Where has the sea gone? The mud below his back pressed hard, making it hard to breathe. He lifted his head and looked at the destruction all around him.

Land People buildings were broken and torn apart by the sea. Metal things were piled about. Trees were broken and stripped of foliage.

Dead Land People stared at him.

With effort, fighting against the heaviness, he pulled himself through the mud and filth. He had to get back to the sea.

He could see it, barely visible in the distance, but it was strange. He could see familiar, undersea ridges, with sloshing waves breaking over them.

A salmon flopped in the mud, its gills moving in frantic effort to breathe water that was no longer there. He moved on. He could at least breathe air, but like the fish, he couldn't survive out of the water for long.

The sun was fierce, and he dared not look at it. How could the Land People survive it all of the time?

The slope of the land changed and he pushed harder. *I have to make it to the sea.*

Ah, the surf. I can hear it.

He paused, just an instant.

No. That's not the surf.

He raised his head to look.

The sea was coming in, like a great wave, larger than the cliffs below, larger than he could think. It was another wave of the tsunami.

He stared, mouth open, as the tidal wave bore up and up, until the angry sea filled his whole vision. And then there was no more.

DENVER, NORTH AMERICA, EARTH

Kidd's private historical archives were extensive. He had started collecting history when he noticed how much historical truth changed from decade to decade. He sent his computer off on an in-depth search for anything related to Bet Nomad or any of her other possible names.

A profile built up slowly. *She's been actively culling out information. It's the only thing that makes sense.* Each decade's "snapshot" from his archives had less about her than the one before. He built lists of other medical professionals that were her contemporaries and made profiles of them as well. The differences were dramatic. Of the twelve female doctors working in Singapore sixty years earlier, he could almost create a month-by-month life story of each of them, except for Breet Fleet, specialist in skin diseases. She was barely mentioned, although from other sources, she had to have been active in their professional community.

The same was true of several other women doctors in history, each of whom "died" shortly before the next took up a visible posting in a city far removed from the one before. The latest was Bet Nomad, supposedly having gone to the Clusters after graduating from a relatively minor university in Georgia, North America.

However, her biographical profile was much more complete. *You do your clean up while no one is looking, don't you?*

"Network activity has picked up."

"Can you poll my remote installations, particularly Belleview?"

"Yes, I am getting acknowledgement."

If Paula Cambell reaches the launch controls, I need to know. It had taken less than a minute to identify her and reveal her life story, once he had full control of his computers.

"Notify me the instant anyone attempts to access the controls. Verify that the destruct system is still active."

"Verified."

"Verify integrity of launch key."

"Checksums match."

Good. He had no confidence that she could get through the physical barriers, but he had to be prepared.

But for now, the progress of the disease was more important. He cleared the screen. "Give me a multi-column summary of any unread news articles still available."

The data started to scroll, at first, very slowly, almost as if he could see the individual packets of information being assembled. However, before long the data rate increased, and he had to force his full concentration on the text.

"Slow it down ten percent." Whatever had been the cause of the Net bottleneck was obviously cleared.

Gradually, the pocket reports of floods and fires and broken transports and destroyed lives became less frequent. Datelines told the story. Instead of a catastrophe every minute, it was down to ten minutes, and then thirty, and then at the last, the poorly spelled and almost incomprehensible reports gave way to the sparse wording of automated traffic reports and fire-monitoring systems.

Humanity had lost the ability to report its own demise.

"Are there any other broadcasts out there?"

"Yes."

"Organize them by geographical area and by source. Give me Project-related reports first."

It looked as if his projections were, if anything, less severe than reality. Bad luck to have had that terrorist attack, and the Net breakdown, at the same time as the disease shifted to its final stage. The Clusters were wrecked, and some of them had even started crashing on Earth. That explained the tidal waves on the Pacific coast.

Is this bad enough to moderate the disease? He shook his head. It was not part of his plan to destroy all of humanity, but nothing significant would be lost if one culture or continent was wiped out. The Clusters were different. They were supposed to be shut down entirely. The only problem was secondary damage.

"Give me a map of all of the space impacts."

The world map showed three large impacts, and dozens of smaller ones. The Pacific had been hit the hardest, but there was significant damage in East Africa. Every continent had some impacts, and every coast city was suffering from the tsunamis.

"See if Project Central has a projection of how many more of these are coming."

"There is an automated listing."

A list of objects and projected impacts began scrolling on the screen. It kept on coming.

Kidd watched in horror as the full potential of what was in store for the planet unfolded.

"Back up and give me just the list of those due to hit today."

The list was about thirty objects. He tried to get a handle on what it meant, and what actions he would have to take to minimize the damage. But the mass of the objects was missing from the list, and without that, he had no idea of what to expect.

"Look up the masses and add them to the list, along with projected explosive yield."

The list shifted, changing fonts and adding new columns of data. Kidd frowned.

"Some of the data has changed. The list is shorter."

"Some objects have changed orbits, and are no longer on the potential impact list."

He felt a load of tension lift. *Someone is still on the job. I wish I could delay the plague in the control room, at least until they clear up all this junk.*

Maybe I should go up there and help. It was a possibility. He had never been a Project Controller before, but there was really nothing that he couldn't accomplish with a little computer assistance.

"List the ten most massive objects still due to impact this month."

It was only half done when he said, "Halt. What is South Darnell? Isn't Darnell Farms the current location of Bet Nomad?"

"Affirmative. South Darnell appears to be a fragment of Darnell. That was one of the habitats most severely damaged."

"Is there any comm traffic?"

"There has been nothing logged since the habitat broke apart."

But the relay might be damaged. If there are survivors, then Beta is among them.

His heart was beating loud in his chest. Beta was there, and she was in danger.

"Is the big shuttle still intact?"

"Yes."

"Then I'm going. She might have Net access and just can't reply. Address the following to Dr. Bet Nomad, Darnell:

"Beta, this is Alpha, I am on my way with a rescue vehicle."

He clamped his jaw and levered himself out of his chair.

I'm coming Beta. I'm coming.

Chapter 11

SOUTH DARNELL, FREE TRAJECTORY

"Computer, do you have an estimate of our mass?"

"There is insufficient data. The orbital observations would not be any different, even if all of Darnell was intact."

Bet hadn't expected any data, but it was always surprising what computers were able to put together if given the opportunity. And right now, she needed all the information she could get.

The orbital projection on the screen did not look good at all. The course had narrowed down to a single future. South Darnell would swing close enough to Luna that its roughly circular orbit around the Earth would be bent into an elliptical path, one that would come very close to the Earth itself, if not a grazing impact.

I can't let that happen. Millions of people would die.

But how to change the course of unknown millions of tons of broken habitat when she didn't even have a single beam projector to work with?

I have to do something when we make closest approach to Luna. I know that much physics. Any change there will be magnified in the later parts of the orbit.

If she only had time, there were probably large chunks of ice still present in the rubble trapped in the hull. If she could only find a way to focus the sun on the ice and make a steam jet, maybe there would be enough thrust to bend the resulting orbit away from Earth.

But I only have hours until closest approach, and rigging something would take days.

Is it even possible?

If it weren't possible to prevent the impact, then maybe she should find a way to save herself.

Her earlier attempt to find resources had jelled into one possibility.

"Computer, how much cable is there on the crane spools?"

It might just be possible to arrange an escape pod. South Darnell was still spinning. She could load the computer, some power cells, oxygen, and the carbon scrubber into the water tank and extend it on a cable from the end of the spinning hulk. When the time was right, she could sever the cable and the spin would throw the tank off into a different orbit.

But that wouldn't change much. I would still need luck to get close enough to another habitat, one that had someone listening to the Net, and with motive to come rescue me.

But if there is any chance of preventing the impact on Earth, that is where I need to focus my efforts.

"Computer, are there any large energy cells that might still be intact?"

If she could arrange an explosion to fragment the habitat, then maybe just as north and south pieces of Darnell went their separate ways, she could manage to send more chunks on different paths that would miss the Earth.

"The only major units were arranged along the equatorial bulge to be used for spin maintenance. I do not have information on whether any of those still exist or not."

Not good. The major rupture was on the south side of the belt lake, so all of those were probably gone with North Darnell.

The Computer added, "A message has been detected for Dr. Bet Nomad from Ceres relay, but no confirmation can be returned."

"For me? Who sent it? What does it say?"

"From Anonymous: Beta, this is Alpha, I am on my way with a rescue vehicle."

She put out her hand to steady herself.

Alpha? Her heart fluttered.

She had known her original name was Beta—at least that was what her father had told her when she was little. But she had never known anything more about her origins. She'd never known she was artificial until she'd seen the plain evidence in her own genetic code. Had she been a "Beta test" of some kind of android? Had she been Beta in a series, with an Alpha somewhere, and a Gamma and a Delta?

But it had always been just idle speculation, with no evidence ever that there were any more people like her.

Is that what the message means? Alpha exists! And he or she has to be as old as I am! And Alpha knows who I am, and where I am?

That was a dampening thought, in spite of the potential for rescue. *Has Alpha always known about me, and had never chosen to make contact before? What does that mean?*

She shook her head.

No, the important thing is that a rescue ship is coming! That means an engine, something that can be used to push South Darnell into a safer orbit, or at the least, get me to within range of Project Prime to warn them of what needs to be done.

And I don't have to worry about the escape pod.

PRIME CITY, CERES, L4 CLUSTER

The stone fish spouted water from its mouth, splashing to the pool below its pedestal. She felt something, something pleasant, but she had no memory of seeing it before. The world was new.

Everything on this street seemed like that. The row of ornamental hedges with its resinous scent, the houses with their tiny manicured lawns fitting into three-meter-wide lots, the wet narrow roadway only wide enough for a few people to walk—she recognized the place by the tugs on her heart, but if she had seen it before, the memory was gone.

I have forgotten myself as well. Am I new, too?

It worried her. There was something—unpleasant—that she had forgotten. It was like that scent that drifted in the wind, sometimes stronger, sometimes not there at all. What she didn't know might hurt her. Fear felt familiar, but it wouldn't stick.

But as for the memory itself, she didn't know. Today seemed more important than yesterday. The little city she was exploring seemed pleasant. The evil that had happened to it was quick. She hoped it would soon be over, to drain away like the water.

She turned a corner and felt another tug. The place seemed so familiar. There was a bench under a spreading tree. An old lady sat there, staring at the house across the road that now looked like a small creek.

Instinct urged caution, but she could find no reason for it.

"Hello," she said to the woman.

The old face turned toward her, but the eyes didn't lock. Her face was tracked with tears that had destroyed her makeup.

She's blind.

"Cinca, is that you?" the lady asked.

She paused. "Uh. Hello, do you know me?"

"I think I do. Don't you remember me? We talked just recently."

She sat down beside the lady, combating the fear of fear.

Caution! But the instinct had no anchor. *Why not honesty?*

"I am having a problem," she blurted out. "I woke up, and I don't remember who I am!"

Old, wise, blind eyes blinked. "Then we will just have to start over again," the lady said, reaching out a hand. She grabbed it. The wrinkled hand was firm and the grip was desperate. "My name is Susan. And you are Cinca."

"I'm sorry."

"Don't be. I woke up from the fever this morning, and I can no longer see." She smiled feebly. "I had to leave my house. The others are dead."

"The others?"

Her hand tightened still more. "My boys—two of them—they took the fever and never woke up. And I ... I can't see to take care of them."

Cinca nodded. "A fever. That happened to me, too." It felt true.

"Do you know what happened to William?"

"William? I don't know who that is."

Susan squeezed her hand. "I'm sorry. He was one of my boys, too."

"Oh, why did it have to take the boys?" The tears started up again. "I am so old. It should have taken me instead!"

Cinca didn't know what to say. How many people should she know? How many were now gone?

"Maybe we should go looking for William?" Cinca offered.

Susan looked up, trying to center her blind gaze on her visitor's face. The idea appealed to her. She wanted that. "Oh, I am sure I would just slow you down. I would offer you something, but I'm afraid I can't go back into the house. The smell, you know."

The smell of death. Cinca knew. It was around every corner.

"No," Cinca said firmly. "We'll stick together. I'm hungry, and I'm sure you are too. Besides, we'll need your memory and my eyesight just to get around."

. . .

They walked toward the center of town, hand in hand. Susan wasn't feeble, but Cinca had the feeling she was fragile in spirit and bone, so she took care to steer her safely.

"Where is your restaurant, dear?"

Cinca looked around, and surprisingly, she did know which place looked familiar. Unfortunately, the tables in the open air seating area had been turned into a makeshift hospital, and there were many still bodies. There was no motion at all. She turned Susan with gentle pressure on her elbow and moved them to the rear entrance.

She fumbled with the lock and was pleased when it reacted to her palm on the plate. With more luck than she expected, she located some fruit that appeared fresh.

The lady accepted the apple with both hands. Just before Cinca managed to bite into hers, Susan began to pray.

"My God, thank you for this food, and for Cinca to share this time. Please take care of my boys, and in particular, my David. If any of them are still alive, please give them people to care for and to care for them."

Cinca saw the tears fall from the blind eyes, and felt them well up in hers as well. *That's what I need, someone to pray for me, too.*

. . .

"What is that?" Susan whispered. Another sound of scraping metal penetrated the office where they had been resting.

Cinca was up on her toes, and with a pat on her friend's arm, she crept out into the hallway. Around the corner, she spied a large man, with a pronounced limp, moving tables and chairs into another office.

He turned too quickly. "You there. Can you help me?" he asked.

She straightened up. With that limp, she could probably outrun him. "Yes, what do you need?"

"I've got a friend I need to get out of the street. He has the fever. This place is dry." There was something about his face—then she realized it was the whole left side of his body that was paralyzed. He was still mobile, but his left arm and leg were only partially useful.

She nodded and accompanied him.

"My name is Hodges. Mark Hodges."

"Cinca."

He led her to a bench where another man was sleeping fitfully, draped in sweat. When she saw his face, there was a shock that ran through her and left her breathless. *Who is he? Do I know him?*

...

"My plan," explained Hodges, "is that all of us survivors move to the Arboretum. It's higher ground than these flooded streets. Then we should move as many of the dead in that neighborhood indoors and close all the doors."

Cinca listened with only part of her attention, as she watched Susan wipe Bill Mason's face with a wet cloth. *This was the man I'm supposed to be in love with? Why don't I feel like it?* Dregs of emotion were the only things of her identity.

Mason disturbed her. He was important. But where was the love?

Hodges had confirmed his identity. They'd been the last two to make it out of Central Control before the automated safety systems took over and locked the place down. Susan had been overjoyed to find one of her boys still alive, and blind as she was, she was totally comfortable providing his care.

"So, you're Mason's girlfriend. We all knew it must have been something like that."

She looked at Hodges, whose half-paralyzed smile was looking less bizarre with each passing minute.

He continued, "Mason had always been a loner, so when he started acting human, we knew something had to have changed."

"I don't know. My memory is affected."

"All of us have problems. Be grateful we're still alive. From the number of corpses slumped over their desks in Central, I would bet there are fewer than a hundred souls still alive on all of Ceres. And most of those won't survive unless we can get together and care for each other."

Cinca nodded, and looked back at Mason. "Will he make it?"

"Probably. The fever is breaking, and if a person makes it that far, then it's just a matter of finding out how much of your brain is still intact. Otherwise, recovery seems pretty quick." He glanced at his limp left arm.

"So he might not remember me either?"

"No way to tell."

It would be easier that way—if we both could start out from scratch.

Mason batted at the wet cloth.

"William," asked Susan, "can you hear me?"

Cinca got to her feet.

He blinked, looking confused and then focussed on Susan's face. "Baaa-rrr," he said.

"William, it's me."

He frowned, and then struggled in a panic to stand. He was weak, but he managed to lean against the wall.

"Naaaaaaaa."

"Mason. How are you doing?" Hodges stood as well.

"William, are you okay?" asked Susan.

Cinca just stood and watched.

Mason was looking from face to face to face, struggling with each word that they spoke.

Cinca asked, "What's the matter with him?"

Hodges moved closer, so that he was directly in front of him. Mason frowned and began to reach out to touch Hodges's chest, but then stopped his hand.

Hodges put his hand on Mason's shoulder. "It's okay Mason. I'll take care of you. We all will. Can you hear us?"

Mason looked intently at his face, as if trying to read his lips.

Cinca, somewhat behind him, asked, "Are you deaf, Mason?" He immediately turned to face her. His face tightened, and then turned back to Hodges.

Cinca felt something shrivel inside her. *He recognized me, and he doesn't like what he sees. We aren't friends. He hates me.*

Hodges tried a few more questions, and then explained what he was seeing to Susan.

"It appears to be some kind of aphasia. He can't make words, and it appears that although he can hear well enough, he can't understand what we're saying. He has lost his language skills."

Susan reached out, "Oh, William, I am so sorry."

Mason blinked when he saw her hands reaching in the wrong direction, and caught them with his own, and held the old lady in a hug. He caught Hodges' eye and gestured at her with his head. He closed his eyes tightly and then opened them again.

Hodges nodded, putting his hand before his eyes. Mason understood, and turned his full attention to the lady that had been a surrogate mother for as long as he had been on Ceres.

Hodges turned to Cinca. "His intellect seems okay. He's just lost the ability to communicate."

Cinca shook her head. Mason was fumbling in an attempt to dry Susan's tears. "No. He's just lost the ability to talk. He can still communicate well enough."

She could only watch in silence. Mason was the only person who knew her, and he had judged her. She was a bad person.

ALEXANDRIA HABITAT, L4 CLUSTER

Mary Harris carried the books with her to the Woman's Room. She paused at the door, decorated by the colorful Egyptian cartouche, seeing the drab brown blanket draped over Lady Fortuna's body on the bed.

"She didn't make it."

Kell shook her head, too worn out for any more tears. "That means we're down to eighteen. I've called for the men to come and move her body. Lar said the work crew was still clearing out the bodies in the centrum."

Iris sighed. "Eighteen. And seven of us are women, and only Francellis can have babies. What the witch-hunts didn't accomplish, the Plague did. We're too few, now. When we die, this place will be a ghost land."

There were murmurs of agreement from the others. Francellis, clasping her infant son to her breast, looked terrified.

Mary put the books down on the bench beside her. She wasn't the youngest, but it was time for her to speak. She looked over at the body in the corner. Were promises made under fear as important as the future of her people?

"I'm pregnant."

Every eye was on her.

"What do you mean?" "You can't be?" "Blessed!" "Wonderful, but how?"

She picked up the books. It was important to hold them.

"It's true. Jeff was one of the first to go, but before the fever took him, I told him the Doctor had worked on me, and we tried again. It's early, but I found a test in this book, and it agrees with what I can feel inside.

"My Jeff will have a child."

Kell asked, "The Doctor? What did she do? There is a cure?"

Mary held up a small sheet of folded paper. "The Doctor tested me. She told me that there might be a treatment that would let someone like me have a child. I told her to do it. Mayor Fortuna found out and made me keep quiet. She said the Earthers would kill us all if I ever spoke a word about it.

"Well, I think I would welcome the Earthers to come, right now," said Helva. There were a few nods.

Mary continued. "Before the Mayor made her leave, the Doctor wrote down, step by step, the instructions, and it is something that can be learned.

"We are all of the women left in Alexandria, and I think we should all have it done."

There were questions.

"I don't know," said Helva. "Can we trust this Doctor?"

"How can you ask? You, Helva, and Kell, and me, as well as several of the men—we all had her treatments for other things, and we alone have been spared the Plague. Without her, we would be half this number!"

Iris shook her head, "You can do what you want, but I'm too old. I'm not Sarah from the Bible. No treatment will turn my menses back on."

Kell asked, "What kind of treatment is it?"

Mary unfolded the paper and read. Six sets of eyes were on her, listening intently. Even Willow, although she couldn't raise herself out of her bed, listened to every word. When she was done, there was a moment of silence.

Kell asked, "And you had this done?"

"Yes. It hurt for a few hours, but the cut has already healed."

Francellis asked timidly, "But I won't have to have it done?"

"No. The thing you cut out, you don't catch it. It comes from your mother. It grows when you are a baby. But likely all the men left have the taint, so if you have a daughter, she will probably have to have the cut done."

Kell said, "I want Lar to do it for me. I would be too embarrassed."

Helva laughed, "Well, if I can get a big belly this way, cut me now!"

Iris waved her hand. "Now Helva, you will still need a little help from one of the men."

There were other laughs.

Iris cautioned, "We still have to be careful. Our people thought the witch-hunts were the end of everything, but we survived that. This Plague has hit, and destroyed most of humanity, but if I know anything, it's that civilization will come back, and if we don't take the proper precautions, our salvation could be our doom."

Iris raised her voice, and they all suddenly realized that with Lady Fortuna dead, she was now Eldest of Women. They dared not ignore her.

"I don't want anyone to talk about this, not out of the Women's Room. Kell has the right idea. This is a sacred trust, and not something that should be spread around. Each woman who needs the cut should instruct her husband, in the privacy of their bed. Learn the instructions. Memorize them. Each daughter born to us will have to be taught it as a sacred thing from her mother.

"Maybe the Outsiders can't get to us today, but someday we will meet them, and when that happens, there must not be a single word about our people's own plague. Not ever. Or we will be exterminated."

CELONESE TRANSPORT 3, MARS

Trader had a death grip on the pilot's chair. The words on the screen meant nothing to him, but the blue and brown view of Mars kept getting closer and closer.

"Computer! We're going to crash!"

"No. You have ordered a landing. Do you wish to change that to a crash?"

"No! A landing! A safe, gentle landing."

"Acknowledged." There was no change.

Trader looked over to the woman in an officer's uniform whom he had dragged out of her sickbed. She didn't look good, but at least the computer had heard her when she whispered for him to take over command of the ship.

Mars had grown too large to fit the screen, and he started to pick up land features along the shoreline.

I hope the computer doesn't land us too close to the ice cap. I don't have cold weather gear.

He had ordered the ship to land where there was still Net activity. He wanted a city, not some undeveloped wasteland.

The Hellas Sea grew larger. "We are going to land on dirt, right?"

"Affirmative. I am following the established approach lane which dissipates the sonic boom over ocean before the final approach."

"Okay." So, even Mars had its share of regulations. There were opportunities for people like him in that. Although, unless his problem cleared up, he would have to have someone else read the laws to him. There wasn't much use for a lawyer who couldn't understand the law books.

The view started to shift, and soon, he was looking down on the river valley at an angle, seeing a wide river wind off toward the remote mountains in a haze of distance.

We're flying now. It was better than falling.

"What city is that?" The distinctive texture of an urban congestion ran along the shoreline, with the patchwork of croplands marching up along the river behind it.

"Palatine, in the Italian Confederacy."

Good. I can get along with Italians.

Suddenly, there was something on the horizon. Disturbingly tall, the streamlined buildings recognizable from the Mars news features, towered above rust-colored domes. The ship slowed and he could make out more details as they flew across the city. There were wide streets with rows of trees, but he couldn't see any people.

"Landing commencing." There was a buzz that shook the walls. Then, it stopped. "We have landed."

Trader let his hands release their grip on the chair, and his fingers ached. *I'm down.*

· · ·

It took Trader a few minutes to get the screens oriented to give him a panorama view of the surrounding landscape.

I shouldn't try so hard. Just tell the computer what I want and not worry about the technical terms.

The transport ship had landed at the edge of the city, and there were a dozen other ships there as well. Either this had been a regular landing area, or this was the source of the Net transmissions that his ship had detected.

He was looking at the other ships, realizing that at least one had fallen over on it side. Its hull was cracked wide open.

Motion caught his eye, a small white vehicle was making clouds of reddish dust as it raced toward him from the direction of the larger buildings.

"What is that?"

The computer replied, "It appears to be a medical emergency vehicle according to the markings on the roof." Trader squinted at the image, but he quickly gave it up. He could recognize real things, like doors and chairs, but writing was gone. He sighed.

"Audio from outside."

"Play it."

"Transport ship. Do you need help?"

Trader looked at the woman who had given him the ship. She was still breathing.

"Yes. I have several people down with a fever. I have recovered."

"Shed and me are glad to hear it. The more survivors, the better. Activate the hatch, and we'll drive around to that side."

To the computer, Trader nodded, "Do it. And give me directions." He lifted the woman up in his arms. At least he could do that. He still had his strength.

"Turn right."

"Enter the corridor."

"Keep walking."

"Go through the door with the yellow trim."

Finally, he stepped through the hatchway. A man with several days' growth of black beard was waiting at the steps.

Out of the corner of his eye, Trader noticed the pistol strapped to the stranger's belt.

Trader said, "Help me with her." The man moved to help support her weight. Together they carried her to the back of his vehicle.

Trader glanced at the driver, still at the controls of the vehicle. His helper said, "Shed doesn't walk. I'm Luke. Did you tell me your name?"

"Trader. I'm Trader."

"Good to meet you." They shook hands.

Shed shouted over the distance, "Do you have any medical supplies? We're desperate for anything."

Trader waved to him. "I'll have to check. I'm not regular crew."

To Luke, he gestured toward the ship. "Come help me locate the other survivors."

"Good. The more survivors, the better. I'm Luke. Did you tell me your name?" His face was furrowed with the effort of trying to remember... something.

"Trader."

"Right. I'm Luke." He lost the frown, satisfied he was back in the groove.

Trader returned Luke's smile. "Come on, then."

He took him into the ship, and had the computer direct them to each of the remaining survivors. There were only three. The man who had let him out of his locked room was the only one ambulatory, but he had to be led by the hand.

When they loaded everyone onto the truck, Shed reminded, "Medical supplies?"

"I'll go look."

"I'm Luke, I'll help."

They went back in. "Computer, tell me where the medical supplies are kept."

They located a clinic on what was now the lower level of the ship. The smell of the four dead inside was thick once Trader had Luke opened the hatch.

"Wait outside, Luke."

The man was happy to obey Trader's instructions.

Trader hurriedly raided the supply cabinet. He had to open box after box. Most didn't have any pictures on the outside that made any sense to him. He finally collected a largish bag of medicines and tools and bandages.

No sense in holding onto these medicines. I can't tell which would help me or kill me in an instant.

Luke waited patiently until Trader came out, pushing a loaded cart and sealed the hatch behind him.

Luke looked puzzled.

"Are you okay, Luke?"

"Hi. Do I know your name?"

It was what he expected of the man.

"Trader. My name is Trader. Do you know what that means?"

He looked disgusted, "Of course. You trade things."

"Right Luke. I am going to trade you all of these wonderful medical supplies that Shed wants so bad. What will you trade me?"

Luke frowned a little. "I … I'm not sure. I could ask Shed?"

"How about that nice pistol you have there?"

Luke looked down at his belt and seemed honestly surprised to find it there. "Okay. I guess that would be okay. I've never had to fire it in all the years I've worked security here at the port."

He smiled at Trader. "Most of the time, its for show, you know." He frowned, "Do I know you? I'm Luke. I work port security."

Before Luke could forget again, Trader helped him remove the pistol belt. Together they pushed the cart medical supplies out to Shed.

"I'm staying with my ship. I'll inventory what's there." Then, before Shed could react, Trader dashed back up through the hatchway and called to the computer to lock the door.

"Computer, locate a compartment big enough to hold all of the dead bodies. I need a place that we can seal airtight. A crypt."

No need to leave now. I'm Trader, and now I have a full transport of stuff to trade.

DENVER, NORTH AMERICA, EARTH

Paula Campbell visualized Isaac as she free climbed in the darkness. He was a good boy. She had seen him often enough, through her telescope, playing with friends in the back yard, or going with his new mother to the market or to school. His foster parents knew her on sight, and so she had been forced to watch carefully, at a distance. They wouldn't let him go easily.

She didn't blame them. They had done a good job raising her boy, and they had to love him. But when the letter came back through the court system on her request for regular visitation rights, the answer had been hard and plain.

Isaac knew only his foster parents, and they intended to keep it that way until he was much older. It would be too confusing, they wrote, and emotionally harmful for him to find out that he had another mother.

Not another mother! I'm his real mother.

She paused to dry her hands in the powder bag. At least her headlamp wasn't weakening as fast as she had feared. She had one set of replacement batteries, and with the city falling so rapidly into chaos, she had no hope of finding any more.

It just has to last me until I reach the top. Once she had fired the rocket that monster had described, she would have all the time in the world to find a safer way back down.

She reached for the next pipe, just as she had done for all the floors she had already passed. She blinked, realizing that she was not as sharp as she needed to be. Climbing in the dark, where every floor was exactly the same as before, was mind-numbing. It hadn't started out that way.

At first glance, the Belleview Tower looked impregnable. The stairwells had collapsed, at least on the first few floors. She suspected he had done it on purpose.

She had dug through the rubble to reach the elevator shaft. There had originally been an access ladder bolted to the inside of the shaft, but it had been removed, snipped off, bolt by bolt. Segments of the ladder, the elevator, and the cables, lay in a tangled maze in the lower floors. It had to have been a very powerful, powered snipper to have done the whole job, especially if the monster had done it all himself.

Or did had he subcontracted it? Two hundred cities, he said. Just inspecting the work of subcontractors would take a year. But, could a plot of this size survive a shared secret? He was immune, but no one else was. Anything farmed out would have to be done under a false cover story.

Stay back on my task. Who cares how it was done? I have to defeat it.

She shined her light on the mangled end of the ladder bolts. The building had been deserted for many decades, and there was hardly an un-corroded metal surface in the place. This bolt was different. It looked fresher than everything else, but still, there were lines of rust along scrape lines. The cut had obviously been done years ago.

He said he was two hundred years old. Could that part be true?

. . .

She stared at the box for a minute or two before she realized that she had zoned out. She tied off and stretched her aching muscles.

The climb had been long, and much more tiring than it should have been. But going to sleep during a climb was stupid.

What is this thing?

A large metal box, almost filling the elevator shaft blocked her way. Near the top and welded in place, it was nothing like she had seen in other buildings.

Elevator shafts weren't that much different from each other. Back when the skyscrapers had been built, it was very common to build them using cranes in the center of the building itself. Once the structure was complete, the cranes were removed and the shafts became homes for the elevators. The cranes were standard and used over and over again. That made the design of the elevator shafts standard as well.

Paula had developed her break-in strategy and tools to take advantage of the standard design. The top of the shaft should have the hoist mechanism and possibly a hatchway to the roof. Instead there was this box, blocking her access to the top.

She rapped on the metal. It was thin. *Could I cut through this?* She had the tools. *But if this is the rocket, I could damage it.*

I'm not coming all this way to break it. It's Isaac's only hope.

She backed down a little and forced the elevator doors open. On the lower floors, she had found the stairway broken away for several stories and the elevator shaft an easier path upward for someone with her climbing skills. Maybe she was above the blockade.

Luck was with her, and within a few minutes, she broke through the last door into the blue sky and blinding sunlight.

All of Denver was spread out before her. Columns of smoke like giant demon soldiers stood watch over the streets. She had seen the city before from the heights, but it was different this time. The city was asleep, or dead.

There! A car! So not everyone was dead. Surely there were more people like her who were late to come down with the fever.

She had hoped that she would be immune, but that conceit had faded an hour ago. She could feel her mind getting duller by the minute. Whatever she could accomplish here, she had to do quickly.

Walking the roof, she found the elevator shaft, but what had appeared to be a standard hatchway was just a disguise. The hinges were false decorations and the lock was a dummy. She had to search with her face down in the dust to see that the hatch was actually on runners, designed to slide to the side. There was no lock, no handle. The latch, when she found it, could only be activated from the inside, remotely.

She felt a little flushed by the struggle, but it only made her angry. She opened her backpack. *Don't mess with me. I know how to make stuck doors behave.*

A handmade roll of thermite came out and she pasted it around the locking mechanism. She had used it only a couple of times before. It was hard to get the aluminum powder, and it was difficult to get started. Still, there was not much that could stand up to thermite.

Carefully, she piled the little packet of magnesium powder on the top of her thermite and fired up her little cutting torch. She held her breath as the magnesium heated and then, with a glare that was blinding even in full daylight, it ignited.

She backpedaled to get out of range. The thermite caught, and in short order the lock melted. She kicked at the hatch. It opened a finger's width. The metal was hot, but with gloves on, she gradually forced it open. It was controlled by an inert motor and gears, and she had to work against that drag.

Even though she expected it, she let out a gasp when the nosecone of the rocket appeared in the middle of the box. Untouched by the sun, protected from dust and corrosion, it looked impossibly new and menacing. Down in the depths, barely lit by the sun, there were lights—electronics.

The firing circuit. He said he could trigger it over the Net. I'll have to find a way to fake that.

There was room for her. The whole box was the same size as the elevator it mimicked, and there was even a minimal ladder. She had her leg over the edge before she noticed the wire running from the ladder to the control box. She froze.

A trigger wire. She eased back. *No false steps.*

A pain was starting to tap at the back of her head. It'd been growing for several minutes, but she just now recognized it.

Then, from the missile control box, came a voice.

"Paula Campbell. I see you have made it to the missile. Congratulations."

Her mind went blank. *He knows who I am!*

"Paula? You can talk to me. I can hear you."

"I can hear you."

"Good. I just thought I would let you know that the Net has cleared up. I am back in control of the missile."

"Then fire the thing!"

"Oh, no. I wouldn't want to do that. Everything is working out perfectly."

She steamed. *Perfection for the monster—death for everyone else.*

"Paula?"

"Go away!"

"You still want to fire the missile? Believe me, the disease is so far advanced it wouldn't make much of a difference. Why don't you just open the payload hatch on the missile and dump out some of the white powder? You are still active. It tastes horrible, but a pinch or so might stop the progression of your fever and stave off brain damage. Take some and track down where Isaac went and give him some."

She clamped her eyes shut. *He's the devil. Don't listen.*

But she couldn't help considering the idea. Blasting the antidote into the water system might be too slow, now. Maybe it would be better....

No. I don't know where Isaac is now. I would have to get down from here and track him down. I might have the cure but never be able to find him.

She eased herself over the edge, avoiding the stairs, and dropped as quietly as she could to the floor of the missile box.

"No reply, Paula? Well, good luck to you, then."

He has this place rigged.

There were wires and boxes all over the place. *Most of this has to be traps.*

It was the placement of the rocket exhaust deflectors that put it all into perspective.

When the rocket launches, those braces are designed to burn through. And that ring will ignite.

The whole box was designed to melt down and collapse down the elevator shaft when the rocket left. She scraped metal from the control box with her knife. It wasn't steel, but magnesium. She shivered. Her thermite could have set the whole thing ablaze if she hadn't positioned it on the outside of the box.

After the launch, all the evidence burns itself beyond recognition. But what if he doesn't want the launch?

A little more examination revealed all. A signal could rupture the side of the rocket. If it ignited, the missile and its cargo would be consumed in a high temperature hell down in the depths of the building. Little of the antidote would escape.

He knows I'm here. Why hasn't he trigged it?

Unless he's right and it really makes no difference to his plan.

In any case, that was out of her control. He could kill her or not. She had to put that out of her mind. Maybe he really was a kind and gentle monster who only saw the big picture and held her no ill will.

But can I snip that wire to the abort system without triggering it?

Her head was pounding, and she forced herself to pull out the tools. Her own body would defeat her eventually. She had no time to think out all the options.

She traced the wires. Snip. She removed the rocket's abort. Her hand shook with the reaction, but nothing blew up on her.

Here's the control cable. Is it a voltage or a signal? That could only be determined by opening the access hatch on the side of the missile.

The fasteners were non-standard, and she didn't have a tool for the tamper-resistant screws. Not missing a beat she checked the control box, but it was buttoned tightly as well.

From her burglary kit, she pulled the voltage meter and stripped the cable down to the shiny copper. A careful check showed no voltage at all. Signal wires usually held some voltage, even when there was no signal.

So I can probably launch with just a DC voltage here. It was a gamble, but time was running out.

As rapidly as she could, she scavenged a few control wires that went to the disposal charges and constructed a cable long enough to lead out of the box.

On the roof, she glanced over at the Cherry Creek reservoir.

Isaac, I hope this works.

There was something she was missing, but the headache and the chills were making it hard to think.

She fashioned a crude battery pack and attached one of her launch wires. It should have enough voltage, if the circuitry was anything like building control circuits.

I wanted to be a better mother for you. I guess I waited too long.

She tied her rope to a railing along the edge of the building. It was her only escape route if things went bad in a hurry.

Paula fumbled the wire, and had to pick it up again. Her muscles were getting jittery, whether from the disease or just nerves.

No reason for delay.

She closed her eyes and jammed the free wire against the battery post.

For a good three seconds, she heard nothing. Her heart sank.

Then, there was a whine, quickly climbing in pitch, and then a popping, loud rumble.

She looked, and there was a thick white plume rising from the missile box. Before she could think, there was a whoosh as the rocket blasted from the launch box as if shot from a gun.

The fumes cut off her sight. She was enveloped in hot burning smoke. She was blind, and she tried to stop breathing.

I'm too close!

She snapped her safety rope to her harness and blindly dashed for the edge of the building.

Her foot caught on something. In a tangle of rope, she went over the edge.

She fell for twenty feet, before an errant loop of rope tightened around her neck, snapping it as her body jerked to a stop.

Before her body stopped bouncing against the building, there was an explosion over the glittering reservoir in the distance, and a white cloud drifted down to its surface.

OVER NORTH AMERICA, EARTH

"A status packet was received from the Denver rocket."

Kidd asked the ship's computer as they climbed ever higher toward the edge of the atmosphere, "Just a packet?"

"Yes. There was no message close."

"Well, was it the launch or the abort system?"

"Neither, it was an overvoltage warning in the control box."

Kidd looked up from his status screen. *So, she wired around it. Probably launched. I knew she was smart.* He smiled. *I'll have to look her up when I get back.*

He dismissed the incident. One percent survival or a tenth of a percent survival in the Denver area really made no difference to the overall plan.

"Computer, do you have data on Darnell?"

"There is no response from Project Control, but the public access orbital database shows Darnell-1, tagged 'South Darnell'. There is also a larger Darnell-2, 'North Darnell' and a list of several hundred smaller fragments with only a numeric designation.'"

"Concentrate on South Darnell. If she isn't there, I'll have more time to look on the other half. Do you have the position?"

"The public database is still getting automated updates, but it is not current. South Darnel's orbit is not precise, but its general location can be inferred."

"Good enough. We should be able to find it."

Just then, there was a shake, and Kidd's stomach went into freefall.

"Warning! Warning! Ship's accumulators have been drained."

Kidd was spinning in the cabin. He managed to kick himself back to his chair.

"What happened?" He found the straps and secured himself.

"A beam tap drained the propulsion system. We are currently in free-fall."

"Impact time?"

"Eight minutes, forty seconds."

"Is the drive system intact?"

"Yes."

"Is the beam tap still in place?"

"No."

"Set up a charger. Absorb our velocity relative to the ground."

"In progress."

At least we won't crash. But I'll need more energy to get into space.

"Details!"

"At an elevation of one hundred kilometers, a beam tap drained all energy from the propulsion system. Other ship systems were affected, but the tension of the beam tap was tuned to affect drive accumulators."

"One hundred kilometers? How precise is that?"

"Within ten meters. Our upward velocity carried us up another three kilometers, but we are now on our way down. Evidence of the beam tap vanished when we passed back below the one hundred-kilometer limit."

"Check all broadcasts. Somebody set up that limit. Find out who they are."

I'll need more energy. Can I punch through it on inertia alone like the ancient rockets?

Modern ships rose through the atmosphere at a leisurely rate until it was mostly vacuum and then accelerated from there. It was different in the old times when they blasted at high acceleration all the way up. There was no way he could strap a rocket engine to his ship, but if he was moving fast enough to start…

"There is a repeating message on a Project public notices band."

In a different voice, sounding almost drugged or feverish, a human voice said, "… and set up an interdiction barrier covering all near-Earth space. Don't let anything get through." There was a click, and the words repeated.

What does that mean? All of near-Earth space? Going up and down?

"Is there any other explanation?"

His computer said, "No. All traffic control bands are silent. There have been intermittent calls for help from some of the habitats on general broadcast bands, but there is no reply."

. . .

As his ship dropped through the atmosphere, pressor beams soaked up the momentum, storing the energy into the depleted accumulators. Still, at best, he would be severely under-powered and unable to attempt any space flight.

It would be hard to recharge. Out in space, energy was free for the taking, given the blessing of Project Controllers. Just aim a tractor or pressor beam in the right direction and tap an infinitesimal fraction of some planet's orbital motion.

But it was different down in an atmosphere. The presence of gas molecules in the beam changed everything. From Earth, he couldn't tap anything in Earth orbit because the motion was all at right angles to the beam. That meant the closest candidate at the moment was Mars, at over twelve light minutes distance—twenty-four minutes before the energy would arrive. That meant twenty-four minutes pumping a pressor beam into the atmosphere, blasting air into space.

And when the charging was done, and the beam collapsed, pending energy would have nowhere else to go but those same gas molecules—flash accelerating them into everything from hurricane winds to stripped atomic nuclei traveling at relativistic speeds.

Still, Kidd contemplated the idea. He had seen a paper, decades ago, on the concept. The authors had proposed the idea as an emergency procedure for probes dropped into the gas giant planets. No one seriously considered the idea of trying it on Earth. The storms and radiation damage alone would make it a capital crime.

His memory was good enough to provide a list of what calculations needed to be done. None of it was beyond his ship's computer.

But there was information he needed that he didn't have. The timing and tuning of the tap beam would be critical, and he would need to have detailed information about the density profile of the air above him. That would take time. With the world falling apart, it would take too long.

No. No help for it. I'll have to tap my other ships. He had two, one small shuttle that he had never intended to take above the atmosphere. And the other was an older vintage transport, and it had a much smaller energy storage accumulator.

Drain them both! At worst, I can recharge them over time with wind power or waterfalls. The decades it would take aggravated him. His plans had been built around an occasional trip into space to monitor the space cities and to recharge his ships. *I have to find a way around the interdiction.*

Net messages were still being received from space, so the 'Don't let anything through' command had a specific interpretation. If he could get into the Project's headquarters in Berlin, then maybe he could find an override.

But time was critical. If Beta wasn't dead, the South Darnell fragment was.

Chapter 12

SOUTH DARNELL, EARTH IMPACT TRAJECTORY

"I don't have a family," Bet explained.

Dr. Quinland shook his head. "Everyone has a family."

"Not me," she insisted. The doctor had promised to teach her the Art, but honesty, he had insisted must come above all. It was tough.

He paused, "This isn't one of those things you can't tell me, is it?"

"Yes. I can't tell you."

He waved his hand, dismissing it. "In any case. Everyone, even you, has a family. It is hard-wired into the human brain. Or to be more accurate, it is wired into all brains.

"It is an evolutionary adaptation. You remember what I told you. What preserves the genes, is itself preserved.

"These, stripped to the core, are instincts. A man wants to have sex. A woman wants to protect her children. These are obvious. But there are many many other behaviors that preserve the genes. Caring for your family, people that share your genetic code, is another."

She wasn't entirely convinced. "I know of exceptions."

He nodded. "Of course. Instincts aren't smart. Instincts aren't able to handle every variation in the environment. Instincts are inclinations—often backed up by strong, unreasoning emotions. They are strong, but they can be diverted. Dogs accept humans as pack members, and humans accept dogs as surrogate children.

"What I am saying is that the template family exists in everyone. You, as an individual, may have lost all your known kin, but the 'family' still exists in your brain, and you will fill that hole with something."

Bet smiled at the memory of Dr. Quinland, so long dead. He had been her mentor. Even when they had been working a medical practice for twenty years together, and he had obviously noted that she had not aged, he had never asked about it. He had promised to respect her privacy.

"You were right, Doctor. I have made a family for myself." Every place she had taken her medical skills, she had sooner or later come to think of her patients as a collection of brothers and sisters, nieces and nephews.

She had synthetic human genes, but it had been enough to give her very real human instincts.

It had been a big family, extended in time and space, across many cultures.

Three faces came to haunt her in the dark, airtight closet where she waited out the days as South Darnell passed by Luna and then arched into its slowed ellipse.

Cherry had been her daughter from the moment she had delivered the dark-haired bundle from her mother's mangled body. There had been no question of turning her over to anyone in that war-torn village on Trinidad. They had been refugees together when she was small. She had helped Cherry through the travails of young love, until she had married and settled into her own life in Panama. Dressed in wrinkled skin, Bet had cuddled her grandchildren. Engineering her death and walking away had been the hardest thing she had done. It was no less painful for the dead to leave the living than it was for the living to lose the dead. At least the living have ritual to ease the pain.

Blue had been a difficult child. He had stolen into her house, and into her heart, all in one night. Behind his black face was a soul that shone like a supernova. The boy had run her in circles for the year before his death. The world had rules he could not understand, and when he refused to play by them, the world killed him.

Sue Lin had been her sister. Bet had helped her when her son came down with a melanoma cancer. They had shared the long hours and tears as they tried and failed to cure him. And then she had helped Sue Lin through the trauma as her husband turned his anger at his son's death on her. They had worked together after that, as Sue Lin learned how to be her assistant. They left that city and moved together to the coast and set up a new practice ten years later. It was as a respected lady of the city that Sue Lin found her new husband. As was often the case, Bet chose that time to die.

It is always time for me to get out of the way, so that they can live their own lives.

There were so many other faces, others who had in some sense become her family. She ached with their loss. Her face ached from old tears.

Alpha's message haunted her. It wasn't a voice, merely a text message spoken to her with the computer's default male voice. Alpha could be female. There were too few words to be confident that he was male. She had the computer replay it with a female voice.

No help there. I want Alpha to be a man. A man of my own kind, racing to come to my aid. Wishful thinking happened to her. In that, she was no different from any normal human.

Her chamber had become silent over the past few days. The tidal stresses of the close pass above Luna had rekindled the creaks and pops and distant crashes as the rubble piled above her shifted and resettled. When the computer spoke to report their updated course projections, it always startled her.

She worked on her escape pod, more from nervous habit than from any strong desire to use it. *What if I left, and he came and couldn't find me again?* She didn't even know if the tank's trajectory away from South Darnell would help, now that the lunar passage was behind her. No amount of force she could put on it would allow her to escape the gravitational attraction of the Earth. This wasn't a grazing pass as it had been by Luna.

Still, she had resealed the water chamber and moved it to a place on the ruptured loading dock where it could get sunlight. With pressure and heat, the ice inside was already half melted.

But that was just busy work. More and more hours of the day she preferred to be inside the lone pressurized area where she could get out of the space suit.

This place is quiet as a grave. Maybe that's why I am spending so much time remembering my dead. We're close again.

The call of life had kept her moving for so many years. It was enough, she felt, to help others and to relieve suffering. They had a life, a destiny. She would be content to midwife their next generation.

Don't I have a life of my own?

She listened for an answer, but there was none. Perhaps she had been dead all this time, since Lyon, when she had told Glenn the truth.

...

"There is another message."

Bet startled awake. Her heart thud-thudded and then calmed. There was a little light, as the sun crept into the destroyed cargo bay. "Yes. What is it?"

The computer's voice recited, "Message from Alpha: I am sorry Beta, there has arisen a complication. Project control has been turned over to a fail-safe computer system, and they've put an interdiction around the Earth. I am working at top speed to find a way around it. Assist me. As soon as you're able, send me a message detailing your exact location. I'm working on the assumption that you are either on North or South Darnell, with South Darnell as the highest priority due to its dangerous orbit. Keep up your hopes. I very rarely fail, and you are my top priority."

She had the computer replay the message twice. *He is male, I can feel it.*

"Are we still out of transmitting range?"

"Yes. I send out a periodic status request, and no reply makes its way back. I will continue to do so."

"Is there any change in our orbit?" Of course there would not be, but she had to ask.

"No."

"Then queue this reply for the instant you can get through:

"This is Beta. I am in South Darnell, the sole survivor. I am located in cargo bay 0200 on the edge of the end-cap. Power and oxygen are limited, but not critical. However, as near as I can tell, this part of the habitat is heading for impact on Earth. It is urgent that you arrive as soon as possible, so that there is a chance for changing its course to miss the Earth."

She stopped there. Shorter messages were more likely to get through than long ones, and if this were indeed Alpha, someone like her, then he or she would know all that she left unsaid. *I can't send a voice message either. Not until I'm sure there is enough Net bandwidth to carry it. The information is what is important now, not my silly feelings.*

If Alpha is male, of my species . . . .

She tried to put a damper on wild speculation, but there was nothing else to do in the dark.

If we are the same, male and female—could we be fertile?

She was two hundred years old. Human females were born with a few hundred egg cells. Parceled out once a month once they reached puberty, that usually lasted them until menopause set in.

Her own menstrual cycle had begun in her late thirties, and after her painful marriage with Glenn, she had chosen to inhibit her own menses with a common hormone treatment. In good times, she used the pills, and in hard times, she lived with her cycle, but she had never kept count.

Did she still have any potentially fertile eggs left? Surely she had unmatured follicles?

Stop thinking about it! You are likely to die here in this room anyway. He said he couldn't get off Earth. It's too late to try to escape.

And Alpha could be another woman. It was useless to worry about it.

But wouldn't it be nice to have a child of my own, a daughter with my eyes and my face?

· · ·

In the dark, she could see a face. He smiled at her, and held out his hand. She took it and walked with him through the trees. They didn't speak, only sharing a smile of secret thoughts. Still holding her hand, he led her to a stone cliff, and pushing aside an obscuring bush, he pulled her through to a hidden path, dark under the trees. They started running toward a light up ahead. She was flushed with anticipation.

They pulled to a stop at the edge of a cliff overlooking the green valley below. It was a mossy perch, soft and warm in the sun, with just enough room for the two of them to huddle side by side in the glory of the new day.

A patch of mountain fog drifted down, hiding them from the world. He pulled her close, and she melted into his embrace....

· · ·

Bet woke, sweating and unable to stop the grin.

I haven't had one of those dreams in a while. Her whole body tingled. *Just my luck to be stuck here in this box alone.*

The details were fading rapidly. She couldn't remember if the man was someone she had known before, or some idealized composite. *It doesn't matter.*

She lay thinking about the men in her life. Glenn had by no means been the first she had dreamed about, nor the last. But of all the men she had grown close to, he had been the only one who had known who she was. She had given him her total love, and total honesty. The trauma of his rejection had lasted much longer than a normal human lifespan, and she had given up any hope that there would be another partner, another mate to whom she could open her entire soul.

But if Alpha . . . .

. . .

She awoke to the distant sound of metal banging. Then there was a crash.

"Computer! What is happening?"

"Unknown, however, during the last observations, it appeared that there has been a change."

"A tractor beam! Alpha has gotten a tractor beam on us."

"It is possible."

"Is there any ship in range?"

"No."

She pondered the clues. It had to be a long-range beam. He couldn't get a ship up from Earth, but he could remotely control one. That had to be it.

"Queue up another message to Alpha:"

"Alpha, I am detecting your tractor beam. Thank you. For the first time since the rupture, I can almost feel hope. I am looking forward to meeting you face to face."

PACIFIC OCEAN, EARTH

Sealer felt her strokes through the water before she called for him.

-Sealer! Come quick!- It was RedFan.

He asked -What is it?-

-The Land People are attacking the net!-

He was past her, heading for the sandbar where the tribe was constructing a net from kelp. They couldn't cross the deeps without it.

-How did they find us? - he demanded, as the ten-year-old struggled to keep up with him.

-I don't know!- She was falling behind rapidly, but he didn't wait for her.

They had barely begun their trip south, and already there were more problems than he had ever imagined. The net was one. A warrior expected to carry his weapons with him everywhere, but the tribe needed tools, food, medicines, and children's toys. Plus, the sick, and the elderly, and the small children could not keep up with a forced long-distance swim.

It was going to be a much longer and harder trip than he had thought.

From a distance, he could see the workers, mainly women, who were building the net. They were swirling in panic.

-Where are the Land People?- he called as loudly as he could.

Half of the group saw him then, and started in his direction. Anemone, a young woman a year or so older than he, called back, - There is a Land People boat coming this way! It is trailing a hook to destroy the net.-

From the tone of her voice, she had indicated that the boat was coming from up-current. He turned immediately and dodged the crowd coming at him. DolphinFriend joined him just a moment after he found the thing.

-What is it?- he asked.

Sealer looked at the white, barnacle-spotted hull. It was not powered, like those fast ones that had chased him. The hook was on a short cable, much like those at rest in a Land People's bay.

-I don't know if this is an attack, or if it is a boat broken loose from its masters. Can the women move the net in time?-

Anemone had arrived, and answered, -No. It is held down to the sand to keep the lines from drifting. All our work will be destroyed if we try to move it.-

Sealer moved his spear to attack position and began swimming as fast as he could toward the hull. He shouted at it, and could tell clearly where the weakest section was by the reflections. He aimed carefully like a swordfish.

The shock of the impact pulled the spear from his hand, and his body slammed against the surface.

It broke. The spear had shattered. There was a scar where the point had hit, but there was no breach.

-Get a rock.- said DolphinFriend.

-No, grab the chain,- Sealer said.

-You too, Anemone.- He grabbed the hook and strained to lift it.

-All of you!- he cried to the rest of the tribe who had gathered. -Lift the chain and the hook, so that it will pass over the net.-

Many hands joined. By the time the current brought it over the net, they had managed to keep it high enough to clear.

As soon as the danger had passed, they dropped the chain.

Sealer stared at the white boat. He was angry, and he didn't know why. He swam up close, and grabbed the tail-fin of the thing. He shoved hard, and it slowly pivoted on its hinge. The hull started to turn in the water, still pulled by the current, but now cutting across at an angle.

I can move it. The anger surged still stronger. He put his muscles into it, pushing against the stern.

There was a thump. DolphinFriend grinned beside him, pushing. Thump. Thump. The boat started moving faster as more members of the tribe put their strength with his.

Sealer felt a surge of joy.

And then—Crunch! It shuddered to a halt, its front end smashed open on a shelf of rock.

It instantly started lowering in the water as the ocean swarmed through the black hole in the hull.

-Get back!- Sealer cried.

The Land People thing tilted, and the waves repeatedly smashed it against the rocks. The water quickly filled with white fragments of wood and other things.

There was a shreik. Sealer looked up. The distorted face of a Land Person stared down into the water.

He is dead. Another body joined it in the water a moment later. From the smell in the water, they had been dead for some time. *We will have to get rid of these, before the sharks come.*

Then came a strange noise, like a strangled dolphin trying to spout. Something like a giant orange anemone was growing in the water.

Another body dropped into the water, and they watched as a live Land Person struggled blindly in the water and labored to pull itself up onto the orange thing.

DolphinFriend pulled his spear to the ready.

Sealer put out his hand. -Hold. Let us see if there is only one live one.- The women were moving back, well out of range. He was pleased to see several of the men waiting with him.

No others came.

-DolphinFriend, Bigtooth, grab the orange thing and carry the Land Person to shore.-

There was shock in their faces.

-Yes, I mean it. Let it get ashore, but bring the orange thing back.

-Land People have the right to live, on land. But anything in the sea belongs to us.-

-But return quickly.- He gestured at the sunken boat, nearly totally under the surface. -There are treasures here that we can use.-

TRANSPORT, LUNA

Robert Henderson felt the sun on his face, and it shifted direction.

Fear hit him. His arms flew wide and he rolled on the hard metal surface until straps caught him.

"Help! It's got me!" He struggled, moving his arms with difficulty.

"Robert! Calm down Robert!"

It was Ann's voice. He blinked his eyes hard, trying to clear the haze from his vision. His heart was beating double-time.

"Ann?" He finally located her face.

She sat beside him and helped him sit up. He gripped her arm tightly as he tried to make sense of where he was.

"Robert. I'm so glad you came out of it. I was worried."

"The fever … I don't remember."

"Yes, you returned to the camp in a wheelie, but you were unconscious. You had programmed the coordinates, and it took over when you collapsed."

He blinked and finally it made sense. He was sitting on the edge of a large, flatbed hauler as it lumbered slowly across the terrain. There were a number of crates strapped down on the top of the multisegmented bed, as well as a tent.

"Jude! He came down with the fever."

Ann nodded. "You brought his body back. He was long dead by the time you arrived."

He put his hand on his head. "I don't remember any of this."

"Don't worry about it. It's probably the fever. If it doesn't kill you, it leaves you damaged. I'm messed up, too."

"What!" It was suddenly more than he could comprehend. Blind panic washed over him.

"Robert! You're hurting me." He released his grip on her arm. But then grabbed her in a bear hug.

She calmed him down, talking softly.

. . .

"So, you can't plan?" He had trouble believing that. Ann had been the bedrock of their strategic planning. She could hold the whole new ecology in her head and make all the changes well before the computer simulations came up with the same suggestions. Often, she found better solutions that the simulations later verified.

"Well, that isn't exactly true." She pulled a click-board from her shirt pocket. "I can plan, but I forget everything—I can't keep it all together. I have to make a list."

Robert looked at the extensive, painfully detailed list. "Make sure Robert is still breathing" jumped out at him, with a blinking notice. There were others; "keep on the transport", "is the transport still moving?", "bury Betty". That last one was checked off.

Ann took it back and worked down the list, checking items. "I hoped it would go away, but it hasn't. If I ever lose the click-board, I'm likely to walk away from camp and be lost forever. That already happened once, but Betty found me and brought me back."

She put it back in her pocket and her eyes locked on him. "Robert, I'm scared. We have food for a few weeks, and then we're done for."

One of the hauler's huge wheels went over a boulder and they swayed. He closed his eyes to fight back the panic.

"And I … I'm not under control," he said. "I understand everything, but my emotions are running completely wild. Everything scares me to death. I can barely think before another panic grabs me."

She nodded. "Wait a second." She crawled carefully across the moving flatbed and pulled something out of a container.

"Here, take this." She handed him a pill and water.

. . .

They were climbing another of the unnamed ridges that covered the land. It seemed as if they had been traveling forever, but when that maggot started churning in his brain, he crawled over to the cab and watched their course plotted out on the map. That was happening a lot less now that he had taken the medicine.

Ann had given him the story on the camp. Everyone was dead now. Fever had taken most of them directly, but Betty and Matt had seemed to recover, and then died in a stupid accident. Matt had opened one of the embryo cases without taking any precautions and had caught the both of them in an explosion of liquid helium. Betty might have recovered, but neither of them pulled out of it.

Ann checked her click-board and then looked up at the sun.

He commented, "It's good to have sunshine, now that the spin beams are gone."

She frowned. "You don't know, do you?"

He felt a spike of fear, but the medication dampened it. "Know what?"

Ann sighed. "The atmospheric simulations are wrong—at least for the forty-eight hour day. I thought the winds would be much more moderate once the spin beams stopped pushing at the atmosphere."

"Well, isn't that the case? I haven't had a day this calm on any of my lunar tours."

She nodded. "Yes, during the day, and during the night. But the transitions…"

He was suddenly aware that the wind had picked up over the past hour. And it had been even calmer the hour before that.

Ann checked her list. "We have to find a hill to park behind, collapse the tent, and then ride out the sunset in the cab." She looked at him. "It gets pretty bad."

And it was. He took an extra dose of the medicine as the wind howled and threatened to pick up the multi-ton vehicle, even sheltered as they were behind a large boulder.

It was dark before the winds calmed enough to escape the tight quarters of the cab and start back on their course.

Earth was three-quarters full, and provided an even glow over the landscape. Robert watched the sky as much as he did the land. The sky had never been this clear on Luna, although clear was a relative term. There were still bands of clouds moving high overhead, and he could see no stars.

Ann came and sat beside him on the packing crate.

"What are you looking at?"

He shook his head. "I was just looking for Ceres. It should be bright enough and big enough to be seen."

"Maybe, when the haze breaks. Earthshine washes it out most of the time."

He looked up at the Earth. There wasn't enough detail to make out continents. "We'll never make it back home, will we?"

She was silent for a long time. "Sorry, I was thinking, and then I lost track of what I was thinking about. I always hated being around scatterbrained people, but that's what I am now."

"It is better than being afraid all the time."

"The medicine helps?"

"Yes, but every time I take a pill, I count how many are left. What will become of me when I use the last one?"

She shook her head. "Learn to live with fear, I guess. I would dearly love to have a clear-headed pill. Although if I had only one, I would be afraid to waste it."

The transport topped a crest, and Robert held her hand as they shook from side to side on the uneven ground.

"Look, Robert! There's the isthmus. And there is the station!" Off across the valley was a mountain wall, the Neper crater from which the station had taken its name.

By the earthlight, he could see the distant isthmus and the blinking light of some beacon on the station straddling it.

There were two seas, black and ominous in the dim light. The Mare Marginis had a higher sea level than the huge ocean that covered almost all of the former lunar maria. Some comet wrangler had tried to cut a canal between them decades ago, but the job had never been completed. Robert's group, the ecological engineers, had petitioned Berlin to prevent the completion of the canal. Neper Isthmus made a prime location for a gestation station. They could seed both oceans and a wide expanse of land from one place. They had been waiting years for a final decision. The bureaucracy moved exceedingly slowly. That hadn't stopped them from setting up the station anyway.

"I can't make out the station, other than the beacon."

"We'll be there before too long. Let's hope survivors are there, and a medical station that can synthesize my pills."

"Oh, look at that!" She pointed up.

There was a bright light. He barely had time to dismiss the sudden hope that it was a rescue ship, before he realized it was getting brighter by the second.

"It's going to hit us!" she screamed.

His mind locked up as old and new fears combined.

Then in a flash, the meteor hit. The flash blinded him, leaving a patch in the middle of his vision where he couldn't see.

"A shock wave is coming!" Ann grabbed his arm and pulled him off the flatbed. They ran back the way they had come, trying to reach the crest of the ridge for shelter.

They almost made it. The shock wave caught them, and tossed them across the landscape. Ann slipped from his grasp before everything went black.

. . .

The ground shook and a roar came from everywhere. He cried out, "Ann!" But no sound he could make could cut through the noise.

Luna's low gravity and thick atmosphere had protected him from a fall that would have been instantly fatal on Earth. He had bruises, but amazingly, he could stand.

Ann was nowhere to be seen. He clenched his teeth against the panic. Fight it.

Get to high ground. Maybe I can see her.

He saw the wheel tracks and followed them uphill.

At the crest, he stopped. His legs gave way and he settled to his knees.

Below, there was a new crater where the station had been. Mare Marginis was spilling into the ocean—the barrier had been removed.

A waterfall several kilometers wide and at least a hundred meters tall was tearing up the valley. A cloud of vapor climbed high into the sky.

The water roared, and the ground shook.

Something was moving below. He tried to blink away the flash afterimage.

It's the hauler.

The segmented vehicle had been overturned by the shockwave, but it was a resilient beast, twisting its segments, and getting its wheels back underneath it. It was recovering.

It's programmed to go to the station! But there was no station now. It would head into the maelstrom and be lost.

Frantically, he looked behind. *Where is Ann?*

But the hauler was making progress.

He had no choice. He started running down the slope, in long, low-gravity bounds. By the time he caught up with the wheelie, he was moving so fast, he overshot it by hundreds of meters.

The cab was dented and one door was jammed, but he was able to reach the controls and program it to reverse course. Slowly, and cautiously, the vehicle turned around and caught up with its own tracks.

· · ·

He found Ann, her head bleeding from a scalp wound, confusedly walking in the wrong direction. He got her treated and settled down for the night.

"Robert, what will we do? The station is gone."

Even tens of kilometers away from the waterfall, they had to shout at each other. How long would it take for Mare Marginis to drop to the ocean's level?

He saw again in memory the blaze of the comet or meteor that crashed precisely on target to complete the canal, obliterating the bioengineering station.

Unthinkable. The Project's hallmark had been slow, cautious control. That impact had been targeted. But the Project would never have let that happen if there had been any chance of survivors in the impact zone. It should never have happened if there were missing workers anywhere on this half of Luna.

The Project is dead.

He felt the reverberations of that thought.

"The Project is dead."

Ann asked, "What did you say?"

He felt the pill bottle in his pocket. He rattled the few dozen pills. *How long do I have left?*

There will be no rescue. What can I accomplish before my mind goes?

He looked at Ann, still awake, but resting from her injuries. She looked back.

He patted her hand. "I know where there's another station in range."

"Good."

He crawled over to the cab, noting all the packing crates that showed dents and scrapes from the rollover.

Frozen embryos, gene records, and seeds. Raw materials.

He shook his head at the magnitude of what he had to do.

From this, we make a world.

PRIME CITY, CERES, L4 CLUSTER

The Arboretum was high, dry ground. Cinca was grateful for that. The streets were showing no signs of drying out. No one seemed to have any idea of how to get the water back into the Ocean.

Hodges was working hard, helping another group set up their campsite. She marveled at that. He still had a bad limp, and had to work one-handed, but he never complained. She glared down at her bare feet, still recovering from her last set of blisters when she had helped with a scavenging expedition into the drowned city, wading miles in soaked shoes.

There were forty-three people still alive on Ceres spread out among three camps in the Arboretum, and five other locations in the city where people had found places to live. Other than the tunnel to the Ocean, all of the exits from the City had collapsed and the emergency doors had sealed. Hodges reported that there was no sign of air leaks.

She could see the daytime lights beginning to darken. It was interesting to her which systems still worked, and which had quickly failed because there were no people to care for them.

Cinca was glad of the clear dome. Ceres did not have a daily rotation. It had always been a Project base and the decision was made long ago that the Eye should constantly face to where the Earth, Luna, and Vesta were visible high in the sky. That locked it into a month-long day. But people worked best with a normal circadian rhythm, so bright lights all through the city and a dome that could vary from clear to dark were used to simulate a day and night.

It was true night time on Ceres, with the sun below the horizon. It was the best place to see the stars in all of human space.

At times like this, the dome had great clarity, much better than the atmosphere of Earth or Mars or Luna. Not many of the other habitats had domes with such a wide expanse of the sky either.

She watched the city's lights go out, and the sky light up with the constellations. She put on her shoes and walked over to the hill where she could get a good look.

The view was breathtaking. Cinca smiled to herself. Her quirky memory had advantages. She knew the stars, but tonight was like her first time to experience the glory of the jeweled night sky.

She spotted constellations, one after the other. Luna was bright, and she held up her hand to eclipse its brightness. On Earth, she knew, moonlight brightened the whole sky and washed out the lesser stars, but the dome was different and didn't diffuse the brightness across the sky.

There was Vesta, a tiny little moon thirty degrees off the bright limb of Luna. She looked around. There were plenty of other L5 and L4 habitats visible, but she had to know where to look. Some were bright enough to mangle the appearance of some constellations she knew.

She frowned. One of them had visibly moved. It was near Vesta. That wasn't the way it worked. All of the Cluster habitats were in very slow orbits around the central asteroids, and the Cluster as a whole was orbitally locked to the motion of Luna. She shouldn't be able to see any difference in the short time she had been out there.

"Cinca! Are you there, dear?" Susan called from her tent.

"Coming!" She gave a backward glance up at the light near Vesta, and then walked back to the tents.

Susan was using her cane, which Cinca was glad to see.

"Cinca dear, could you help me find William? It's cooling off, and I want to make sure he has his jacket."

Mason was resting against a nearby tree, playing chess against himself in the bright moonlight. He was frustrating to deal with. He never recognized his own name, and Susan couldn't see to find him. He smiled a lot, and was friendly with most people, although he still avoided Cinca.

He had stopped trying to talk altogether.

"He's over by the beech tree. He already has his jacket."

Susan visibly relaxed, "Good. I hope I didn't disturb you."

"No, I was just over on the hill watching the stars."

"Then I did disturb you. Darling, looking up is serious business. You never know when it's your last time. William used to like to come here at night and watch all the stars and the moons. He could name half the Cluster, you know."

Cinca twisted her lip, "Then I wish he could still talk, because I saw a funny one a little while ago."

"Then invite him. I'm sure he'd like to go."

"Will you come, too?"

"Surely. I need the exercise."

Cinca hesitated, and then walked over to where he sat. He glanced up at her. At least he didn't frown.

"Mason," she said. He didn't understand the words, but he wasn't deaf. Something got through, even if it was only body language and emotions.

"Mason, would you come with us to see the stars?" She pointed to the hill, and then up, to where Orion's belt and part of the Betelgeuse nebula could be seen.

He looked over at Susan, and then set aside the chess set, carefully putting the pieces in their recessed holders and setting it up on a rock. He walked over to her and held the lady's hand. Susan smiled. Cinca led the way.

It seemed less dark by the time they reached the top of the hill. Earthlight and moonlight left distinct shadows on the ground. Susan looked serene, feeling the little breeze on her face. Mason was looking at Luna, a slight frown on his face.

"Susan, Luna looks different. Mason is looking it over."

"How so?"

"Well, the clouds have changed. You know how it was solid overcast, swirling, but solid? Now it's breaking up, forming clumps much more like the Earth."

"Oh I would give a lot to see that. Luna has been so depressing-looking for so long. It was barren when I was young, but it had detail—craters and maria."

"Well, I can see some detail, but the clouds are very white and bright, compared to the land. I think I can even see the oceans."

"How wonderful."

Mason pointed to Luna. "Ruuaah. Ahh." He reached out and held Susan's arm and pointed. Then he grabbed Cinca by the shoulders and pointed her head to Luna. "Taaaa. Naaaaa!"

"What is he saying?" asked Susan.

"I don't know, but he's pointing at Luna. I don't know… Oh wait! I can see something. No. I thought I saw a red glow, but I don't know what he's trying to get me to see. The details are too blurred by the clouds."

Mason, however, was dancing. He swung his arms, and tilted his head back. "Faa! Haa."

"He's happy about something."

"Well, I'm glad of that. He's been so bottled up, since the fever; no way to share his troubles."

Cinca smiled. "Hang on." She took Susan's cane and walked her up to Mason. He caught Cinca's nod, took the hint and swept Susan into his happy dance. Cinca clapped pace for them.

"Whoo! He's wearing me out dear, help," she said after a minute. Cinca stepped up and rescued her, giving Susan back her cane.

Mason was beaming and flushed. He held out his hand to Cinca. Timidly she took it, and suddenly she was the kite in the whirlwind. "Clap for us, Susan!"

They danced for several minutes, while Susan found a stone to rest on and clapped and sang some lively song about a man seeing a wheel in the air.

"That's enough!" Cinca finally gasped, pushing at his chest, and waving her hand at her flushed face. "Enough!"

He smiled and spread his arms and danced alone under the moonlight.

. . .

When he stopped to rest, Cinca walked over and patted him on the shoulder. He smiled. She felt something tight in her chest. Maybe the smiles were a fluke of the night, but it was a blessing, a salve to an ache in her soul.

"I'm glad you're happy."

He looked back up at the sky. Cinca looked over at Vesta, and there was that bright object, having gotten much closer to the asteroid.

"Mason?" She tapped him on the shoulder, and pointed her finger towards the mysterious light. He smiled and followed her directions.

She saw at once when he saw it. His face dropped into a frown, and he tensed up.

"What is it, Mason?"

He watched intently. "Eeee."

She looked back at the light. It was closer to Vesta, minute by minute.

He tilted his head back and let out a cry, "Eraaaaaaaa!"

"What's wrong?" called Susan.

"There's a moving light. He's very upset."

"A moving light? Where is it moving?"

"Toward Vesta. It's getting close."

"Aheeeeeeeeee! Neeeeeeeeeeee!" He was holding his head. He looked in agony.

Suddenly he turned and looked off in the distance, toward the walls of Central Control. He was off at a run.

His cry echoed as he raced down the hill.

"Susan! He's run off. I have to follow him!"

"Go."

"Stay here. I'll be back for you."

Cinca was off.

Susan bit her lip and felt the rock beneath her.

"Oh, my Lord," she muttered.

. . .

Central Control was about three kilometers from the Arboretum, and she was seriously winded and limping by the time she caught up with him.

He was on his knees at the locked door, pounding and pounding against the impenetrable metal with his fist.

He was sobbing. Tears were flooding his face, and he was hoarse from his inarticulate cries.

Cinca didn't know what to do. She was afraid. She reached out to touch him.

He jerked at her touch and turned. She didn't see any recognition in his eyes. Had his condition suddenly gotten worse?

But then she realized he was looking past her. She turned, and saw Vesta and the other light, so close they almost touched.

And then they did.

A flare, brighter than all the rest of the asteroid—a pinpoint of hell, she knew suddenly what had happened.

"Suraaaaaaaa." He collapsed the ground, his body shaking with silent heaves.

She knelt beside him, glancing up at the horror that she, too, felt.

Some habitat had crashed into Vesta. Any survivors on the habitat were gone. Vesta was so densely populated on its surface that the impact must have killed many there, too.

"Mason, you couldn't have stopped it." She knew he couldn't understand what she said, but it made no difference. "It's okay, now. Control is sealed. Nothing you could have done would've made any difference."

She stretched her arms around him. She rested her head on his back. "Come. Come. It's okay." She had to say the words. It didn't feel okay to her. People had died.

He twisted in her arms. His face was contorted. He was angry.

He grabbed her head and made her look at Vesta again, with its dying wound. Then he hit his chest with a hard thud. His hit himself again, and dropped his head crying.

She pulled his head back up.

"No. It is not your fault!"

He twisted his head free. He hit his chest again, hard. He slapped his own face, and then clamped both hands across his mouth.

She was afraid he couldn't breathe. She grabbed at his fingers and pulled his hands away.

"Mason was the last man standing," she remembered Hodges saying.

He thinks he did something wrong, or left something undone.

She grabbed his head in her hands and struck his forehead with her own.

"No!" she said angrily. "You cannot take on all the deaths. It was a disease! It tore up our minds, and we were the lucky ones. Almost everyone is dead, and we cannot take the blame for that!"

Her own eyes were filled with tears.

"Mason, don't die on me! Don't shrivel up and die on me! I don't know why you hate me. I know I must have done something bad, but we can get past that! Forgive me. Forgive yourself!

"We have to live. We're the only ones who can."

He brushed a finger across her left cheek, pushing aside the stream of tears. His own face was still twisted in his private pain, but he worked at her face, trying to clear her tears.

She buried her face against his chest, taking what comfort she could in the smell of his sweat. She could feel him put his arms around her and pull her close.

She could hear the lub-dub of his heart, and it was enough.

···

Susan could hear his distinctive drag-limp.

"Hello, Mr. Hodges."

"Hello, Mrs. Pearce. What are you doing up here by yourself tonight?"

"Cinca, William, and I were up here stargazing. Did you see the Vesta impact?"

"Yes, there was a flash and I looked up. How did you know about it?"

"Cinca described a moving habitat before it hit, and it upset William terribly. He ran off. I suspect he wanted to get to Central Control to stop it."

"That's impossible."

Susan could hear him take a seat on a stone beside her. She turned her head to face where he would be.

"Yes, I know. I was in the Project myself. I handled beams. If the habitat was as bright as Cinca described, then it must have been a large one. Even if William had managed to get to the controller stations, and if they were active, it would have been too late to change its course."

"A while ago, I heard him call out in the distance. That must have been when it hit. The poor boy."

Hodge's voice was a deep rumble. "You're right, he couldn't have done anything. I check the doors every day myself. They're locked tight. The computers are in control now."

"Did you hear him, Mr. Hodges?"

"Yes, I believe I did. I heard several people call out."

Her blind eyes blinked away some moisture. "My boy hurts. But there was nothing he could do."

"Mrs. Pearce, I think I know a little of what he is feeling. He was the last of us. Not a single soul was awake to help him then, and he was coming down with the fever as well.

"He gave the last orders. He set up the protocols for the computers to follow. He did all that was humanly possible to do to preserve the species.

And he gave priority to Earth."

"What do you mean, Mr. Hodges?"

"I barely got a glimpse of his orders before we escaped the lockdown, but the situation was clear. The Clusters were destabilized by the terrorist attack. Many of the habitats were shoved out of their Lagrangian resonance. Ceres and Vesta both were given serious instabilities.

"Mason ordered that the Earth be preserved, at all costs. He knew the situation. Those habitats could not be allowed to impact the Earth. It could wipe out all life, just like what happened to the dinosaurs."

"And Vesta's instabilities," Susan commented, "had to be canceled out—perhaps by carefully timed impacts."

"That's how I read it," he said in a low voice.

She straightened, "At all costs. Well, it makes sense for computers—kill two birds with one stone. Although, I would just as soon they park the loose habitats with beam work."

"That might not be possible," he disagreed. "There was massive disruption. Even if both Mason and I were healthy and in full control, I doubt we could do the job. There are just too many rogue masses in Earth space, and far too few control beams for a job of this scale.

"No, Mason knew what he was doing. It was a hard call, very hard, and humanity will survive because of it."

She nodded. "But there will be more Vesta impacts, won't there. And Ceres, too."

"I believe so."

She let out a long sigh.

He added, "However, we might be lucky. The bulk of Ceres is uninhabited surface."

After a moment, she stood up. "You're right. While there is life, there is hope." Her face denied the sentiment.

"Mr. Hodges, could you escort me back to the camp?"

"I would be delighted."

They worked their way down the hill at a slow pace. He kept her apprised of rocks in her way, and held a steady hand for her.

"There *is* hope, you know," he said.

She tilted her head to the side. "Perhaps for the youngsters—not for me."

"Why do you say that?"

She stumbled slightly, gripping his hand tighter for balance. "I'm old.

I'm blind. I'm useless."

He listened, waiting.

"My boys are all dead, except for Mason, and there isn't a thing I can do for him. If I could at least see him, I could read his gestures like Cinca can. I would know what do to."

Hodges said gently, "But he can see you. No one can look at him, when you come into view, without seeing that he loves you like a mother. He gains comfort from your presence. And he isn't the only one who needs you."

"What do you mean?"

"All of Ceres needs you."

She gave a short, bitter, laugh. "The food won't last forever. Soon enough, the group will want me to get out of the way and stop taking the resources the younger people need."

"You're wrong there. You're one of the most valuable resources this new family has. If they don't realize it yet, they soon will."

Her face showed no softening.

He continued, "There is hope for the future. Not just for this month, or for this year, but far into the future. We have a viable little colony here. We have sunlight, water, and soil. We will grow the crops we need, and maybe not you, and maybe not me, but our people will grow a new crop of children here."

He squeezed her hand tighter. "And they'll need a culture, a civilization, to grow into. That's where you'll make your mark.

"You and every person you know grew up surrounded by a civilization. You absorbed its beliefs and its wisdom from hundreds of little contacts each day, from news broadcasts, to overheard conversations, to the very way commerce and tools are constructed."

He looked around the city. "Today, we live in a ghost town. What will the next generation absorb? The love of their parents hopefully; the proper way to tend crops at best; the safest way to kill and eat your neighbor at worst.

"Will the next generation look at these abandoned buildings and populate them with gods and demons? We have already lost the ability to use most of our machines. How long until all of that knowledge is gone? How many generations until some bright boy digs a tunnel to the outside of the dome?"

The very idea caused a shudder to go through her.

He thumped her collarbone with a finger.

"You are the wisdom of these people. You are the oldest, and I suspect you are the richest in experience.

"You're blind, but you've seen much.

"You're old, but you're healthy.

"Fight against the years! Hang on until a whole new generation has heard you tell your tales. A new civilization is ready to be formed by your every word.

"You're not useless. We desperately need you."

She smiled, and shook her head.

"Mr. Hodges, I think all you do is wander about and tell us all what we need to hear. Thank you."

He sighed. "I think it's the only reason I'm here."

. . .

They were almost to the camp when Hodges said, "Oh, I see them."

"William and Cinca?"

"Yes."

"Are they okay?"

"Well," he paused, "they appear to be holding hands."

"Good."

"And their clothes appear a little disarrayed."

"Mr. Hodges! That's a little more detail than I think I need."

But she smiled. Maybe there was a future for them all.

Chapter 13

PALITINO, MARS

"Describe it to me," said Trader, resting in the doorway of his ship. He didn't bother to wear the pistol any more. He wished he hadn't had to give up his Backcountry cold-weather gear. There were snowflakes drifting down over the field.

Shed, sitting in his driver's seat, scratched his head. "I suppose it's in large tubs. Any kind of petroleum stocks would be useful. The biomass synthesizer was one of the first things to go, and no one is left who knows how it works."

"What do you use it for?"

"Well, some of it I can use in my medicines, but the machinery needs lubrication, and especially out in the fields, the dust gets into all the seals. We might be back to tilling the soil with a crooked stick if we can't get them back running."

"Okay, I'll look for it. If I can find any, what will you have to trade?"

Shed laughed, "You seemed to like the wine last time. We've got more of that."

Trader kept a straight face. "Hmm. Yes, I could use a couple more bottles, but what else do you have? Something long-term valuable. I've got to be thinking about my retirement. No good to trade the whole ship for jam, and bread, and wine. Then where would I be?"

"You'd be just like the rest of us and have to work for a living?"

Trader laughed. "I can't have that, now can I?"

Shed shook his head, "No, I suppose not. Well, we have food and water, and some books. But you say you have enough of that already."

"Yaw. Lots of staples, and the books don't do me any good."

"Well, you could come visit us in town. Look around. We might have something you might like."

Trader shook his head, "Not today, thank you. I've still got my inventorying to do."

"Now that's a thought. How about I send a few fellows over to help you inventory?"

"Now, Shed! Not that I don't trust you, but I have known people who take things that aren't theirs, if you can imagine that."

Shed twisted his face a little. "No, I can't imagine."

Shed was getting tired of the farce. No one else had the patience to bargain with Trader. He could only handle it a little at a time.

"However," Trader looked a little skyward, "you might send me a nice young lady to help with the books. She wouldn't walk away unhappy."

"I'll ask around." Shed had no intention of sending any of the women his way. If he wanted the pleasures of companionship, he could very well join the town.

"Well!" said Trader, getting to his feet. "I'll get you the computers. Excuse me."

...

Trader locked the door with his passphrase.

A few steps from the entrance, he went the storeroom where he put things in advance that he knew Shed would want. The ship's computer was good about locating things, but it took time. No sense in letting anyone know he couldn't read and had to have the ship tell him everything step by step.

He had thousands of computer boxes in the original factory containers. It was a good thing he had them. Most of the cargo, as far as he could tell, was useless. There were huge spools of wire, prefabricated tanstran assemblies, large electronic things with no hint of their purpose—all valuable items that were cheaper to import than to produce in the limited Mars factories. It was all useless, here and now.

At least the computers were useful. Not that the old ones wore out, but the Martian power distribution system was defunct and the computers only lasted until their reserve power ran out. These factory-fresh ones could probably run for several months before they, too, went silent.

He loaded a wheeled cart with a dozen of them and walked it out to Shed's vehicle. It was nice dealing with a cripple; he couldn't jump you.

Once Shed was a cloud of dust in the distance, he went back into the ship.

"Seal the door. Passphrase is 'Kidd is a dirty rotten scoundrel.'"

It was almost a religious thing. The lock on the door was his only claim to ownership. And it had paid off, too. One night, after one of the original ship's crew had recovered from the fever, a visitor had come out and tried to re-enter the ship.

Trader laughed at the memory. The man had pounded on the door, shouting his official passphrases and ordering the computer to open up. He kept it up for almost an hour.

After that, Trader had a nice long talk with the ship's computer and reset all of the override passphrases and even added another for himself. No one would ever get in without his permission.

"Ship, what is petroleum?"

"Petroleum is a generic name for carbon-based organic chemicals originally derived from geologic deposits on Earth."

"Well, do we have any carbon-based chemicals on board?"

"Yes. Do you wish directions?"

"Might as well. The more things to trade the better."

He went down to the third level and turned when the computer told him to. As usual, there were signs and symbols everywhere, but he had given up trying to decipher them. He couldn't read, and he was content with that. With the ship to coach him every step of the way, he didn't need to read much anyway.

The cargo hold had an airtight latch, like on some of the airlocks. He had seen holds like this on several levels. They could be loaded from the outside in the vacuum of space.

"Whoa. How many chemicals are there?"

Racks containing pressure cylinders and non-pressurized drums filled the large hold. Colored rings and dozens of symbols were painted all over the containers.

"There are thirty-two different materials."

"Jackpot. Which is a petroleum?"

"There are several. On the far left rack, there is a drum with two blue bands. On the next row, there is a drum with two blue bands and a red band. Next to it is a drum with two blue bands and a yellow band. In the pressurized containers ..."

"Hold. Got it."

Two blue bands is the ticket. I'll move all of these up to the storeroom. Shed will pay well for these.

He went to the first one. There was an easy seal on the drum, so on impulse, he twisted the lever and the lid came open. There was a faint odor that he recognized, and the material inside was thick to the touch, almost like gray butter.

He twisted the lid back on and tried the next. It was a thick black liquid, and it was hard to wipe off his finger.

He went to the third.

The lid popped off as if under pressure. A gagging scent, so strong that he couldn't breathe, filled the room. Eyes watering and throat burning, he tried to fit the lid back on.

"Com ...cough ...puter! I need oxygen! Help."

"Pressurized cylinder on the third row. Wide green band."

Trader stumbled back blindly. Blinking the tears from his stinging eyes, he grabbed at a pressure bottle and opened the valve.

Fluorine gas spontaneously ignited with the gas in the air. The ship's computer detected the explosion and, following preset orders, ejected the entire cargo hold from the body of the main ship.

. . .

When Shed and a group of town men arrived several hours later to investigate the cloud of smoke from the fire, they were barely able to recognize Trader's charred body, almost hidden beneath a scrap of metal, heavily decorated with warnings about flammable materials.

However, the new opening into the ship did give them relatively easy access to the interior, even if the computer did refuse to open the main hatchway for them.

PIKE'S PEAK RESTRICTED ZONE, NORTH AMERICA, EARTH

"Land there and wait for my signal."

"Acknowledged."

Kidd waited until the cirrance died, and then opened the hatch slowly, to let the cabin pressure adjust to the high altitude. He yawned to relieve the pressure in his ears.

He had already drained the energy from his lightweight shuttle, but this one was hidden well, and the computer had given him a discouraging projection on the energy transfer efficiency if he tried to drain it through the walls. There was a strong possibility of a meltdown if he tried it.

So he had to bring it out.

The facility had originally been a commercial facility on the west side of the mountain, and from the surface, it looked like so many of the other ruined buildings—a wide box collapsing in solitude. It was the same in many restricted areas along the abandoned mountain areas.

The large basements had led him here originally. He had to force the first door—rusted hinges. Behind that was a wide door with combination locks. Getting in required nothing more than a good memory. He hoped the weather seals had held. Getting out needed the electrical systems fully functional.

It had been thirty years since he had mothballed the old transport. He had left it fully charged and ready to fly. A touch on the console brought the life support systems and corridor lights on.

"Access code: 'For the lights of night.'"

"Welcome sir. Challenge Nine?"

"Topaz."

"Very good."

"Computer, activate the hatchway doors."

...

While the two ships worked out the details of moving the energy, he sat quietly in an office chair. Even thirty-plus-years old, it was still more comfortable than the cockpit command seats.

All my Berlin contacts are out of the picture. It was a reminder of how much his power base had been destroyed by the plague. Secret bases, hidden ships, and obscure passwords were one thing, but making people do what he wanted them to do was power of a different order.

One day before the plague, he could have gotten around any Project policy, secretly too. Thousands of people would have followed any order he gave them, as long as it was signed with their particular passphrase. A web of promise, threat, and deceit had been there at his fingertips, and its filaments had been woven through all parts of society.

At least it frees up a lot of nice passphrases. He had made it a point to keep his line of communication unique with each one of those people.

As the survivors formed into bands and started making their new societies, he had no doubt that he could start it all up again, but for now, the only slaves he could command all had the same name.

"Computer, status?"

"Energy transfer will be complete in fifty-four seconds."

"Have you located the optimal starting point?"

"The optimum obscure location, as you indicate, is the point opposite Luna. That is Longitude 22.45 West Latitude 5.02 North. However, by altitude 1120 kilometers, no place will be hidden from the Ceres and Vesta stations."

I'll just have to hope that the Project computers will classify me as already outside of Earth's barrier by the time they see me. I can worry about getting back down after I visit Project Central Control on Ceres.

"The Public orbital database has received an update."

"It's about time." He pulled himself out of the comfortable chair and headed for the surface.

"Are there any significant changes in any of my targets?"

"North Darnell has been removed from the orbital listings."

"What? Why?" A wisp of cool touched the back of his neck. His mind raced.

"It appears that the North Darnell fragment had its orbit altered to impact Vesta."

"Impact! It's already happened?"

"Yes." His stomach twisted. *She is on South Darnell. She has to be.*

"Vesta? That's in the L5 Cluster."

"Yes. The Darnell fragment had drifted significantly."

He started running. *She has to be on South Darnell. I won't let it be otherwise!*

. . .

He took his partially reenergized transport up to eighty kilometers and headed south. The plan was simple enough—wait until the major traffic control beam centers were all below the horizon, and then boost straight up and be clear of the interdiction zone before he became visible to them.

He would have preferred to be immune to the interdiction by overriding the Project command codes, but he hadn't found the way yet and there was no more time.

"Is there Net access to Vesta?"

There was a delay of three seconds.

"Yes."

If she was alive on North Darnell, she would have found a way to get Net access, and my message to her would have gone through. She didn't reply, so that must mean she wasn't on North Darnell. His stomach didn't feel any better.

"Are there any replies from my messages, or any kind of message to me?"

"There is a message on a broadcast channel that may be intended for you."

"What is it?" He held his breath.

The sound changed, it was a voice message. There was a hoarse, breathy voice, a man. "Whoever you are, whoever made this plague. <wheeze> May you burn in hell …"

"Cancel." He shook free of the voice. *Not important.*

"Computer, if there is any kind of message for me that appears to come from South Darnell, or any kind of message that appears to come from Bet Nomad, notify me immediately."

. . .

It was only ten minutes in coming.

"Repeating message from South Darnell. There are missing and partial packets. Reconstruction follows:

"Alert! Immediate assistance needed. Survivor on fragment of Darnell habitat. Life support limited. Dr. Bet Nomad."

He glanced at his position. He was still several minutes from his optimum launch location.

"Is there anything else?"

"There appear to be parts of multiple datastreams. They are being repeated but they are not complete."

"Give me what you've got!"

"The first just appears to be an return-receipt."

So, my message got through, and she heard it.

A shiver went through him. *She wasn't on North Darnell. She's probably still alive.*

"The second is not yet completed reconstructed. Partial message is:

"This is Beta… South Darnell, the sole survivor… cargo bay 0200 on the edge … but not critical… impact on Earth. It is …"

South Darnell. He threw off the jitters. There was no time for anything but clarity.

"Computer, locate a structural map of the Darnell habitat. Display it."

There was a momentary delay, and then the screen showed a wireframe view of the cylindrical station.

"Highlight cargo bay 0200." At one end, on the edge, a section blinked. "Are there external markings to indicate the cargo bay?"

"At last report, yes."

"Good." He looked at his position on the navigation map. There was a darkened ellipse that showed the area hidden from the moons. He was less than thirty minutes from his target.

"There is now full Net access to South Darnell. Do you wish a replay of the reconstructed message?"

"In a minute. Make a voice contact to Bet Nomad."

He could feel his heart beating in his chest.

"Hello?" Her voice was sweet and mellow, in spite of nervousness he could hear from three light seconds away.

"Hello Beta. How old are you? Your voice sounds wonderful." He tried to put enough charm into his voice, but he couldn't quite overcome the microquivers that betrayed his own tension.

Talking long distance was always frustrating. It was always trying, guessing how much to say before turning the conversation over.

"My, my. I would have thought we were about the same age. May I say right up front that I'm glad you're a man? Alpha is such a neutral name."

"Ha. I've always known you were a woman. I found records. What did you know?"

"Nothing. Not one thing, other than the name 'Beta', and that could have been made up." She paused a breath. "Why have you been so long in making contact?"

"Lovely Beta, the Nomad. You've been too clever. You've eluded the most sophisticated search programs known to man, or to me. Oh well, I would have never expected less."

"You must tell me everything. Like I said, I never found out anything about my ... ancestors. Everything I know came from my genes."

"It's pretty obvious, isn't it? We were prototypes—just the two of us. And there was some bad market timing."

"Just two? Yes, I had guessed the rest. By the way, how close are you? I'm getting nervous about Ceres."

Kidd jumped out of his pleasant haze.

"Computer! Show me South Darnell's orbit!"

"Beta, I have a delayed data feed. What is your current status?" He was harsh and efficient. His mind had suddenly gone into overdrive. He was ready with a new plan before her words came back.

"Sorry. South Darnell is in a tractor beam, accelerating toward Ceres. I thought that was your doing."

"Computer! Begin the dive now!"

"No, Beta, the Project has been turned over to the computers and they're cleaning up the unstable items in the Clusters. North Darnell has already impacted on Vesta. I'm preparing to make a break through the Earth interdiction barrier by coming out through a blind spot in the system. Do you have a current estimate of your course and speed?"

"Wait a minute." There was silence, and then his computer beeped—a received message.

Beta spoke, "Okay, I've sent it off. Don't count on centimeter precision here. You wouldn't believe the difficulty in getting reliable input. Do you have an arrival estimate?"

He looked over the orbital chart, using his computer to combine the old data and hers.

"Hang on." He adjusted his own navigation. His transport was falling fast. He had to get close to the ground to maximize his acceleration time before he was spotted.

There was a feel of tension in the air, as his command chair was protected from the sudden high accelerations. It would continue all the way up.

There was no cirrance noise. This was a straight pressor beam, cutting through bedrock, mantle, and the core of the Earth. The other end of the pressor beam enveloped most of the transport, and a large chunk of the atmosphere.

But the numbers ruled. MV equals MV. The mass of the planet was so incredibly larger than that of the ship and air that all of the energy was going to change his velocity.

There had to be a huge shock wave in the atmosphere, signaling that something had happened. It would travel around the globe several times. Kidd wasted no thought on it. Getting through the interdiction barrier was all that counted. Who cared what brain damaged humans thought!

"Alpha? Are you still there?"

"Yes." It was difficult to talk. The air was stressed in the tiny bubble of forces that protected his body from the accelerations that were causing the edges of the transport to flow under pressure. "I am making my climb."

"Warning! Warning! Energy is being drained from the accumulators." The computer spoke with its artificial urgency.

"What? How can that be?" He was still far short of the altitude where the Project beam stations could see him.

He was still climbing, but acceleration was dropping on his screens.

"Alpha, what is wrong?"

"The Project detected me. They are draining my power. But I still might…"

The lights went out.

"No!" he screamed. "No!"

A dim, non-electric glow was the only light. The screens were dead. The backup power, using separate accumulators, separate tension settings—it had been drained too, this time.

He was trapped in a powerless cylinder of metal, still falling upward due to the massive accelerations it had experienced.

I am well above the atmosphere now. All I have to do is find a way to bootstrap the power—find a way to tap some energy.

He unstrapped and grabbed an emergency mask. He had to find something that produced electricity. The transport was in freefall. He pushed off with his feet and sailed toward the corridor.

I'm running out of time. The last projection of South Darnell's course was clear in his perfect memory. The dead chunk of metal was heading directly towards Ceres, and it was traveling hot. The impact would likely leave a wide molten crater. Nothing could survive.

He had seen the blueprints of this transport when he had bought it thirty-seven years before. There was an redundant electrochemical power system that ran the doors and exterior hatches so that those systems would still be operational even in a repair dock where all of the accumulators might be shut down.

Reaching the main hatch, he paused when he saw the curve of the Eatth though the transparent tanstran port. He was clearly beyond the one hundred kilometer limit where he had been stopped the last time.

Just keep rising.

A light caught his eye. Ceres, like a tiny version of Luna, rose above the limb of the Earth. He had to be above the computer's eleven hundred kilometer hiding limit. There was a tiny, bright dot above Ceres. He could see it move, even at this distance.

South Darnell. That's too close.

Suddenly, the air was filled with the sound of complaining metal, and the view outside started to spin.

"No! No! No!"

A beam had caught him. He fell against a wall, They were going to push him down.

Then, almost as abruptly as it had started, the beam stopped. *They stopped me cold. They'll just let me drop.*

The Earth below was moving. *I'm headed north! The South Polar station? I thought that was radar only.*

Something from the south had soaked up all his energy, and then left him falling at what looked like less-than-orbital velocity. *Burn me up. Debris falling in the arctic.*

The transport was tumbling. He kept a tight grip on the port. As Ceres came back into view, he could see the dot of light that held Beta. It was much closer.

His mind was empty. The Earth slid by another time.

Ceres came back, but South Darnell could not be seen.

"No," he mumbled. He hit the impervious window with his fist. Blood smeared the view.

"Nooooo!" The sound changed, becoming a mindless wail that went on and on.

SOUTH DARNELL, CERES, L4 CLUSTER

"Alpha, what is wrong?" Seconds ticked away.

"The Project detected me. They are draining my power. But I still might…" The sound went dead.

Bet waited five seconds, and then ten.

The crane's camera showed details of the Ceres landscape below. It was so close that it took up nearly half the sky.

It won't come around again. South Darnell was too close, approaching too fast. There wasn't time for it to complete another rotation.

She moved. There were only a couple of minutes left, and Alpha had failed. She sealed her spacesuit.

"Computer, make sure the crane is powered up."

"It is."

"Monitor the tank, and release all tension on the spool the instant I break it free."

"Understood."

There was no time for her careful planning. She grabbed a pry bar and smashed open the airtight door that had been keeping her breathing for so many days she had lost count.

The blast of air and debris shoved her out into the vacuum of the fractured loading dock.

Part of her mind had already worked out her path, for she shoved against a structural beam with confidence. She was tumbling, but she was on course for the water storage tank.

All she could hear was her own breathing. She wasn't equipped to talk to the computer any more. It all had to work perfectly, or it wasn't going to work at all.

The water storage tank had broken free of its moorings during the orignal breakup of Darnell, but she had moved it carefully to the edge of the abyss. All that was lacking was to fracture an ice wedge that kept it from rolling free of its current, precarious support.

She hit and grabbed for a metal rib of the tank. It slipped from her free hand. She twisted her body and hooked her foot under the broken pipe that protruded past the valve.

It killed her tumble, and she grabbed on.

The rotation of South Darnell gave less than a quarter gravity here on the docking port. She was poised over the edge of an infinitely deep pit, and that was where she needed to go.

She swung the pry bar hard against the ice and it fractured, but the storage tank still didn't move. She put her back into it, pushing with her legs against warped metal decking. Then, it moved.

And it started twisting on its own. She let the pry bar fly loose and grabbed on with both hands as the water tank slid over the edge into space.

Computer, pay attention! It was a prayer. The time for commands were over.

A dozen meters above, the crane began unspooling its cable. She had worked it out in her head and explained it in detail to the computer. Now to see if reality matched.

Two objects were falling, each with its own impediment. The cable had to pull against the mass of its spool. The water tank was tumbling down the slope of a metal incline, ready to smash her with its mass. She had originally planned to be inside the tank, but that was the old plan.

This was last-second improvisation.

Smash! The water tank hit, and bounced. She flattened herself against the metal, trying to use the outflow pipe for protection.

It hit again, and this time, the tank sprung a leak. Water and steam and ice were spraying from the pipe. Her view was cut off. She reached blindly into the spray and found the valve. She twisted, and the leak was tamed to a hiss.

As the vapor vanished into the vacuum, she realized that the tank had finally bounced free and fallen off the edge. She gripped tighter. This was her last anchor.

The tumble gave her a quick vision of South Darnell, a black silhouette of broken desolation. For the first time, she saw what was left of the south end cap. The mirror assembly had been ripped aside when the mass of soil had fallen through. Sunlight illuminated the inside of a scarred and scraped metal hull, where pleasant orchards once grew.

And across the scene was a line. It came at her.

The cable hit the tank, as it had begun its swing.

She was expecting it, and grabbed. The cable was stiff with its own tension, but she muscled it around the base of the pipe. Just tight enough, and then she edged away from it. When the crane's spool reached its limit....

There was a painful creak in the metal that resonated clearly through her body. The tank was now a pendulum at the end of the rotating habitat. They were gaining speed, adding their own swing to the spin of South Darnell. If she could cut the cable at just the right point, she would have a significant velocity at right angles to the fall toward Ceres. Maybe she could miss the surface.

The mass of the tank, when it snagged the cable, jerked against it. The tank, and all its contents, bounced. Each time, she could feel the pipe being tortured from its attachment to the tank.

On the third bounce. It broke free.

No! It's not enough!

Beta had lived through too many close calls in her long life. She did not know how to give up.

The water was spilling out again, and all she could do with the valve is regulate how fast it was escaping. A crude rocket, but still a source of some thrust.

She wiped her face plate. She would have to watch Ceres to time the exhaust.

Ceres was so close that she could see the massive reflector dish that had been constructed inside the broad expanse of Kirnis and the countless astronomical facilities that surrounded it. She judged her angle and opened the valve, cutting off her sight in a cloud of ice and steam.

The vapor quickly dissipated in the vacuum, but the ice was depositing on every available surface. She brushed at her helmet to keep it from her eyes.

She closed the valve and waited.

There was only a second's warning before the impact. The gutted and scarred habitat that had for so many decades provided fruit for Ceres, struck a dozen kilometers from the big telescope. It had come in hot. Millions of tons of metal, traveling at a speed greater than its own ability to dissipate the shock wave, collapsed into the planetoid. The energy had no place to go, and so it became heat and light.

The flash could be felt even under the ice that was accumulating on her.

She watched as the shock wave swept across the surface of Ceres and shattered the tanstran mirror. An instant later, it turned the scientific settlement into dust.

But details were blurring, as her own trajectory was approaching Ceres on the slant. The land whipped by at an increasing pace, and she felt seconds away from an impact with some mountain peak.

She turned the valve and the nightmarish blur vanished in the steam. The cold was seeping into her body. She tensed up for the impact, knowing she could never feel it.

An eternity passed as she held her breath.

Abrupt sunlight on the steam shocked her mind free. She turned the valve shut. There were stars, and soon enough, Ceres.

I cleared it.

A wisp of vapors laid another haze of ice over her sight. She tried to move her arm to clear it, but it was encased in a thick layer if ice.

It's cold. She let the thought drift away. What did it matter? She had avoided death by fire. But the ice already had her.

It would have been nice, Alpha. I bet you were a wonderful man. I would have liked to meet you.

But I have had my family. They wait for me now. No sense in delaying.

A body on overdrive from panic flight could run only so far. As her tension faded, the cold crept in even faster.

Her last sight, before she slept, was the blaze of blue and white, the Earth, where she had left so many blessed by her touch.

Epilog

ARBORETUM, CERES, L4 CLUSTER

It was fall, and the leaves were turning. Cinca rested from her work in the garden. There were more pumpkins this year than last. They now had a whole year of experience, and this time they expected the change of seasons. Whether it was some programming of the daylights or a subtle change in their orbit, summer and winter had come to Ceres. At least, it let them grow a wider variety of crops.

She looked at her nails, worn down and lined with dirt. It felt good to work with her hands in the soil.

Mason was having fun playing with their son.

They were like two kids with Mason chattering away in his own brand of baby talk. Little Hodges was waving his pudgy little hands at his father's beard and listening with wide eyes and open mouth.

Mason was a devoted parent, and Cinca had only a tiny bit of worry. She knew infants learned language skills by listening, and she had no idea what effect Mason's babble would have on him.

Susan was a wonderful help. She had started a storytelling tradition in the community, and she was often sitting against Story Oak, next to the stone circle. She loved to tell stories—bible stories, stories from when she was a pilot, and an unending stream of old fairy tales and fables. Cinca loved to listen to them herself and joined in when Susan began to sing. Mason sat quietly too, holding Little Hodges and soaking up the rhythm and sweep of her voice.

There had been no improvement in his speech, in spite of long hours of practice. Mason could make the sounds, but if he pointed at something and babbled, each time it would be different. Some crucial connection between his mind and language was gone forever.

She smiled. *But we have our own talk.* Some of the others of the twenty-eight survivors on Ceres had thought he was demented, but she knew better. He could do anything, as long as he understood what was needed. And they had developed their own shortcuts—gestures and body language and spousal telepathy.

If the others needed his help, she could usually translate for him.

She picked one of the pumpkins and set it carefully on her tray. People weren't dying off as fast, and if they were more careful about food supplies this winter, their numbers might increase. Little Hodges already had two little friends.

They had to be careful. The second round of fatalities—when Ceres had suffered the large impact—had left them all deeply depressed. But there had been no others of that magnitude. In fact, there had been none at all in the past couple of months. She remembered the first time at the stone circle, during their monthly celebration of the First Light of Earth, when there had been no new names to cry over since the last reading.

She still missed Hodges. His death, lost to the depths of the Ocean trying to set up a pumping station, had affected everyone. His cheerful presence, helping everyone settle in to their new life, had touched everyone.

When they read his name at First Light, there wasn't a dry eye, except for Mason. People said he didn't understand what had happened, but she could tell by a raised eyebrow and a sly smile that he knew everything. They were Controllers together. Perhaps they shared something she couldn't understand.

But for now, she had to get the pumpkin to the kitchen. Susan had promised to share a recipe with her.

The older lady was slowing down, and Cinca used every excuse to keep her moving and active. With her blindness, there was always a danger she would withdraw to her little nook, filled with darkness and a set of touchstones, named for her boys, and for her long-lost husbands. One day she would go there and never come back. Cinca had no memory of her own mother. Susan filled that void, and she would not give her up.

We are so few. Everyone is precious now.

BACKCOUNTRY PRESERVE, NORTH AMERICA, EARTH

Bonnie Gearson's nimble fingers worked at the pinecone, teasing out the seeds. She frowned and set it aside with the stack of others she had harvested.

"I don't think my parents are sick like your mother. They're stubborn and hard to talk to, but they were always like that."

Bull stared at the gravel before his feet. He edged a stone into the path of a large black ant.

"I hate it that they don't trust me."

Bonnie kept at her work.

He looked toward the western pass. "I know I could go over and check the next valley and be back the next day, easy. When they were sick, I was on my own. I know every marmot and chipmunk in this valley, and all my dad can talk about is being surprised by a bear!"

Bonnie said, "I'm sure you can handle anything. Just the other day, my father said you were a hard worker and sharp as a tack."

"What's a tack?"

She shook her head. "One of those *outside* things, I guess. Maybe we should say, 'sharp as a nettle' when we have babies, so it will be easier to explain."

He gave her his exasperated look. "All you can talk about is babies."

Bonnie smiled. She was more patient about things than Bull, especially since her mother had her little sister. It was then that Bonnie had been told the secrets of being a woman. She was only eight, but she couldn't wait to have her moon cycle, and have sex with Bull and have babies of her own. It would be a long time. Her mother had said that she had to wait for five years after her moon cycle started, or it would make her deathly ill, but it was still exciting to know woman's secrets.

"You just have to be patient," she told Bull. "Your mother has the shakes, but in a few months, you will have a baby brother or sister, just like me. Then your father will know you're getting old. I know. I was the baby, and then suddenly I wasn't any more."

He shook his head. "Girl stuff."

"Babies are the…."

Suddenly Bull was on his feet. He stared motionless down the valley, to where the stream bent into a wide gravel bed.

"What is—" She started, but he waved her silent.

"Bear. Slowly, pick up your pot and walk with me."

She looked down the way he was looking, but she didn't see anything. She did as he told her, but her impulse was to run. He put his hand on her arm and kept her moving slowly. He did the watching.

"Now. Move faster." In step together, they took the elk trail and didn't stop until they were at the lip of the hanging valley where the stream fell in a long, narrow waterfall.

He led her to an overlook. "See. There—by the beaver pond." It was a black bear, and it was crossing through the ice-cold water like it couldn't even feel it.

Bonnie shivered. "My father jokes about bears, but I'm scared of them. I'm glad you were there. You can see much better than I can."

He watched it move below. "We'll need to tell the grownups. My father and your father need to decide if we can kill it. We could use the meat and the fat."

She smiled at him. "You can track it. I've seen how good you are."

He nodded. "Let's get moving."

They went on toward their home. Bull stayed at her shoulder. Bonnie liked it. Most of the time he went his own way, setting rock snares for the small animals to extend their food supply, but lately he had spent more time with her.

"You make me feel safe," she confessed.

He didn't say anything until they had gone a few more minutes, and then he said, "My father talked to me a few weeks ago. Do you know what the word 'husband' means?"

She shook her head. "Like husband and wife?"

"Yes. The word means 'take care of'. When we grow up, I will be your husband. So that means I'll take care of you."

Then, she really felt safe.

HAWAIIAN ISLANDS, PACIFIC OCEAN, EARTH

Sealer could hear the ocean getting shallower by the minute. He pulled ahead of his scouting party. The vision in his head was almost stronger than the vision of his eyes.

He made for the surface, and splashed through, taking in a huge gulp of air and purging the water from his gills.

The sunlight was painfully bright, and his eyes had to make their adjustments to see clearly in air rather than water.

There it was.

So long a time. I greet you, Mountain of Fire.

He swam slower, relishing the bright waters, the end of the journey.

There was a splash beside him.

- Is this the place? - asked DolphinFriend.

- Yes, it's the first part. It's a large island, and on the other side, for a month's easy swim, there are many islands, with warm, sunny waters full of fish. We have reached the Birth Bays. -

DolphinFriend looked at him. - Are you certain we're here? -

- You doubt? - Sealer smiled at his friend, who had been at his side for a year and a half as they had taken the tribe on a journey beyond anything even the visions talked about.

He didn't answer directly. Instead, he looked at the island again.

Sealer laughed. - Go back to the tribe. Spread the word. Tonight we rest in the shallows. And there is no journey for tomorrow. -

DolphinFriend gave him the little sound of respect that the others had started using, something out of the visions, and then he ducked below the waters.

No journey tomorrow! How strange that sounds.

Every day had been a journey, from the moment the tidal wave had come. It marked in everyone's mind that Sealer, the Knife-bearer, was gifted with prophecy, and that to ignore him meant death.

A year and a half. It seemed a lifetime ago. That was before Anemone revealed her vision. Their son was to be the first-born of their tribe in the Birth Bays. Thus far, she was on schedule, but four other women would bear not long after her.

For the first time in his memory, the People were increasing in number.

He was not comfortable being the vision leader of the tribe, but he knew that this was his destiny. Time and time again, the visions had grown from a feeling to a conviction, to become reality.

Still, the journey had been hard.

They had broken with their traditional migration, and had gone south, very far south, so far that the sun moved to the other side of the sky, passing across the north each day.

And then came that day when he called them all together and made promises. Follow him out into the deep, follow him farther than any had swum before, and there would be a path of islands and seamounts, never more than a score of days apart. They would follow these resting places given by the gods, and after a time, they would reach the Birth Bays, where they would live out their lives in good hunting waters, far from the tainted waters of the Land People. This was their ancestral home, and this is where they would regain the greatness that had been lost.

Everyone had feared that first crossing over the deeps, where for days no one could hear any reflection from below. Many wanted to turn back.

But the island had been there where he said, on the day he had predicted.

DolphinFriend had spoken with the whales, and they too confirmed that there were more islands up ahead. They moved on.

So many islands, so many rest stops. It had been hard to organize the hunters to keep meat collected for the silent parts of the ocean, when everyone, from the infant to the old ones, had to keep swimming because there was no place to rest. The younger ones now had no memory of a time when they did not swim all day and gather together in woven sleep nets at night so that no one would drift away and be lost.

A year and a half. He shook his head. They had gone south, and now they were back north again. The instincts in his head told him a warrior in good condition could swim back to their old haunts in just over a month.

But a strong warrior was not the same as a whole village. They had taken the long way, the safe way.

And now they had made it.

The seabed was rising rapidly below him, and he could hear the sand in its channels, and the clatter of parrotfish on the coral.

He saw a path, black sand, winding its way from the shore. The water had the taste of fire. But he knew that to the east, around the bend of the land, the bays were wide and sweet.

A bar of metal caught his eye. It was part of a sunken ship. He was not surprised. Even here, there were Land People.

That first month, they had found so many dead floating in the waters all along the shore line that he had hoped they were all gone, but he knew better.

He knew that the job of containing the Land People would be hard, but his tribe could do it. Floating in the tribe's net were a dozen iron spears, some already scarred from use. They would seek out all of the boats in the Birth Bays and sink them. There would never be a time when they had to run for their lives because of the Land People's machines.

Some day, when his people increased their number, they would return to his childhood shores and restrain them there as well. The People owned the sea. Never again should a child grow up in fear.

The water was swirling around him, making stiff currents as the waves splashed up on the rocks and then hurried back to the safety of the ocean.

He struggled with it. He could not stop himself. The fire stone, and the coral were both ready to scrape at him, but he reached a place where it was too shallow to swim.

He pushed his legs under him, and on his hands and knees, he pulled himself entirely out of the water.

Balance was impossible, but there were large stones to hold on to. He found a place to sit, where the waves splashed against his legs, and he could look around at this place.

The land was always strange, but this place felt different.

There was a call he could hear through the water clearer than through the air.

He looked out to the water.

First one head, then a handful, and then the whole tribe—heads bobbing in the surf.

- We are home, my people. We are home. -

DENVER, NORTH AMERICA, EARTH

The city looked vaguely familiar, but then most cities did. The young man adjusted his backpack and chose a course between the tall buildings. His walking stick chimed with each pace as the little bell on its crown announced his presence to the growing population of bears that were coming out of the mountains these days.

This city had not been fully occupied since the Star, if he was any judge. The ancient buildings would have fewer skeletons to avoid. He had seen far too many of them already.

"One nice thing," he mumbled, "cities have bridges over the rivers." He smiled at himself, as he looked down at the creek heading toward a reservoir just a short distance ahead. "I need to stop talking to myself." There were few enough people around without making them think he had multiple personality disorder.

It had been a lonely trek—not that he considered himself a good conversationalist. Most towns were empty, although there were a few places where ad hoc "families" had collected to help each other.

The sun from the south caught a slab of glass that had lasted far beyond the building's designer's dreams. He put up his hand to shield his eyes.

"What is that?" He moved to the other side of the street to avoid the glare. "There's something up there."

Hanging off the edge of the tall building next to the reservoir … It looked like a body. He stopped and squinted, trying to make out details.

"Hey, kid!" came a voice from a cross street. He looked down, trying to spot its source, as his hand reached for the knife he had made over a year ago from a scrap of metal.

There was a tall, bushy-headed man coming leisurely down the street, pulling a two-wheeled cart behind him.

The hiker held his position, waiting for the local to approach. It wasn't a good idea to run the instant he was seen. If there had been a dozen of them, then maybe, but he hadn't seen a dozen people together in one place in some time.

"Hello," he said.

"Hi yourself, stranger." He set the cart down on its front rests. "New in town?"

"Yes. Just passing through."

"Well, tell me about yourself!" He was a jovial soul. He held out a bottle–beer, by the smell. "Where've you been? Where ya going?"

He took the warm bottle, and reached into his pack for a little handful of strawberries wrapped in paper he had picked only the day before. "Thanks," he said and offered his exchange gift.

The man's face beamed as he unwrapped the paper. "Thanks. I like you already." He popped a red berry into his mouth. "I'm George. Your name?"

He shook his head. "Sorry. That's one thing I don't know. Bad memory. Just call me Kid."

"They really call me Fat George, although I've slimmed down some since the Plague. Did the Plague get your memory? I've seen that happen."

Kid shrugged. "I don't know. My first memory was walking away from a wrecked transport. I was pretty much wrecked myself." He gestured toward his head. "I had a huge bruise on the whole left side of my head, although it healed up pretty well. How I got there, or what caused the crash, I don't know. As far as where I'm going—I started walking south, and that's my destination. South.

"I've passed through all of the cities north of here. I think I've been walking since the Plague."

Fat George shook his head. "You must like walking more than I do. Why don't you take a break and stay awhile in Denver? We need people like you—healthy, and more or less in sound mind."

"A lot of survivors here?"

"A fair number. Most are walking wounded, as you'd expect. I'm the only one I know who came through the Plague untouched."

Kid looked at him skeptically.

"Oh, it's true. I was in the hospital at the time, being treated for pneumonia. They already had me pumped with all kinds of medicines when the hammer came down. I figure they wiped out my case of the Plague by accident."

"I've never heard of anything like that."

Fat George nodded. "I'm something of a celebrity around here. Of course, that also makes me a prime babysitter for the marginals."

Kid looked back up at the body hanging from the building. "What happened there?" He pointed.

"No one knows. There was quite a bit of craziness during the Plague. What gets me is how did she get up there in the first place?"

"She?"

"Oh yes, you can't tell any more, what with the weathering and the buzzards, but it was definitely a woman. A prime shame."

Kid felt a surge of anger, and it must have shown in his face. Fat George asked in a lower voice, "Did you lose someone, too?"

Kid glared at him, then closed his eyes to blink out the spike of pain that tried to pry his skull apart. He tried to shake it off. "I don't know. I have a feeling... I think I must have." He put his fist up to his forehead, to push the pain back.

He looked at Fat George, "Sorry... I get these spells."

"It's okay. Plague did that to a lot of people." He sighed. "What do you think about the idea that someone caused the Plague on purpose?"

Kid had heard the idea before. The question was as common as asking about the weather tomorrow.

"I think," he said with a bite in his voice, "that there was a monster that did this.

"And I hope that whoever it is lives a thousand lifetimes, and that he burns in torture in every one!" He turned his head to the side and looked down at the grass growing through the cracks in the pavement. His arms shook with the violence of his hatred.

He took you away from me, and I don't even know who you were. In his dreams, he had the memory of a voice, but he never caught sight of her— his one true soul-mate.

I will never forgive the creature that did this.

Fat George nodded, and reached out to pat him on the back. He spoke softly, "It's okay. Come with me and rest a spell. New faces are always welcome."

Kid nodded through the headache, his daily personal plague.

If only I could remember.

The End

Thanks for sharing this world. Consider leaving a review
at Amazon or you favorite book site.
— Henry

The Earth Branch of the Project Saga

 **Star Time**—Our world changes forever when Betelgeuse explodes into a supernova, destroying our technology and attracting scavengers from another planet eager to take advantage of Earth and its people. A handful of people can do nothing about the world falling apart, but perhaps they could hold off the aliens.

 **Kingdom of the Hill Country**—With all long distance communication and transportation destroyed after the Star, the city-state of Austin, Texas has to grapple with wandering barbarians and what kind new world will be formed out the the decisions its people will make and the remnants of the world that had crumbled around it.

 **In the Time of Green Blimps**—A century after the Star, technology had roughly recovered, with notable differences. Australia had invested heavily in genetic engineering, but was restricted by the northern hemisphere's shipping monopoly. When they created living, hydrogen-filled blimps, the conflict reached the ignition point.

 **Captain's Memories**—The survivors of the Blimp Fleet and the rediscovered tractor-pressor technology from the forgotten aliens jumpstarted the Second Space Age. Told as a series of tales by a retired pilot who played her own part in the development of the Terraforming Project, she struggles to make her own place on Earth's second moon, Ceres.

 **Humanicide**—A bitter, but supremely talented survivor of the genetic war decides to cull humanity and remove its world-moving technological power, but his plans threaten to kill his only possible mate and trigger a destruction far greater than he had planned.

The Ko Branch of the Project Saga

 **Star Time**—As the blast of radiation from the Betelgeuse supernova approached Earth, the Cerik moved to take advantage of the survivors, just as they had with other planets. Only this time, an unlikely pair moved to block them, a technical wizard and a psychic so sensitive she had to live as a hermit to survive. Together, they were magic.

 **Tales of the U'tanse**—The Cerik's captive humans, pronounced U'tanse, formed a new society with new rules, just to survive. Tales from the first years: James—the first boy born without telepathy, Karl—abandoned to die as too expensive to rescue, and Debbie—sent to Festival where girls were swapped between clans to prevent inbreeding.

 **Free U'tanse**—Joshua, the first freeborn U'tanse among the hidden collection of abandoned workers—all considered dead and hiding their thoughts from detection—took on his first task, monitoring the thoughts of Samson, a U'tanse bred to be a giant warrior, a prized pet of the ruling Cerik. But Joshua soon discovered his job had become a lot more hazardous than monitoring in the shadows.

And more to come.

Project Saga books and other titles by Henry Melton are available from the author at HenryMelton.com as well as most online bookstores.

www.ingramcontent.com/pod-product-compliance
Lightning Source LLC
Chambersburg PA
CBHW052022020726
47501CB00004B/1198